I0631400

CITY
of
WIZARDRY

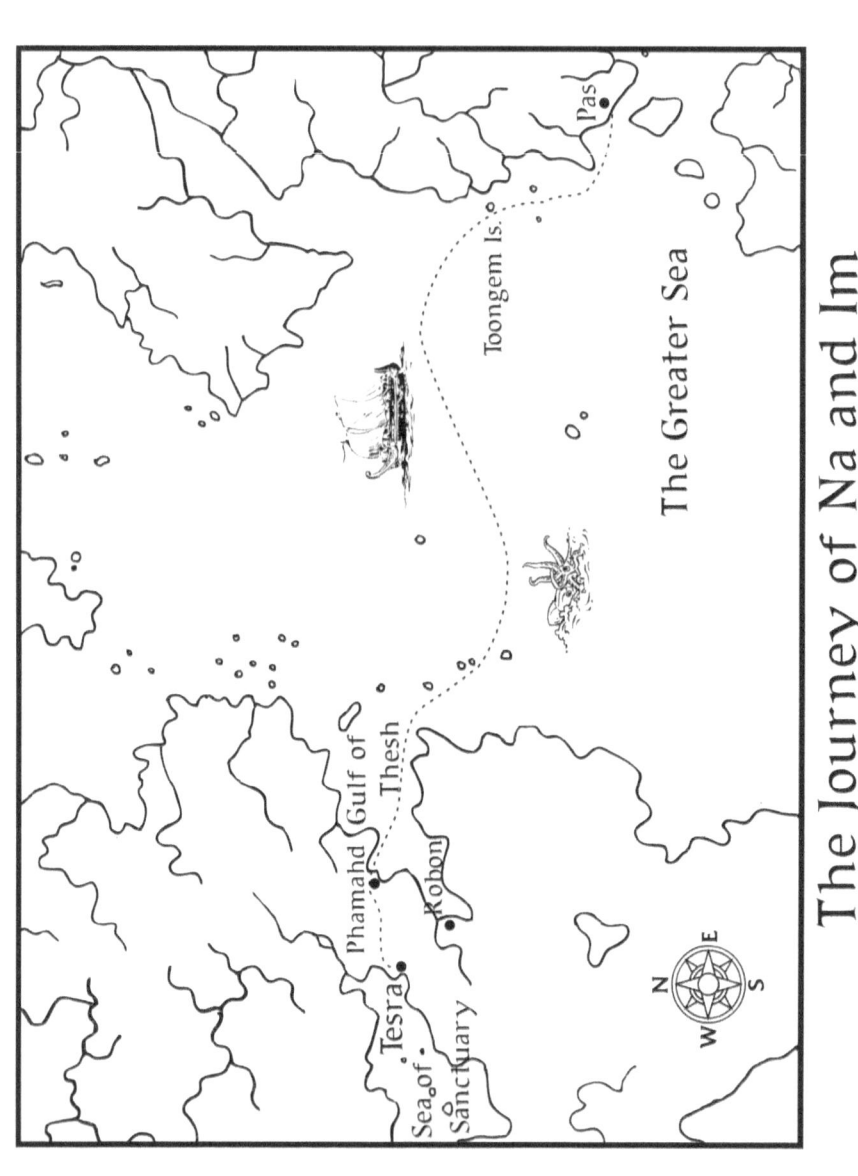

The Journey of Na and Im

CITY OF WIZARDRY

STEPHEN BROOKE

Arachis Press 2020

She could have all she wanted here, couldn't she?

City of Wizardry
©2020 Stephen Brooke

All rights reserved. The text, art, and design of this publication are the copyrighted work of Stephen Brooke and may not be reproduced nor transmitted in any form without the express written permission of the author or publisher, other than short quotes for review purposes.

ISBN 978-1-937745-73-8

Arachis Press
4803 Peanut Road
Graceville, FL 32440
http://arachispress.com

1.

THE SORCERESS NA HEAVED AGAIN, but nothing remained of her breakfast. Drat that Im, she thought, how can he be unaffected by this weather? Na suspected magic—but surely he would share it with her, wouldn't he?

The boy sat by the golden statue of Qu'orthseth, conversing cheerfully with the sailors. Not all of them looked completely comfortable either.

Yes, you know Qu'orthseth is not really a statue, if you have listened to my earlier tales of Na and Im. Now don't spoil it for the others!

For the most part, those sailors seemed of the same race as the two sorcerers, even though Tesra's towers rose in another world from that in which Na was born. She had explained some of this to the city's chief wizard, Holos, speaking from afar as wizards can and do.

She might attempt contacting him again later, when she felt better. If she felt better, perhaps that was. The air here on the deck was definitely preferable to that of her close cabin, and surprisingly warm. The ocean water, not so much, and she was drenched by the spray blowing off it.

The captain picked his way between the goods lashed to the deck. There was little wasted space. He stood by the man at the steering oar for a minute or more, looking to the sea, to the sky, to his own sails.

"We have a strong southerly wind," spoke Captain Mak at last. "We'll let it carry us up the coast as long as we can."

"But it means a winter storm to come," warned his first mate. The only mate, to be honest, for the crew was small.

"With any luck we can turn far enough north for it to carry us to the far coast and into port at Phamahd."

A quick crossing of the Great Sea was always desirable, Na was sure. She certainly would welcome setting her feet on solid ground again! This was but the third day since departing the Ildin port of Pas and the passengers had been warned it might require two weeks or more of sailing to reach their destination.

All around lay only the gray heaving sea. For a time, an equally gray shore had been visible to their right—Im insisted on calling it the starboard—but that had faded into the mists of distance. Na knew they still paralleled that unseen coast.

A voice roused her from her reverie, a voice only in her head. Or another world, to be precise. *Na.*

Xit? Not that she didn't know. She went to their meeting place, a little dim-lit room in that other world. *It's about time.* Na was entirely willing to scold anyone, even a god. A small and rather human god, to be admitted, but Xido was a god none the less.

I've but returned to the shrine of Banat, he explained. Xido did not sound in the least apologetic. But then, did he ever? *All is well with you? Atima is anxious for word of her Im.*

So why didn't you call to him?

Because he would be just as anxious for word of his Atima. I'd rather not deal with that.

Hmmph. Tell her Im is doing fine. Better than me. I intend never to cross this sea again, no matter what awaits in Tesra.

It is not wise to say never, advised the god.

Very well. I'll never do it again. I've been meaning to contact Holos but I haven't quite felt up to it. Many times in the past several weeks had she spoken to the chief wizard of Tesra from afar. It was at his invitation they sailed toward the fabled city.

Then let us call to him now, said Xido.

Why not? Na reached out, called to the wizard before Xido had a chance. She felt, somehow, she should be the one dealing with him. After all, Xido was going to be far away while she would be in the same city as this powerful sorcerer. No immediate answer. Was this the wrong time of day, when Holos might be sleeping or in his bath?

For all she knew, he might have a wife or wives or whatever to keep him busy from time to time. Na had to admit she knew little truly of the chief wizard of Tesra. Ah, there was the sleek sorcerer materializing, swathed in silk, his curling gray beard hanging to his ample stomach.

Na, my greetings! The man's chuckle was warm and seemed sincere. *You called as I sat at Prince Huenoziles's table. It is not so easy to slip away at such times, though the ways of wizardry are well understood in Tesra. Lord Xido! I greet you as well.* He did not sound quite so happy about the god's presence.

We are on our way, Na informed him. *Somewhere in the Greater Sea.*

Holos knew Im and she had intended to sail soon, had been informed when they left the temple of Banat, their refuge high in the hills above the Lantabee River. *I shall send a deputation to greet you at Phamahd and escort you across the hills.* Then he seemed to think on this. *I might come myself.*

This port is near Tesra? Na's knowledge of geography beyond the sea was sketchy. For that matter, so was her knowledge of geography anywhere in this world. There had been no need for the subject in the empty desert world where lay the Hirstel of her birth.

A journey of four days or so if one hurries. Somewhat longer if we choose to dawdle.

I would advise against dawdling, spoke Xido. *Torut surely knows something of what is going on and may choose to strike.*

To this Na added, *I suspect he knows we sailed from Pas. He had spies there.*

Hmm, yes, the Wizard-Lord must be considered. Holos attempted to appear no more than thoughtful about this but Na could tell there was more going on in the man's mind. She did not doubt that Xido could sense this too. The god and she must confer again soon.

Then there is no more to be discussed now, said Xido. *Call me when you approach your port.* With that, he left the two sorcerers.

And I must return to the prince, spoke Holos. *I regret I haven't the time to chat with you today, my lady.* He too faded out.

Na regretted it herself, as she returned to the tedium of the little ship and the empty seas. It would have been diverting to hear the latest gossip of Tesra. She had heard enough already to almost think she knew the city.

2.

THE TESRAN LANGUAGE DID NOT differ greatly from Na's native tongue, which these Tesrans persisted in calling Ancient Zikem. Na had picked up enough of it to understand most of what the captain said to his crew, and he rarely deigned to address his passengers in Ildin anymore. That was just as well. Soon they would be in Tesra itself and would have to use the city's language.

For the most part, the sailors did not speak to her. Na's repute as a mighty sorceress might have something to do with it. These Tesrans were people who knew of magic and respected its practitioners—and had a healthy fear of them. That Im was also a wizard did not seem to matter so much. The boy looked reassuringly harmless. She chose not to enlighten them that his powers were even greater than hers.

Yes, Na recognized this and, yes, it rankled some. But she had a healthy and well-earned regard for her own powers.

As well she should. Do not make the mistake of underestimating the wizardess Na!

Na also knew that being a somewhat attractive woman, the only woman within many leagues, cast its own sort of spell. The only woman on this lonely ship in this vast sea. Yesterday, it had passed between two islands, both distant but large enough to glimpse. The captain seemed pleased.

"We'll turn her nose westward soon," he announced. "Near Toongem Island, I hope."

"Reckon there'll be any ships there?" asked the mate.

"Maybe a lumber-boat but it's late for that. And let us pray to any and all gods there be no pirates about."

"Late for them too," was the mate's opinion.

"Lumber-boats?" wondered Im. "Aren't there any forests around

Tesra?" Na was more interested in the pirates Captain Mak had mentioned but chose to hold her tongue.

"Aye, much larger vessels than this little ship of ours."

"Practically barges," chipped in the mate. "Not suited to heavy seas."

The captain acknowledged this with an amiable nod of his head. "But it's more convenient to carry wood across the water than over the hills, so the shipbuilding at Phamahd and the other Tesran sea-towns tends to use lumber brought from this side of the Great Sea."

"They land mostly well to the north and cut it themselves. Toongem is a convenient rendezvous before striking east for port."

"And a cold rock this time of the year," said Mak.

"Any time of year."

"Aye."

Mak had called his vessel a small ship and Na believed him readily, though she had never seen one larger. All ships would seem small on this empty expanse of water. She felt more vulnerable than perhaps ever she had in her near hundred years of life.

"I see you carry some lumber yourselves," remarked Na. It was hard to miss, stacked neatly and lashed securely to the deck. Not very much of it.

"Valuable woods from the southern lands," said Mak. "We traded for it in Pas."

"For furniture and such," offered the mate in further explanation.

"Not our usual cargo but I keep an eye open for good deals. Mostly our hold is stuffed with bails of the raw silk the Ildin produce."

"From worms," added Im. He had been somewhat fascinated when he discovered this. "I saw them at the shrine of Banat."

Na had not been particularly interested but the boy had filled her ears with what he had learned of silk production and the reason for mulberry trees around many Ildin villages. She felt she knew quite enough on the subject.

"Land!" came a cry from the bow. The sailor stationed there pointed northward or maybe a bit east of northward. Na had no clear idea of directions on the open sea but Captain Mak had said they sailed north, hadn't he?

"Toongem. I see no ships," said the Tesran skipper, before squinting into the overcast skies. "Wind is coming more westerly. We'll see a shift to the north soon." Without further word to his passengers, he set his crew to shifting sail and went to the steering oar himself.

"Captain is adjusting our course," the mate explained. "We'll have to work into the wind some now." He left just as abruptly to tend to whatever duties fell to a ship's mate.

"That will slow us down," proclaimed Im. "The sailors said we would be turning against the wind soon."

"That would seem a good time for pirates to ambush one, wouldn't it?" she asked.

"I suppose it would. An insight or have you been having secret trysts with Mak?"

She ignored the jibe. "It just seemed logical." No sailors had informed her of anything. "I would guess our Tesrans are aware of it."

Im only nodded and gazed out toward the island, already falling away into misted distance. It seemed good sized, almost a mountain rising from the sea. "It might have been nice to set foot on land a little while," he said, his voice but the least bit plaintive.

"Better to get where we're going as soon as we can and be on land permanently," Na replied.

"Permanently for you, maybe. What's that?" He pointed toward the fading Toongem. "Captain Mak, is that a ship?"

Na peered but could make out nothing. Mak came to stand beside them. "Aye. Lying behind the isle and up to no good, I fear."

The Tesran boat didn't seem much of a prize for pirates, if pirates those were, felt Na. But it and its cargo might not be their target.

"We'll continue on our course," the captain decided. "Mmm, no, turn a bit more northerly while this wind holds."

"It'll come around soon," his mate reminded him.

"So it will."

Na thought it would be more sensible to put this brisk wind behind them, even if it meant heading back whence they came. Surely these sailors knew their craft, didn't they? The sorceress was quite willing to admit she was ignorant of such things. Some of the sailors had gone below at once, to man the oars. These had been unused since they had eased out of the harbor at Pas.

Im stood staring toward the other vessel. "They are gaining," he said at last, his voice flat and matter-of-fact. "I think they have many rowers to help beat against this wind. Far more than we do."

"Then we need a better wind, don't we?" the sorceress replied. "We could take turns pulling one in."

"Better let Captain Mak know what we intend first."

The Tesran skipper heard them out. "I've heard of wizards doing such things," he admitted, though he sounded more than skeptical. "I'll need warning so I can set the sails properly. When you let up, too." He gave the pair a long look. "Very well, give it a try. If we can keep ahead of them through this day we might lose them in the night."

"Um, maybe not." Im appeared reluctant to speak but continued. "Someone over there may be able to locate us anyway." Of course, he was not going to tell Mak that it was the demon Qu'orthseth—currently disguised as a statue—that was likely to draw their pursuers to them.

The captain might well toss it overboard. If he doesn't toss us over, Na told herself.

For a moment, she thought Mak might be considering just that course of action. "Don't try to give me a wind that blows against what we have. We need something that works with it."

Im turned to his companion. "Let's go look for a nice breeze."

"First to our usual meeting place," replied the wizardess. It would be best to start from a world they knew before sending themselves out together among the unnumbered universes in search of their wind. A moment later the two of them were in a little twilit room somewhere in the infinite.

Where now? asked the boy, with a bit of grin. Na had no better idea than he where to seek. Then—an idea.

There were always winds blowing in the desert about Hirstel, she said. *We know it.* Any place they knew, that they could picture, they could find instantly. Other worlds took longer. *But how do we know which direction the wind is blowing?*

Im laughed. It was irritating. *We need only put it at our back there and point toward the sail here,* he said. *Open the way and let it through!*

Oh. Of course. She tried to sound gracious.

But we know better, don't we? Nu should no doubt be commended for putting up with much from the young upstart wizard. More than you and I would, I think!

They went at once. A cloudless yellow vault rose from distant horizons, above the bleak and empty desert. Only sand and faded broken rock lay about them. *Not near the city,* remarked Im. He had let Na lead the way.

Better so, I think. Not that she had actually planned it. Im needn't know that. It was likely they were in fact close to Hirstel. Yes, those rocks over there marked one of the gates they had passed through when they first left their home. *Let's get to it. And hope no demon policemen show up!*

That would be inconvenient, agreed Im. Some of those demons had followed them the last time they visited Hirstel in this manner, intent on destroying Im and thereby releasing the bonds that held Qu'orthseth to him. They very much wanted to take the great red criminal into custody! The pair of wizards were quite capable now of handling them but it would be, indeed, inconvenient to need bother.

There, said Im, pointing into the hot wind that howled around the rocks. *We should take turns opening the way for it.*

Yes. Let's get back. It was not necessary but to leave a small part of themselves here, only enough to keep the way between worlds open. Their minds were needed on the ship.

All this would have been done with hardly a thought had one of them been working alone. They would have simply reached out and taken that wind, brought it to another world. Im now did just that. Not a great wind did he let through, just a modest breeze to assist that which blew off the sea, and directed toward the pair of square sails. He should be able to maintain that for some time before needing relief.

Na gazed toward the other ship. It had been drawing ever closer but no more. Perhaps they were even gaining some on their pursuer. She could just see the oars rise and dip, mostly by the foam and spray they created. There on the deck—a glint of a dark metallic blue in the cold, wan sunlight? She knew at once that one of those demon policemen stood there.

It wouldn't be able to step foot on their ship, not with the wards Xido and Banat had put in place. No demon could break through the protections placed by the pair of gods. Men could.

Through the midday and into the early afternoon, Na and Im took turns letting that wind blow from another world. It was nearing sunset in that other world, for its time was not the same as theirs. Stars began to faintly show at the darkening horizon. The wind would die down soon, both sorcerers knew; it was ever the strongest in the afternoons, when the hot air blasted from the desert and up the stony hills and escarpments. Fortunate it was they had tapped it then.

Here on the Great Sea the winds continued to shift, growing more westerly. Mak persevered into the face of it, his ship struggling on north of west. "Without your breeze we might not have made it," he said. "Soon we'll have both darkness and a wind moving around to the north. With winter's gale behind us, we'll run for port and no one can catch us!" He gave the wizards an appraising eye. "Can you manage another hour?"

We must look tired, Na thought. She certainly felt tired. "We'll try," she told him. "There might not be much of a usable wind soon anyway." Im was not party to this conversation; his attention was on keeping the way open.

She should spell him soon. As the young wizard, she kept a way open to the world of their origin, the world of the lost city Hirstel. Just a tiny part of herself remained there, not as much as Im at the moment, ready to take over when needed. More of her went there now, and her consciousness, there where some part of her physical being already was.

Hirstel was just off that way, wasn't it? Na felt a sudden nostalgia for the city, a desire to glimpse it once more, though she knew she would never wish to return to her narrow life there. When it grew dark she might be able to see its lights. Would the Prince-Sorcerer, Piras Tindeval, her rival and sometime suitor, have rebuilt his high tower by now?

The tower Im had caused to come tumbling down. She marveled still when she thought of what the youngster had done. A furtive sound caught her attention, brought her from the depths of her reverie. Was something moving about out there on the sands? No creatures lived on this world, none outside the walls of Hirstel, save in the depths of the slate-colored seas.

A pack of snarling, bestial man-like creatures came bounding out of the dark. *Break your link!* she cried out to Im. *Break it now!*

3.

"WHAT WERE THOSE THINGS?" GASPED Im.

"Ghalun. They lurk near gates and ambush travelers."

"Like sphinxes?"

"Exactly, except they travel in packs. You're too young to remember the last time they showed up in our world." Our former world, she reminded herself. "Why they came now I do not know." She could suspect, however.

"Nor is there time to worry about it," said Im. "We may have trouble enough in this world."

"I think I'm too exhausted to go look for wind somewhere else. You too," she decided.

Im looked about. "It's gotten awfully dark. It isn't nighttime already, is it?"

"I wouldn't think so," said Na.

The captain enlightened them. "Winter storm-front moving in. See the clouds banked up north, there?" He waved an arm toward what Na assumed was that direction. "Reckon we might not need your wizard-breeze after all."

"That's good, because we're certainly not going back for more of it," proclaimed Im. "Though," he continued, now turning to Na, "I don't think there was enough of our substance over there for those ghalun to harm us."

Neither did Na. "Maybe they could have come through the way we opened for the wind. I know too little of ghalun."

"Ghalun on my ship? Fasenais forfend!" croaked the captain.

"From a different world," stated Im, "we might have blown some birds through with the wind. There are none of those in the world of Hirstel, nor even insects."

"All of which would have popped back to their origin eventually, as will the air we've been pulling in," Na added. "That's no concern right now." She turned to scan the sea for the pursuing ship. When she turned back, failing to have caught any glimpse, Mak had left them to busy himself with the sails.

"We could pull through some hail to pelt yon pirates," suggested Im.

"I'm not sure where their ship is now. Better to rest in case we're needed later." Na needed rest and was certain Im did as well. What they had done for hours was not easy. It was not easy even when done for minutes.

She felt too tired even to go down to their tiny cabin. Na sat down on the deck, leaning back against the stacked lumber, and watched the sailors busy themselves with the sails, those not manning the oars, a bank of ten on each side of the vessel. Im took a place beside her. "We'll be out of everyone's way here," he remarked.

"Mm-hum." Na's eyes closed. Then, with a great shiver, she reopened them. "The wind is getting chilly."

"And it's turned northerly, I think," said Im. "More northerly." A moment later cold rain drove against the deck. The stack of wood provided them little protection. Fortunately, the squall lasted but a few seconds. "I'll go get my cloak," he said. He rose slowly to his feet, revealing a weariness the boy was unlikely to admit to. "Want yours? We'll need them if we stay up here."

"Yes. Thank you, Im." She did want to remain on deck, to see what was happening. The ship had turned, Na was sure, no longer working its way into the wind. Who could tell what direction was what in this gloom of impending storm?

The gloom of night would follow soon. A voice cried out. She rose and turned to see a mass loom suddenly from the darkness. The pirate ship! Its crew seemed as surprised as theirs for frantic shouts arose and it veered suddenly. None the less, it grated along the flank of the Tesran merchant, entangling and sheering the oars of both ships.

"Enough!" said Na. Perhaps she only said it to herself; she was not certain after. What she did remember clearly was reaching out into the infinite and finding fire. A world of fire, with a great volcano belching lava down its dark desolate slopes. Lava wouldn't do. Too difficult to bring, though it was certainly possible, with enough effort. But ash—

A moment later, hot volcanic ash rained on the enemy vessel. Only for a few seconds was Na able to hold the connection and let it through. That was enough. Its sail—it had but the one—burst into flame, and fires sprang up here and there on the deck. More devastating was the toll it took on the crew.

She averted her eyes from the mayhem she had wrought. Where was Im? Oh, he had gone to fetch cloaks. Safe below deck, no doubt.

Captain Mak approached. It was hard to read his face as he glanced toward the burning pirate ship and then back to Na. "Young Im went over the side when yon pirates jolted us," he said. "I fear he is lost to the sea."

4.

AT ONCE, NA SOUGHT HER young companion. Would that he had enough presence of mind enough to meet her, to speak to her from afar! Assuming he were conscious or even alive, for that matter.

Did the boy know how to swim? Na didn't but Im had spent time with the god Xido who, being a crocodile in his other form, certainly did. Maybe he had taught Im something of the art when they bathed in streams and rivers.

I am—here, came his voice. She saw only darkness. *Where?*

Under water, I would assume, she told him, keeping her voice as even as she was able. *Don't you see anything?*

A light. Yes, above me. Damn, it's hard to remember to keep my mouth closed here when I talk there! Im's form appeared, hazy, his arms and legs milling.

Swim to the light, boy! Surely he was seeing the burning ship. *We'll watch for you.*

At once she returned to Mak. "Im is alive," she reported. "We must wait for him."

The captain's demeanor betrayed a certain doubtfulness—for which Na blamed him not at all—but he nodded an agreement. "Hold position," he called out. Na could only hope they had not drifted too far already. The sails flapped in the wind but were not properly set to drive them forward after their collision. The burning enemy vessel still sat fairly close by, to their starboard. Im would like that she remembered to call it that.

They seemed to be getting the fire under control. Again she sought Im but he did not acknowledge her call. She looked out across the churning water, lit by the flames. There! Something bobbed up from the surface.

"Im," she called out, pointing. He was about halfway between the two ships.

"I'll fetch him," offered a youthful sailor. "Give me a line!" In seconds he had the rope secured about his waist and leaped into the waves. Im seemed to appear and disappear among those waves. Could he keep himself afloat long enough?

Over on the pirate vessel stood a man with a bow, also scanning the water. Beside him rose a bulky figure, a head taller. Its silhouette was enough to tell Na it was a demon of Qu'orthseth's world. Too far away maybe, too dimly made out, for her to attack efficiently. Nor was an arrow likely to reach them here on Mak's ship. Im made a more likely target. It was he the demons wished to destroy.

More burning ash? Na didn't want to take a chance of raining it on Im and his rescuer. Smoke to obscure the archer's vision? No, the winds would whisk it away too quickly. Pulling in shadow was difficult and more so at a distance. Im could probably do it.

The increasing rain might do the job for her. The sorceress reached out again to Im, and found him. *Tau is swimming out to you with a line*, she informed him. *Can you see him?*

No, but I'll yell, he replied and broke off, apparently to do just that. Na saw the distant archer release an arrow but was sure it fell nowhere near either swimmer. Rain and darkness, wind and heaving seas would surely prevent anything but a lucky hit. But people sometimes were lucky.

Hey, is someone shooting at me? came Im's querulous voice. *That was close! Oh, here's Tau.*

"Tau has reached him," Na relayed to the captain.

"If they both have hold of the rope we can pull them in."

Na asked, was answered in the affirmative. "Pull away," she told

Mak. A couple minutes later—surely no more though it seemed so to Na —two drenched boys shivered on the deck.

"Let's get out of here," ordered Mak. "Sails only. We've a good wind to drive us on now!" What flames still burnt on the pirate ship faded into the storm and the night behind them.

"You were under the water for quite some time," said Na, once Im was dry and settled into their close cabin. "Could you hold your breath so long?" It seemed unlikely to her.

Im looked sheepish but admitted, "I pulled air from another world to keep from drowning."

Na considered this. "You may pay for that later."

"Yes. Any trace of that air that remains in my body will be pulled away to its own world eventually. I should breathe deeply and get it out of me!"

Im was probably joking. Still, some of that air would have gone into the tissues of his body, into his blood. It could be uncomfortable when it departed.

"Better than drowning," was all she could say about it. She could fill him in on the battle, on the demon presence, later. The young wizard needed sleep now.

Na left him and found her way back to the deck. Though the cabin was always spoken of as being 'below' it was in fact almost at a level with the deck, only a couple steps down and across a narrow passage from Captain Mak's cabin. Both lay near the stern of the ship, with the steersman and his oar stationed just above them.

Cold and dark and driving rain greeted her as she stepped up. The mate spied her at once, from his place by the steering oar. "We'd best get a line on you, my lady," he called out. "Don't want to lose anyone else overboard."

"How long will this last?" she called back.

"Not long, were we staying in one place. But we're traveling with the storm tonight."

"Or aslant to it," spoke the pilot. "The storm front is moving southeast and we go southwest."

"More or less," the mate agreed. "You may see sun tomorrow."

Na could see both men had ropes about their middles, and that a line was strung down the deck, from her position to the two masts and on to the prow. The sailors' cabin was up there and most were wisely under cover. There was but one sail up and it was partially furled.

"Captain Mak is in his cabin if you seek him," added the mate.

She did not, but there no reason to say so. Na pulled her cloak more closely about her and stared out over the black waters. Lightning flickered occasionally, but not close. "I'll just watch from here a while," she said. Maybe speech from afar with Holos or even Xido would be good right now. Na felt restless, unsettled, after the day's events, and not ready to settle down in her cabin.

Moreover, she had given Im the bed, the bed in which she usually slept. She was not about to stretch out on the floor as was the boy's custom.

No, perhaps tomorrow she would call out to someone. Or she might feel no need by then. Two hours later, when the captain came up to take his watch, he found her asleep on the steps.

5.

NA REMEMBERED SOMEONE BUNDLING HER into bed. Little more. She opened her eyes and sat up. This was not her cabin.

There was only one other cabin on this ship, the one currently shared by the captain and the mate, Na and Im having been given the mate's customary space. She had been in here before. She recognized it and the few little homey details Mak had added. Her cloak, still damp, hung from a wooden peg on the door. Na took it over her arm and stepped out into the passageway.

It seemed the storm was past. A thin light slanted in from above. Was Im up and about? She cautiously pushed open the door to their cabin. The youth was in bed, apparently asleep. Mak and an older gray-bearded seaman sat beside him.

"Ah, you are awake," spoke the captain. "When I tried to help you to your cabin last night, our young friend was raving so I put you to bed in mine. I hope you do not mind."

Na shook her head. "Im was sick?"

"Taken badly," said Mak. "He seems well now."

"He had the bends, he did," declared the grizzled sailor. "I've seen it in pearl divers in the south."

"Maybe so," felt the captain. "This seemed different, some."

She could guess what it was, just what Im had been concerned about after breathing too much air drawn from another world. Na saw no point in explaining that to these two. It might, though, be interesting to discuss with Xido or Holos, and learn whether they had heard of it happening.

If not, it should most definitely be added to the great libraries of magical lore that were reputed to exist in Tesra. Learning all that knowledge existed had been the deciding factor for Na when it came to voyaging across the sea. The limited texts at the shrine of Banat frustrated her.

Soon now, she would be in the city of wizardry itself, great Tesra, founded by folk of her own heritage. Folk who had not chosen to run off to another world as had Na's ancestors. "I am hungry," she announced, and then laughed. "As I am sure Im will be as soon as he wakens."

"Let's go on deck," said Mak, rising from his cross-legged seat on the floor. "You," he told the sailor, "stay with the boy."

The sorceress followed him into the open air. Broken clouds scudded close overhead but there was no more rain. A frigid wind pierced her. Na did not think she had ever felt so cold.

And it is most likely she hadn't. Our sorceress came from a desert city, hot in day, cold at night, but nothing like a winter wind howling over the Great Sea. One can live to nearly a hundred and still find new experiences. So don't think you know everything, my fine audience!

"We are sailing toward the southwest currently," Mak told her, as they made their way to the bow. She could see all the sails were up again and filled with the wind. "I am not sure of our position but expect we will make land somewhat south of Phamahd. Best to make speed now and worry about accuracy later."

"To put water between us and that pirate ship." Na could understand this. "Do you think it pursues?"

The captain shrugged. "Most likely not. Ho, Stewmeat, have you any grub left?"

A small, balding, squinting man lounging in the doorway regarded them. "Y' always tells me not t' feed latecomers, Cap'n," he said, grinning. "But I reckons I can scrape a few plates and put somethin' together."

He disappeared into his tiny galley. "He's not Tesran, right?" Na had noted this before but the opportunity had not arisen to ask it.

"A Tesran citizen and that's all that counts," replied the captain. "Not all our ancestors came from the legendary Valley of Visions."

"It is legend where I was born too," she replied.

"In a desert beyond the mountains."

"Yes." Na stifled an urge to giggle. That the desert lay in another world was not something this man needed to know, though she was tempted to tell him anyway.

"The Wizard-Lord is said to dwell in a desert beyond the mountains," he continued. "A different desert and mountains, I assume."

"Undoubtedly." She was unwilling to offer more than that.

"I also assume he may be after you two." Mak held up a hand. "Not that it is my business. I only agreed to take you across the sea. It would have been nice to know of your enemies first, however."

Stewmeat stepped out and handed them plates of hard bread and hot fried pork at that moment. He had obviously fried the meat for them and definitely not scraped it from someone else's plate.

Captain Mak continued once both had taken the sharpest edge off their hunger. "I have no, ah, resentment, you understand? If you go to aid Holos in the defense of my people, then I am pleased to be of aid. And," he added, with a bit of a chuckle, "I was also pleased by your treatment of those pirates. Ho, what have we here?"

Na looked up to see Im nonchalantly crossing the deck toward them, his sailor nursemaid at his heels. "Is there more of that?" he asked.

"No, this is the last," Na immediately told him. "And Captain Mak does not permit meals to be served to those who are late!"

Stewmeat stepped out and tossed Im a chunk of the bread. "Y' can gnaw on that, m' boy. I knows y' don't eat no meat."

Na felt momentarily guilty. She too had sworn to be vegetarian but it had been difficult to maintain that stance aboard Mak's ship. And there was no point in wasting this meat after the cook had gone to the trouble, was there?

She could go back to it when they reached their destination, Na decided. When they started a new life in a new city.

The ship sailed swiftly to the southwest all that day, through rolling seas, and the sun came out for a few brief minutes before nightfall.

6.

"I DID NOT THINK I would come up again," Im confessed. "I might not have without your help."

"I've lost track of how many times we've saved each other."

"I must count them up sometime. Seriously, I was considering attempting to enter another world so I might breathe, even though I knew I would be pulled back eventually."

"Still in the depths of the Great Sea," Na pointed out. "And we would have sailed away by then."

"I didn't say it was a good idea. Neither was bringing air but I might have died without it."

Na nodded solemnly. The boy had brushed closer to death than ever before. "We need thank Tau as well," she said.

"Yes, he's a good kid." Na avoided cracking a smile. Tau was at least as old as Im. "He's almost, well, too devoted. He wants to be around me all the time."

This time, the smile could not be denied. "I believe he has a crush on you, Master Im."

Im was taken aback, and sat silently gazing at the boards of the cabin floor for a minute or more. "What can I do about it?" at last came from his lips, almost too low for Na to catch it.

"Don't encourage him. I'm used to men sniffing after me and I know it's something that happens, whether we want it or not." She frowned. "Usually I didn't."

A slight smile from Im. "Like the Prince-Sorcerer."

"Yes, like the Prince-Sorcerer. I might even have given in to him someday, had I remained in Hirstel. I certainly had nothing better to look forward to."

And Tindeval wasn't a bad sort, though she had resented being second-best to him. It would be best if she didn't go into the affairs she had allowed herself in that city. Not now, maybe not ever. Im needn't know any of that in a new world. "Shall we get out of this cabin? If we're late to breakfast Stewmeat won't feed us!"

Im rose from the floor in one graceful motion. "Get your cloak," he said. "It's likely to be cold."

Cold it was, with a strong wind from what Na made out to be a little east of north, going by the position of the sun. She realized that her guesses about such things were not to be relied upon. There was a clear sky and bright sun; if one moved out of the direct wind it wasn't bad at all. She pulled her cloak close and followed Im toward the bow. Many of the crew were there, with not much in the way of duties at the moment.

Some ate; some simply squatted on the deck, doing nothing. Mak approached the two, noting Na's appraisal of his men. "Lazy bunch but I'll allow it after the past couple days." He scanned the group himself. "Most, you understand, aren't much in the way of sailors. They're here to handle the cargo or man the oars, if needed."

"I'd like to learn something of handling a ship," came unexpected from Im. "Sails." He looked up at the billowing sheets. "I'd like to know sails."

"I could show you something," said the captain. "Or," he went on, giving Na a broad wink, "I could let Tau show you."

"I have some concerns about what Tau might show me," was Im's offhanded response. "Is there any fruit this morning?"

There was, some sort of compote reconstituted by Stewmeat from dried fruit. Na thought she recognized mulberries but was uncertain of the rest. Im slathered a good quantity of it onto his usual bread. Na, after a moment's hesitation—spent looking longingly at the bacon and perhaps sniffing some as well—decided to follow his example.

Mak returned to the subject of their conversation when the two returned to him. "There are many small sailing craft plying the inland sea by Tesra," he told them. "If you do want to learn the craft, you'll have opportunity enough at the city."

"An inland sea," repeated Im. "I saw that on the maps. Named, um, the Sea of Sanctuary, right?"

"So it is. Calling it a sea is perhaps a stretch. A big lake, I would say, I and others who sail the Greater and Lesser Seas."

"I know the name was given by the refugees who first beheld it, those who founded Tesra," spoke Na. "It seemed to them they had at last come upon the sanctuary they sought. Um, Holos told me of it." She had felt slightly reluctant to reveal that.

Mak apparently knew better than to inquire of the doings of wizards, especially those of the chief wizard of Tesra. Im, on the other hand, grinned and said, "Na has an admirer too, I think."

She only scowled at the boy and busied herself with breakfast. Yes, Holos seemed interested in her but that could be for many reasons. The interest was not mutual. No, of course not. He reminded her altogether too much of Piras Tindeval.

"I'll be adjusting course later today," spoke Captain Mak. "We've run before the wind long enough and can start turning more easterly."

"We're safe from the pirates now?" asked Im.

Mak gave a shrug, a resigned half-smile. "There may be the danger of other pirates now, Bazu corsairs out of their coastal cities to the south."

"Those we encountered were of another people?"

"My people," responded the captain and spoke no more of it.

Soon after noon, he did begin to change course. The winds held steady, but lessened. Many drowsed on the deck, Na and Im included.

"A whale!" The cry awakened them, them and others. Many looked where the sentinel pointed, hoping to make it out.

"No whale I've e'er seen," claimed one seasoned crewman.

"Nor a shark neither," stated the mate. "One of you rouse the captain from his cabin. He should see this."

By the time Mak appeared, the sea creature had moved close enough for everyone to realize it was no beast any had spied before. The captain squinted in its direction, hands below and above his eyes to block the glare of the sun. "I've heard of sea monsters in the far southern seas," he said. "The kraken, the shadow-lurker. Maybe one of those strayed here." He did not sound at all confident of that.

Red, it was, or maybe more purplish, and barrel-shaped. It moved directly toward the ship and then veered off. Twice more this was repeated, before it fell into a course parallel to their own.

"The wards are keeping it at a distance," said Im. "It must be a demon of some sort."

Na was in agreement. "Or at least not of this world."

Another cry rose, pulling their attention from the swimming monster. Arms pointed skyward. "Rupa!" swore Captain Mak. "Never have I heard of them this far from their home crags. Break out the bows!"

Winged humanoid figures, maybe a dozen of them, wheeled overhead. These were definitely red, though their appearance seemed to constantly shift, as if going in and out of focus. "Stand ready!" called Mak to his few sailors who actually were ready with bow and arrow. But these strange beings—all females, Na could see, as they were naked—also veered away after approaching.

They seemed baffled and agitated, shrieking to each other as they made attempt after attempt to dive on the ship, only to be repelled. "They'll be carryin' no honest seamen home to father more of their kind," remarked an old sailor standing close by Na. It was he who had helped attend Im when he was briefly ill.

She told herself she would have to learn more of these rupa when Tesra was reached. So much was there to learn.

Mak and his sailors seemed baffled. A pitched battle, possibly a losing battle, was what they had expected. An arrow or two was loosed toward the circling creatures, with no apparent harm, before they rose, hovered a few moments as if in council, and then sped off into the west. The sea monster remained, doggedly following.

"If yon creature came from another world, it will be pulled back in time," Na whispered to Im.

"But that might be days."

True enough. Both turned their attention back to the thing, whatever it might be. Remaining mostly submerged, it was hard to make out much of its form.

That was about to change.

7.

IT WAS MOTTLED, IRIDESCENT BLUES and reds and purples. There were tentacles and what might be fins or even wings. A great maw gaped. All this could be seen as its misshapen mass rose from the water, hurtled itself into the air, to fall back heavily. The wave its plunge created swept across the deck.

"Anyone go over?" called out Captain Mak. The ship rocked in the aftermath of the attack.

"Don't think so, Captain!" called back the mate. "Hang on! It's fixing to do it again!"

Once again the monster rose and fell, sending another tall wave across the vessel. "Do you think we could send it back?" whispered Im.

"Let's look," Na said, despite her doubts. If that creature were sent —or pulled—from another world, they might be able to make out the link that yet bound it to that place of its origin. There, a faint line of—of what? Energy? That didn't seem a completely accurate word to the sorceress. Not important. If it could be severed, the name didn't matter! There were intricate bindings woven into that link, bindings meant to deter just one such as she. With time, maybe—

No! Na was not going to waste her efforts attempting to unravel them. She returned to herself and then immediately went off to other worlds, seeking, seeking, until she found what she wanted. The sea monster was again hurtling up from the water when she opened the way, allowing a great bolt of lightning through from a world of churning storm, wrapped in a poisonous atmosphere, a world where no man could survive. It struck the creature fully.

An horrendous bellow echoed over the waves as it winked out of their world, leaving naught but a stench nigh unbearable. Im gave her an irked look. "I would have undone the link in another minute or two."

"No doubt," she replied, coughing. Some of that poisonous air had come through with the lightning. "That smells worse than Stewmeat's cooking." Indeed it did. Na had never smelt anything to rival it.

Nor have you, my friends. Imagine thousands of burnt fish rotting, and you will have no more than a hint of its true stench. Chances are, the beast didn't smell all that good before being hit by a lightning bolt, either, but we are fortunate that its kind lurk in another world.

A good wind carried the stink away, as it did the ship. Na noted the occasional dark look from some of the crew. It was to be expected the sailors would be divided when it came to the two sorcerers, some grateful they had delivered them from several misfortunes, others seeing them as the source of those misfortunes. Some holding both views at once, perhaps. Did Im note such things? She knew politics and human nature as he did not. He might need guidance when they reached land.

Mak had promised to soon have them safely there. It didn't matter until then, but it did feel good to remind herself she was better than the boy at something. The next morning they spied an island, quite a large island, apparently. Na must take the seamen's word for that.

The captain gazed at it looming ahead and shook his head. "Much further south than I had expected. No matter." He called to the mate, "We turn north at once." They passed well north of that island and an hour or so later a pair of smaller isles—though not small, she was made to understand—went by to the starboard. Mak remained vigilant, perhaps in anticipation of those Bazu pirates he had feared. Na knew better than to bother him about it.

Im learned things, though. The boy listened and was not reluctant to use Tau as a source of information. "We follow a chain of islands now," he told her. "They run parallel to the coast, south of our destination. And crawling with pirates, I am told!" His smirk told her he was not completely taken in by the sailors' tales. That boded well.

Now he continued, more serious in tone. "The men claim the Bazu are unlikely to be in league with the Wizard-Lord. They are a fierce people but have their own code of morality."

"Which wouldn't prevent them stealing Mak's cargo and slitting our throats."

"Oh, we would be sold into slavery. Some Bazu captain would make you his concubine!"

Na had but the sketchiest concept of slavery. It had existed neither in Hirstel—if one didn't count demon servants—nor in the Ildin lands they had known in this world. But she did recognize one thing. "If they knew we were wizards, they would put us to work on affairs magical."

"We may find ourselves in no better a position in Tesra," said Im and left her abruptly.

Perhaps so, she thought. Had that been a concern of Im? For that matter, was she going too trustingly to this strange city? And dragging the boy along with her. That might have been a disservice to Im. He might have been better off remaining on the other shore of the wide sea.

Ah, but Im had chosen to come. None had forced him. To be sure, Holos and others in Tesra hoped to use two powerful wizards against Torut, the reigning Wizard-Lord. They were unknowns to that mighty sorcerer, possible threats, best eradicated swiftly. Well, mad Torut had failed in that. So far, at least! And he had antagonized them in the process, Im in particular by attacking his beloved Atima. Im had indeed chosen to come, and with good reason.

Progress was slow for they no longer had favorable winds. They beat up the coast the rest of that day and into the next.

She awoke to find Im sitting on the floor. "I was restless during the night," he reported, "and went on deck for a while. We passed another big island before dawn which I was told marks the entrance to the gulf where our port lies. We'll be there today, maybe." He sounded as if he were trying to be cheerful about the prospect but Na knew him well enough by now not to be fooled. The young wizard had his trepidations about this new land they were about to reach.

As did Na. "Get out of here, boy, and let me use the pot. I'll come up later." She snickered. "And you can come down and empty it."

"I have had enough of bad smells on this voyage," he told her. But he did leave.

Today. Captain Mak would tie up his vessel at the quays of Phamahd today. Na assumed there were quays though she had seen but one port in her life, the Pas from which they had sailed. And Holos would be there. Or might be there. He hadn't promised, had he? She finished her morning toilet quickly and hurried up the steps.

"There you are at last," spoke Im. "Captain Mak refused to fill me in until you showed." The peevish tone fooled neither her nor the captain, who stood at the boy wizard's side. "Oh, and I got you breakfast," he added, holding out a wooden platter. No meat. Maybe that was just as well.

She took the proffered plate. "So, fill poor Im in, will you?"

He gave her the slightest of bows. "We have entered the Gulf of Thesh." Thesh, of course, meant the East. Gulf was one of those words that did not derive from the older Zikem but was borrowed from some other tongue. "Phamahd lies at its western end, as well as some other ports. It is an easier, if longer, road across the hills to Tesra from there."

"That's the way your goods will travel, right?" interjected Im.

"For the most part. In the city, some name this gulf Bar Theshac, the Eastern Gate."

Na could make out a distant coast to their left. To their port. She might never use those nautical terms again after today. Cliffs? "Then we'll get there today?"

"The wind is good. We might make harbor by mid-afternoon. And," he added with a light laugh, "we are quite safe from pirates here."

"How about sea monsters?" Im did not attempt to keep a straight face while making this query.

"If any show, we shall depend on Lady Na to deal with them." Mak might have been more serious in his reply than surfaces suggested. Na recognized they had gained a great deal of respect from the captain. "I'm unlikely to spend much more time with you. A deputation awaits your arrival, I understand?" Both wizards nodded though they had no more knowledge of it than Mak. "And I'll be busy with the unloading of cargo and other business. My wife will want some attention as well!"

"Then we must thank you now for getting us safely across the sea," said Na.

"Rather than throwing us overboard," added Im.

"You could have tossed him," said Na. "I wouldn't have minded. Oh, I suppose I should get myself cleaned up if there is someone official waiting at the docks." She wasn't going to mention it might be Holos himself.

"I was never tempted to give you the heave," objected Captain Mak. "Perhaps your image over there. I recognize it had something to do with all this." He nodded toward the golden statue—as he still thought it to be—lashed before the main mast. "It has been my pleasure," he said, again giving a little bow, and strode off to attend to his duties.

"He couldn't have thrown Qu'orthseth overboard," whispered Im. "The wards that kept the demons out would have kept our demon in."

That was true, wasn't it? Na had never considered it. She didn't betray that fact to the boy. But another thought came. "How will we get it off the ship?"

"You and I must undo all the bindings. Xido gave me instructions as to how before we left. Shall we start?"

Na sighed. Practicing magic—and hard, fatiguing magic, at that—was not how she had wished to spend her last hours before disembarking. But it had to be done.

8.

Phamahd was not impressive. It was large, yes, or at least larger than any town the two wizards had ever before seen in this world, spreading up smoothly-rounded, treeless hills from the waterfront.

"When do you want to speak to Xido?" asked Na, as the ship was rowed toward the dark wooden docks. And Atima, of course.

Im only shrugged. "Has Holos made any contact?"

"None."

"Then let's call Xido right now and let him know we're here." Na felt that was a good idea. Both went off to another world, calling to the god. He showed up almost immediately.

Anything wrong? were his first words.

We're across the sea, answered Im. *Thought you should know.*

No contact with anyone here yet, Na added.

We had adventures.

I had an idea you might. We can speak of those later. You can speak to your Atima later, too, when you have settled in.

You are with her? I mean at the shrine?

So I am. Once you have had a chance to speak I must go away for a time but I shall return to teach her, as I promised. A smile came to Xido's dark and somewhat ugly face. *And I assure you she is well. I shall tell her the same of you. You are well, aren't you?*

I am.

Na snickered. *Now he is. That's a part of the story you'll want to hear later.*

Yes, later. Xido became alert all at once. *Someone is attempting to break into our meeting. Not—no, not Atima. Nor your Holos. Torut, is that you? Ha, he has slipped away, finding himself incapable.* His attention came back to the two sorcerers. *And I shall slip away now. You shall be busy for a while, I am sure.*

Na returned to the ship. "I sensed no other," she said.

"I did," said Im, and no more.

"Hail, Captain Mak!" cried a stout man from the docks. His long robe of blotchy indeterminate color was pulled up and tucked into a wide leather belt, making a tunic of it. The fellow tugged on a full dark beard and regarded Mak's vessel. "The last ship out of the east this season," said he. "Or so I would think. All others I know of are safe in port now."

"He doesn't look very Tesran either," Im confided. "Not what I expected Tesrans to look like." In other words, like Na and himself. Or Captain Mak, for that matter, though his hair was dark, not straw-colored.

"We shouldn't expect anything," she told him. "Tesra will surprise both of us at times. Of that be assured."

Im chuckled. "As has this whole world."

"Hail, Master Lumus," Mak called back. "Last in, eh? Not unexpected. Say, are there important people in town? Wizards, maybe?"

"I've heard tell of them. Haven't seen any sign myself." He squinted up at the captain. "You have business with them?"

Mak swung an arm toward his pair of passengers. "These two do. Send someone to let them know they've arrived, will you? Now, which warehouse should I use?"

For the next hour and more, they watched Mak's crew methodically empty the holds. Many bails of raw silk came out of the dark, but that was far from being all his cargo. Each item was called out and written down as it appeared, so they were able to keep track as they sat and watched. Im seemed somewhat fascinated; Na's interest did wander after a while, occasionally to the brawny shirtless workmen. It had been too long since she parted with Xido. Surely he did not expect any loyalty.

Na certainly expected none from the god and did not think it would be at all in his nature.

It might be in hers, though. It might be good to settle down, whether in Tesra or elsewhere, and be a wife. Maybe even a mother. If Im weren't so thoroughly in love with Atima, she might even have considered him as a mate.

Turpentine came up from the hold, and barrels of pitch. "Lots of marine stores come out the Ildin lands," Im informed her. Where he had learned that she didn't know, and didn't care enough to ask. The exotic lumber she knew about. Raisins? Na wished she'd known of those. She might have climbed down below deck and filched some. Hides. From what animal was not announced. Horn, too. Ah, the tubs of sulfur that had surprised Xido.

"I have some gems and ivory in my personal store," the captain told the man who had first greeted them. Apparently Lumus was in some way in charge of the docks. Or maybe the warehouses. Na wasn't sure and no one had bothered to introduce them and that was probably just as well. "Stuff brought up from the south and traded in Pas."

"Will you want me to take charge of it?"

"No, better to keep it in my own house. You can look it over first if you'd like. Picked up some glass that took my fancy, though I don't know if anyone would buy it."

"You were ever the curious one, Mak. I believe those are your important men coming," he said, looking toward a group slowly progressing in their direction. "Important women too, it seems."

"The high priestess of Fasenais! And that is the chief wizard Holos himself at her side, isn't it?"

"Could be." The dock master was not easy to impress. These weathered boards were his domain and here he was lord.

Na, however, felt like running and hiding from these people in their rich robes, with their air of command. Holos she recognized, having spoken with him from afar on several occasions. He might be a little taller than she had realized; that had been hard to judge. Every bit as plump, however. The wizard was swathed in a yellow robe and carried a long staff. He did not seem to need nor use it as support.

He stood looking at her now. No, staring at her. His eyes slid to Im momentarily, before he turned and whispered a few words to the tall woman at his side, a woman clad in enveloping robes and hood of sea-colored silk. There was not enough of her visible for Na to make even the most reckless of guesses as to her age.

It would be best to go down to them and get off this ship at last. She and Im had brought little and that they carried with them now. The boy seemed as hesitant to go down to those great people as she was. "Together," she murmured, linked her arm in his, and the two descended the gangway to the docks of Phamahd.

9.

"IT'S HEAVY. YOU MAY NEED several men to fetch it," warned Im.

"I would suggest an ox cart, sir," offered Mak. The sailor had been endeavoring to make himself noticed as little as possible. Na and Im were not so readily awed by the likes of Holos, now they were close to the wizard and his companions. Had they not journeyed in the company of gods? Yes, and did more than journey with them, Na said to herself. The reminiscence brought a smile.

"Dock-master," spoke Holos. "Can you attend to this?"

"I'll have some men take it up to your place, sir," said Lumus and left at once, apparently to arrange it. After a moment's hesitation, Mak followed.

"You needn't remain, need you?" asked the chief wizard, returning his attention to his guests.

"I trust Mak to see things done right," Im told him. "Um, I took a man into my service. Is it all right if he comes along?"

"Certainly, young sorcerer. Have you an attendant, Lady Na?"

She shook her head. All this was news to Na. Maybe I should have someone, she told herself as she saw Im wave a grizzled sailor to them. It was he who had nursed the boy for a few hours. Name? She wasn't sure.

It was good to have someone to trust nearby. Im had done well to think of it before they left ship. The man fell in behind as they strolled up the docks. Holos and his companions—most of them lackeys of some sort, she assumed—seemed in no hurry.

"Mec Arana, may I present the Mistress Na and Master Im," Holos said to the tall woman. "The mec is high priestess of the goddess Fasenais."

"I greet you, visitors from beyond the sea," said the woman. Her voice revealed no more about her than her looks—it too seemed veiled. "Or from beyond our world, if I am to believe my friend Holos."

"Yet our ancestors were your ancestors," Na replied.

"Cousins, then." There was at least a hint of amusement.

"So we are. I do not know your gods, however. Never have I heard of Fasenais."

"Captain Mak swore by her now and then," said Im.

"So are sailors wont to do, for she is the Lady of the Waters, among other things. I will gladly speak to you of her later, should you wish."

"Speak on and on," said Holos. "Not that one ever minds, my lady." He gave her a short bow. The group turned from the docks onto a broad cobblestone street that ran straight ahead for some distance, rising gradually.

The woman Arana only laughed. "Know, Mistress Na, that wizards and priests are ever rivals in Tesra. I know not how it is where you were born."

"There are no priests there," Im put in. "Nor gods, really."

Holos raised an eyebrow at that bit of information. "Know also," said he, "that the priests and wizards of Tesra work together, whatever little disagreements may arise at times. We face a powerful mutual enemy."

"Of whom we would as soon not speak right now, Lord Holos. Our guests need hospitality first, food and rest and talk of pleasant things."

"Indeed so, Mec Arana."

Buildings of two or three stories rose on either side, mostly of stone. Na thought some were stone but the stones were small and evenly shaped and reddish-brown in color. She had never seen such. Windows were few but doors were wide. Warehouses, she decided. Buildings for storage looked much the same in Phamahd as they did in Pas as they did in Hirstel.

These thinned out as they progressed, giving way to shops. I should pay attention, she scolded herself. Holos is gabbing away and I'm letting my mind wander. I'm surprised he and the priestess don't use litters. This is getting to be a long walk.

Demons would have borne her litter back in Hirstel. She missed being able to easily call them up, to have them serve in whatever capacity her whims required. It just didn't work in this world. Not without more effort than made it worthwhile.

"My villa is on this hill," Holos was saying, as they turned to the left, up a steeper side-street. "Naught but a little place I stay when visiting Phamahd."

"Ain't been here in years, I thinks," muttered a hoarse voice. Na glanced to see Im's new attendant close behind her. She dropped back even with him.

"We may need to depend on your knowledge of such things, my friend," she whispered to him. "Im did well to choose you."

The weathered face gleamed at the compliment. "And I was thankful of the chance he give me. Zerc is gettin' too old for the sea."

Zerc. Yes, Na had heard the name used. She couldn't resist confiding, "You know the boy has no money to pay you." Nor did she, for that matter.

A chortle from Zerc. "Friends in high places is good enough promise. None higher 'n those two." He nodded toward Arana and Holos. "Save the prince himself."

Im walked between those two powerful Tesrans, chatting with them about who knew what? He was proving the better politician than she, at least on this day. Their path wound up a hillside. Low houses stood here and there, most somewhat hidden by ornamental trees. No walls. Maybe that was considered unneighborly. Or unsightly, she decided on a second thought.

"The captain's place is somewheres up here," Zerc told her. "He's made his fortune, he has. Mak is sharp."

A pathway led between two spreading trees, not overly tall. A few pink blossoms showed among the dark glossy leaves. Late in the season for them, Na thought. Not so long ago she would have had no knowledge of such things, not trees and flowers, not seasons. A sprawling house of roughly dressed stone, but one story tall, appeared beyond a garden and small pool. Water lilies floated, as did a pair of ducks. Na doubted the fowl had any purpose other than ornamentation. It was growing dark, the sun disappearing behind the hills, the long shadows becoming one great shadow. Flickering golden light shown through the windows ahead.

Glass! She had not seen glass windows since leaving Hirstel, not even in Pas nor the shrine of Banat. Tesra went up a notch in her regard.

One of the servants who had accompanied them from town, one of Holos's men, Na assumed, edged close to Zerc. "Come with me, mate, and I'll show you where you can get a meal." He gave Na a wink. "I'll take good care of him, my lady."

"Just get him back to us later. To Master Im."

"Will do." The man gave something of a sketchy salute and led the sailor away. Na suspected he and his fellows might want to pump the sailor for information about them. Many of the group had already dispersed to wherever they belonged. With those who remained, Na entered through bronze double doors. There were figures of some sort on their surface, in shallow relief, but it had grown too dark to make them out.

"You will remain the night, Mec?" she heard Holos ask.

"I must return to my sisters at the shrine," the priestess replied. "You may have the honor of feeding me first, sir." She threw back her hood now and Na got her first real look at the woman. Arana could certainly have stepped from the streets of her own city. Older than Na. Well, no, she couldn't tell with a Tesran. Most were not so long-lived as her people. This she had learned from Holos, and from books. Na might actually be her elder but the high priestess would be thought of late middle-age in Hirstel. Golden hair, turning gray, hung curling about a face as dark as hers or Im's, and with the heaviness of the brow typical of their race.

The wizard Holos turned to a robed man standing attentively at his elbow. "We will have a light supper in, oh, a quarter of an hour. Please show our guests where they may freshen themselves. And these two," he said, with an amiable nod of his head toward the Hirstelites, "are those who are to stay with us. Their rooms are ready?"

"They are, sir." He waved a subordinate forward, only to be distracted by noise from outside.

"There's a cart with a big bronze statue out here," said a man who came to the door. "Should we put it somewhere?"

Holos's steward gave his master a questioning look. "Anywhere," said the wizard. "The stables. No, let me get a look at it first." Na and Im followed him out.

Holos gave the golden statue a moment's sharp scrutiny. "There is more here than meets the eye, I think. Is it safe to leave it overnight?"

"It is," stated Im, and turned to speak to the seeming inert image. "Stay put till morning and we'll work things out then," he said. Holos did not appear overly surprised by this.

"Morning then," agreed Holos as he led them back into his house, "when Arana is well away from here."

"And we've had a good night's rest," Na murmured. She didn't know whether Holos heard nor did she even care.

10.

A GOOD NIGHT'S REST INDEED had Na, in the widest, softest, most comfortable bed she had known since leaving Hirstel. Last night was mostly a fog—a light meal, some inconsequential conversation, an early bedtime. Things would become more serious today. Of that she was certain.

She did not realize how soon that would be.

Darkness outside. What had awakened her? A noise? No doubt there were many noises in a house such as this, servants about their duties while others slept. Ah, she might as well get up. Na went to one of the two narrow windows, peered out through diamond-shaped panes of distorting, rippled glass. Rosy light along the horizon. That must be eastward. The sea, the docks. This house was not so high, but high enough she could see the town laid out in the half-light, spreading down to those docks.

Behind her then lay the high hills, and Tesra on their other side. Beyond Tesra, what? Somewhere far to the west lay the realm of the Wizard-Lord, Torut.

Figures moved below her. Furtive figures, keeping to shadow and concealment. Three perhaps? And skulking toward the chief wizard's house. She should tell someone. Im was in the next room; that she knew. Na ran and pounded on his door, then tried the latch. Not locked. She burst into the room.

Almost did she laugh when Zerc sat up in the bed, bewildered and blurry-eyed. "Where's Im?"

"Dunno." The sailor's eyes swept to a pallet by the wall. "He was sleepin' on the mat over there."

It was like the boy to let the old man have the bed. Im was a good kid. He must be up and out already. "There is mischief afoot. Keep an eye out and warn your master if he returns."

To his credit, Zerc became alert and rolled from his covers at once. What he did after that, Na did not know for already she stood in the hall again, trying to decide on a direction. How did one get out of this rambling house?

Hmm, they reached Im's room first last night so they came from that way. Was anyone else awake?

"There's the boy," someone hissed from the gloom ahead of her.

"Him first," came a croak of a reply. "That's the orders. And take the woman alive if we can."

Na stepped into what she recognized as Holos's banquet room. Im sat at a table, an ample breakfast before him. She might have known! The backs of three shrouded men were to her; they spread out, knives in hands.

"Im!" she cried in warning, and then, "Help! Help!" as loudly as she might. Did Holos keep guards here? Were there any defenses at all? Maybe she could pull something from somewhere—

Im had been a step ahead, there. Shadow at once enveloped him. But these assassins seemed to know of such tricks and continued to creep calmly upon the place the young wizard had stood—and stood still.

Something brushed by Na, something large, something fast. Something red. It made not a sound as it fell on the trio. Skilled though they might have been with the knife, they proved no match for the sudden and unexpected onslaught of an eight foot tall demon. Even a demon whose powers were noticeably diminished in this world.

Yes, of course it was Qu'orthseth. You knew it would show up eventually, didn't you? And in time to save our heroes; that you should have suspected as well! Now stop interrupting during the exciting parts.

Qu'orthseth careened into his first assailant, knocking him heavily to the ground. The next turned, brandishing his knife, while the third plunged into the wizard-drawn shadow, intent on completing his mission. Na ran toward him with no idea what she might do.

The demon had its man by the neck, lifting him from the ground even as he slashed at the smooth, shining, red skin of the thick arm. In a second or three he slashed no more but hung limply. Qu'orthseth flung the body aside. Bits of ichor rolled down its arm. Na was not certain whether the demon actually felt pain. She did know such wounds were of no great matter to it.

The shadows Im had raised were already dispersing. The assassin lay sprawled on the floor, a knife protruding from his chest. "He came rushing blindly right into my shadows," the youth explained, a bit sheepishly. "Practically all I had to do was hold the knife out in front of me."

At that moment, Holos appeared at the other end of the room, accompanied by a younger robed man. Na sensed he was a wizard as well, too caught up in the moment to guard himself. A pair of men carrying broad-bladed spears followed. The chief wizard gave the room and its contents a quick survey. "The wards I had set in this place told me there was a demon about."

"They would be more useful if they warned you of assassins," remarked Na. It might have come out a little more sharply than she had intended.

"They should have," was the wizard's reply. His eyes returned to the great red creature in the center of his dining room. "Akorzef, isn't it? So it was you they hauled across the Greater Sea."

"We call it Qu'orthseth. And there are reasons, sir," piped up Im. "We'll explain later if you wish."

"We need an easier name for the big guy," Na suddenly decided. "Or big thing. I'm going to call you Cory from now on."

"As you wish," came the incredibly low-pitched groan of a voice from somewhere within the demon's body. "Men could not pronounce my true name anyway. Not without damage to themselves."

Yes, Cory had a sense of humor though one might not guess it at first. And its expression never gave anything away, in that it had no face.

"I like it," agreed Im. "Cory you shall be. Now who were these people with knives?" He looked over the bodies. "Tesrans?"

"They were speaking Zikem to each other, not Tesran," Na suddenly realized. "Isn't that one alive?" She pointed toward the first Qu'orthseth had crashed into. He lay groaning on the carpet.

The younger wizard squatted beside him, felt here and there. "Several broken bones," he reported. "Ribs busted up pretty bad and probably the same inside. I doubt he makes it."

"Not that he could tell anything worthwhile," said Holos, pondering the assassin's form. "Well, get him out of here. Give him drugs to make his passage more easy, if you will." He turned away and seemingly gave the man no further thought. "Let us breakfast outside while they clean up in here. You can tell me all about your friend, ah, Cory, here."

11.

"I SENSED THE DANGER AS they entered the compound but it takes some little time to regain my form. As you know."

Na and Im did know. The demon had once demonstrated the process for them. It had to unfold, so to speak, from the compact shape in which they had brought it here. Like a bud opening into a blossom they had joked, and that was not so far from the truth.

"And you are under some geas to protect Im?" asked Holos, helping himself to another sweet pastry.

A subterranean chuckle erupted from the crimson monster. "It is under a geas to slay me," stated Im. "But if—"

"When," corrected the demon.

"Yes, when it fulfills this duty, it will be whisked back immediately to its home world." The young wizard grinned at Qu'orthseth. "A place it does not at all wish to be."

"Only prison to be looked forward to," it admitted.

"And the police of its world would very much like that, so they are trying to kill me."

Na had to snicker. "He's an impediment to justice."

"My sort are sticklers for such things," said Qu'orthseth.

"So Cory here is going to protect me and remain free. But it has to at least give lip service to the idea of killing me some day."

"In the meantime," said Na, "it seems your Wizard-Lord had made some sort of arrangement with the demon magistrates. He wants us dead too." She frowned. No, Torut wanted Im dead. These intruders were supposed to capture her if they could. This she did not understand so she said nothing of it.

Holos nodded and made no comment for a while, sipping a hot fragrant drink and staring into the distance. "We must ask the governor to assign some soldiers for our journey back to the city," he said at last. "I did not realize the agents of Torut had grown so bold."

"When Holos asks, others see it as a command," spoke the Mec Arana, stepping out onto the veranda. "Do bring me a plate," she told a servant and took a seat between Na and Im. "And you two must tell your story, now we are all here. The complete story." Her eyes went to the red demon. "It should prove interesting."

So they did. It took the whole of the morning and truly hit only the high points of their experiences. Holos, to be sure, had some of the tale already, mostly from speaking afar with Na. Qu'orthseth stood unspeaking, seemingly oblivious, throughout.

Recharging, most likely, thought Na. Connecting with the sun of its own world. She wondered whether it had been able to when diminished to a seeming statue. Did it even need any energy in that form?

But whether 'asleep' as it was now, or as a statue, it remained aware of Im and any dangers to the boy. It had bells, so to speak, attached to him. Cory was only a demon and such are not greatly skilled, as a rule, but it had some magic.

The morning had been clear and somewhat cool. Now it was quite pleasant; certainly much better than the weather they had met on their crossing of the sea. "I shall go into town after our lunch to arrange some things," said Holos, when their tale was finished. "You are welcome to come or remain here to rest."

"Off to Tesra tomorrow, then?" asked the high priestess.

"I should hope so. That will be convenient, Mec?"

"Quite. I'd as soon be home." She rose, saying, "I must arrange things at the shrine and shall be ready to go in the morning. A most interesting story," she said to Na and Im, gave a nod, and swept into the house.

"The Mec Arana is accustomed to command, is she not?" asked Na.

"Too accustomed, perhaps," agreed Holos. "We've been eating all morning, have we not? What say we forgo lunch here and be on our way? The governor might well feed us if we get there soon enough!" He gave his two guests a quick looking over. "Those clothes will do."

"They'd better," said Im. "We've scarcely any others."

"Hmm. Then we should shop as well. No need to worry about money. The prince is paying. Ah, here is our escort."

The escort included four carrying spears and with short swords on their belts. They did not look much like fighters to Na but were undoubtedly better than nothing. "What of Cory?" she asked. "I don't think it could accompany us, Im."

"And I'm sure it will not approve of me going into town without it."

"But we can not have a great red demon stalking the streets of Phamahd," felt Holos, stroking his beard in a most thoughtful manner. Na had decided this was an affectation.

"Then I'll stay," Im decided, dropping back into his chair. "Ho, Zerc, fall out."

The sailor turned attendant had unobtrusively slipped into the group of servitors and guards. "You do need some new clothes, sir, if y' don't mind me sayin' so."

He's already badgering the boy, thought Na, with an inner smile. Just what he needs.

"We'll let Na pick them out." The matter decided to his satisfaction, he yawned and closed his eyes.

I know exactly the person to help me with that, thought Na, and her inner smile grew wider. Without further word, Holos began walking and the entourage followed, carefully giving the seemingly inert form of Qu'orthseth a wide berth before continuing around the house and toward the trees arched over the entryway. She hurried to catch up and walk beside the sorcerer.

Apparently there would be no litters again. Said Holos when she reached his side, "We shall have to deal with your demon—Im's demon, no?" She nodded only. "Im's demon, in the future."

"It is usually good at hiding itself," she told the wizard. They could worry about that later. She was more interested in where they were right now. This Phamahd was a good sized place. Almost as large as Hirstel, the city of her birth, felt Na. Spread out, which gave an illusion of size, but with none of the tall and massive buildings that rose above that lost home of her people.

"You were unhappy the priestess Arana saw Cory, weren't you?" asked Na.

Holos gave her a tight smile. "So you can read me, Lady Na? Indeed, I would rather she had not known of it. Not yet."

"Surely she can be trusted?"

"I have, ah, misgivings about the mec. Not suspicions, you understand. We are rivals, in some degree." His momentary frown meant only that he was gathering his thoughts. Na knew this by now. "And there are differences in our attitudes, the way we see things. Arana is aristocratic, you might say, though there is no official aristocracy in Tesra."

"And you are not." She voiced it as a statement, not a question.

"My birth is somewhat more humble." A note of pride slipped into Holos's statement. That was understandable enough from a man who had risen to chief wizard. A small vice and one Na felt entirely willing to overlook.

"The governor's house lies over there," Holos continued, pointing out a dome rising above the warehouses. "We should turn up this street. He expects us. He expects me, I should say."

"Surely he would know Im and I arrived," replied Na. Any man in charge would be kept aware of such things.

"To be sure, to be sure," said the wizard, adding to his thoughtful expression by both slowly nodding and stroking his beard. "I would think the admiral would be there as well. His galley is in the bay."

Na followed his gaze toward the water but the ships lying there looked all the same to her. "This admiral does not remain here?"

"The bulk of the fleet is stationed at Robon, further south. That's a more suitable harbor."

Na did not bother to ask why. Holos went on after a pause. "Tesra does not maintain a large presence in the Greater Sea."

"You have an inland sea."

"Three of them, in fact. Ah, here we are." They stood before the governor's palace. It was not nearly as impressive seen close up, not at all comparable to the monumental towers of Hirstel. It didn't even rival the shrine of Banat, across the sea. Holos surveyed his followers. "No need for you to loiter about here. Feel free to amuse yourselves for an hour or so. Yes, you too," he told his four bodyguards when they seemed to hesitate.

"I am sure I needn't have brought any of them along. Let us go in." Na followed him through the arched entry. There seemed to be quite a few arches in Tesran architecture. The building itself was undoubtedly stone, but with a skin of white stucco.

A steward took charge of them at once. As they followed the servant down a barrel-vaulted passageway, Holos leaned in, whispering, "Don't be surprised at the deference I receive here. I am considered an important man."

Na thought to make an answer, but held it in. Yes, she knew he was important. More than that—powerful. One of the most powerful people in all the Tesran realm. Second only to the reigning prince himself, it had been hinted.

But the priestess Arana was powerful too. Na could recognize that. She'd only wanted to come here to learn, not to become involved in politics. But she had best learn as much as she could as quickly as she could about that too. The governor, a large man with a bland face, rose to greet them. He was as dark as Im and Na, and had their blond hair. This Tesran could have walked the streets of Hirstel.

Though graying now, Holos had been dark haired. His beard had some iron to it still. "Governor Azil, I present my guest Na, just arrived from across the Great Sea."

"Lady Na." The voice was deep and mellifluous. Azil gave her a grave bow but his face revealed nothing. "And may I present Admiral Mursoazes."

A small, squint-eyed man, with a great unruly beard streaked with gray, sprawled in a well-cushioned chair. His loose turban of blue silk sat lopsided on his head. "Captain Mak told me of you," spoke the sailor. "Quite an eventful voyage, I understand. I welcome you to Tesra, my lady. Holos! Rarely do events budge you from your comfortable haunts in Tesra."

"Rarely have we such guests. I felt the need to greet Na and her companion."

"A boy, I understand?" asked the ambassador, motioning them toward seats. Liveried servants appeared at once with pitchers and goblets and trays of food.

Holos propped his ever-present staff against the closest wall. "Yes, just a boy," agreed the wizard. "They are of an, um, isolated nation who fled the Valley of Visions as did our own ancestors."

"True *nanem* then," mused Azil. The unfamiliar word seemed to make no impression on Holos but Na noted Mursoazes's quick scowl. Nanem? The word literally meant a group of wanderers. It surely had some other implication to these men.

The remainder of their luncheon passed in polite and impersonal conversation. Gossip, it must be admitted, and most of it meaning little to Na. Nor did the meal hold much interest for her; Stewmeat had served as tasty fare on their recent voyage. There was meat, perhaps from some fowl, and fish. She hesitated but decided there was no harm in having a little.

There were likely to be many meals set before her in Tesra. She couldn't refuse everything not to her liking, could she? And if she kept her mouth full she wouldn't have to talk.

This meal was nothing more than a courtesy, Na decided, expected when important men were in town. She wished an important woman were about, too. Arana's presence might have been welcome, to relieve some of the tedium.

She took another overly-sweet pastry and pretended to pay attention.

12.

"I'll walk down to the docks with you," said Mursoazes as the three stepped from the government house.

A brisk, cool breeze swept up the street from the gulf. "This should revive me," remarked Na. "I fear the governor's voice was putting me to sleep."

The admiral chuckled. "Azil says a great deal of nothing, very beautifully."

"That is his job," said Holos, somewhat more soberly.

"He governs, what, this city?" asked Na. "This port?"

"All Tesra's seacoast, all the land that lies on this side of the hills, down to the edge of the Great Sea. That's where Mursoazes takes over."

"Or the Greater Sea. Those who sail it name it so, for we know the Lesser Sea, aye, and other seas as well." The admiral gave Holos a grin. "Those who call their landlocked puddles seas know no better."

These two were surely old friends. There would be time enough to learn of such things, or it might not matter after this day.

"Some in Tesra call it the Eastern Sea," said Holos. "Most know it only by repute. The city's eyes have ever turned the opposite direction."

They were not passing down the wide central street of Phamahd but a narrower alley a couple blocks north of that way, shadowed by warehouses. There were only a few small doors, most shut. Rear entries, Na supposed. No large wagons would be passing through here.

Yes, I see some of you shaking your heads now and telling yourselves what a fool that Holos is. Dismissing his guards? Passing through dark alleys? I can only say that the wizard, despite his venerable age, was woefully ignorant of such dangers. Allow him to err, my friends, and me to continue.

From a darkened doorway stepped two hooded men. Na at once looked back over her shoulder to see another pair emerge behind them to cut off any escape. She was getting too good at knowing what to expect.

The men drew short swords, blades readily concealed under their cloaks. She felt for her knife. Did Holos even carry a weapon? The admiral's own short sword had hung openly at his side. Now he held it ready.

Na suspected pulling in concealing shadow would work no better than it had with Im's would-be assassins this morning. Im—did they realize he wasn't with them? Was she the target?

No more time to think. Holos abruptly raised a hand. A stream of liquid, seemingly coming from thin air, shot toward those who stood in their path. Alas, it fell short to form a hissing, steaming puddle in the middle of the street.

Acid from some other world. The wizard must know of such places to draw upon in need. Maybe he should have practiced more with them. The advancing men grinned and advanced further, cautiously, not rushing. Ah, to have a demon to call upon! Na would have made short work of this back in Hirstel.

Hirstel, the world she knew best. She reached into it and found a sword, just where she remembered it hanging. It was an old weapon, made of bronze, brought to that world by her ancestors. There had been little use for swords in the city since then. Without a moment's hesitation, Na charged the men before her, swinging the weapon.

No, she knew nothing of sword-fighting but the concept was simple enough. One hit ones opponent with the sharp edge! They ducked, as she had expected, rather than fight. These men, as those earlier, might well have orders to take her alive.

A clash of metal behind her. Mursoazes had engaged one of their assailants. The sorceress wheeled about, ready to charge again—or should she run for it? The way was open.

No more than a moment did she consider it before running in again, blade swinging. And then not swinging as it disappeared from her grasp, pulled back to Hirstel. Na had not at all expected that to happen so quickly and almost fell, thrown suddenly off balance. One of the men grabbed, got her about the waist, began to drag her toward an open doorway. She glimpsed Holos with his back to a wall, defending himself rather expertly with his staff, and Mursoazes hurrying toward the group. He must have dealt with his man.

Shouts from down the street. The sound of running feet? Na heard her captor curse under his breath. "Kill the wizard!" he cried. "Quickly! The other doesn't matter!" His attention was too fully on the fight and on whoever was coming toward them. It should have been on the woman he held.

Na's sword might be lost but she remembered her knife. The man hadn't even bothered to pin her arms. She slipped it from the sheath within her robe and slipped it as quickly into the encircling arm. He howled, releasing her and backing away. With an oath, he sprang through the open door. Na turned to see the other attackers running as well. All save one who sprawled in the street, the red pooling beneath him.

"Ah, Tuthinos!" called out Holos. "You made good time."

The assistant wizard stepped forward. The four guardsmen and a pair of other attendants stood there. "Only because we were fortunately nearby, sir." There might have been a ring of disapproval in his voice.

Na recognized what had happened at once. "You called him from afar as soon as those men appeared, didn't you?" she asked Holos.

"That I did. And, indeed, it was fortunate they were near." He turned to the admiral. "I don't suppose there would be a chance of catching the others, would there, Murso?"

"Doubtful. They'll be well away before we could rouse any

wardens." He contemplated the body lying on the cobblestones. "We will have to explain him to someone."

"Not the first body you've left lying, my friend," replied Holos. Na was more than willing to believe this. "I wonder how they knew we were coming through here."

"A spy in the governor's house, maybe?" conjectured Mursoazes.

"Maybe." He gave Na a long look. "And they hoped to capture you, my lady."

"As did the ones this morning," she told him.

"Indeed? Ah, well, that's no puzzle we'll solve standing here. Let's get on down to the docks. One of you men stay with the body until we can tell someone about it." Without further word, Holos started off.

Mursoazes and Na had no choice but to follow after, the rest of the entourage behind them. Then, a voice from afar. "Hold up," she called out. "It's Xit. Xido, I mean. Do you want to join us, Holos?"

The wizard nodded. A moment later, both were in a room somewhere in another world. Not only was the god Xido there, but the young prophetess Atima and Im as well.

Well, here she is, said Im. He glanced at Holos but made no comment.

Xido chuckled. *These two want some privacy, though I must remain with them for their safety. For Atima's safety, anyway.* He regarded the girl for a moment. They all remembered how mad Torut had nearly destroyed her mind when they had once spoken like this. *I will leave this shrine soon and wished to give them a chance to talk first.*

But you'll go back, right? Im asked.

As I promised. There is much yet Atima may learn. First though, I wished to make sure all was well with you. You needn't stay in Tesra, you know.

Atima perked up at that. She would very much like to have her Im back beside her.

We're going to see it through, proclaimed Im, adding with a lopsided grin, *We've only had one attempted assassination since arriving.*

Two, Na told him. *We were just attacked in the street.*

And I must hear of all of this in time, spoke the dark god. *But now, knowing you are alive and reasonably well, I think we should give Atima and Im their time together. Holos, take good care of them.* Xido gave them a nod of dismissal.

A moment later, Na and Holos were facing each other in the streets of Phamahd.

13.

"Your sword appeared to be of bronze," said Mursoazes, "though I but caught a glance of it. Pulled from another world, I assume."

"You know of wizardly ways?" Na asked.

Holos smiled. "All Tesrans are familiar with wizards. Furthermore, Murso is a wizard himself, though he is more adept at sailing a ship."

The sailor grinned in return. "I'm not even very good at that speaking from afar you find so easy. Pulling weapons from another world?" He shook his head, somewhat theatrically.

"It was from my world," said Na. "The world from which I came. There were no iron weapons in Hirstel. None I ever saw."

"That makes sense," spoke Holos. "Our ancestors arrived at Tesra carrying weapons of bronze. They knew nothing of iron when they left the Valley of Visions, nor did any of the peoples then thinly scattered around the Sea of Sanctuary."

"Those still used tools of polished stone, it is said," spoke up Tuthinos. "There are examples in our museum."

"Yes, you will have to visit it. Tuthinos here is a bit of an historian. He must take you."

The younger wizard gave her an embarrassed smile but went on. "The mining and smelting of iron was introduced to us from the Bazu of the south."

"So it seems," put in Mursoazes. "From whom the Bazu learned the art, we know not. Some say the Ildin carried it with them from wherever they originated, and the Bazu brought it across the sea."

Holos gave her a broad wink. "The dwarfs like to claim they are responsible but few believe them." The wizard knew of her past troubles with dwarfs.

"I wouldn't," sniffed Na. "Are there always so many ships in the harbor?" She surveyed the vessels crowding around the docks. The water sparkled beyond them; though the breeze was cool the sun rode in a cloudless sky.

"In for the winter," Mursoazes told her. "The ports will be closing down some with its onslaught. I doubt I venture beyond the gulf myself."

"That's Mak's vessel, isn't it? I'd like to see him before we leave."

"So we shall, my lady," said Holos. "Then, let us repair to the street of tailors and outfit you and Im."

Said Mursoazes, "I'll come along to the docks. It's on my way." A grin split his homely weathered face. "And you two may need my sword again."

"Those were naught more than common ruffians," scoffed the chief wizard. "Certainly not skilled in the ways of assassination and abduction."

"Except maybe the leader, he who grabbed Lady Na. Here we part. Give my greetings to Captain Mak." The admiral gave Na a slight bow and rolled off, up the docks.

Mak's ship lay tied up at the end of the quay on which they stood. "We'll await you," said Holos.

Na walked out to it and looked the vessel over. A handful of men were on deck, busy about their tasks. Getting everything squared away for winter, she realized. No more sailing for them until the seasons changed. For a moment, she wished she could sail back across the sea right this moment, leave the politics of Tesra behind before she became further enmeshed.

"Lady Na!" Captain Mak stood near the prow, on the raised deck there. "Come aboard! Have you need of something?" he asked as he stepped down and strode toward her.

Na crossed the gangway to him. "Only to say goodbye to you and to give you our thanks, once more, and, um, maybe to steal one of your crew."

The captain raised an eyebrow at this. "Another?"

"For me this time, not Im. There is a certain boy who might make good attendant."

Mak tilted his head at her. "And would jump at the chance to accompany Im?"

She smiled. "Even so, Captain."

"There is little for Tau to do around here for the next two or three months. No sense in him sitting idle." He turned toward his crew, hesitated and then turned back. "If he does wish to go with you, that is."

Na only nodded. "Ho, Tau! Come join us." The young man left whatever business he had with a coil of rope and hurried to them, perhaps more so than necessary. He gave the pair a salute but spoke not, as his eyes went from one to the other.

"Would you like a job?" Na asked at once.

"It's okay with me, boy," added Mak.

"My personal attendant on my trip to Tesra," the wizardess went on, "and perhaps after."

Tau looked at both again and nodded. He was perhaps attempting not to seem too eager.

Na intended to keep things business-like as well. "Get your things then and come with me. I need your help shopping this afternoon."

14.

"WHICH HORSE WOULD YOU PREFER, my lady?"

Na regarded the tall beasts with some alarm. "We've never ridden before. Neither of us."

"Not even in a cart," added Im. "There are no large animals where we came from." Carts, drawn by oxen, stood waiting among the assembling travelers. These seemed for the transporting of luggage rather than people.

Holos regarded the pair thoughtfully. He does that awfully well, Na told herself. It took an effort not to crack a smile. "The Mec Arana travels in a litter," he said. "Perhaps we can find ones for you."

"So we move only as fast as her litter bearers? We might as well walk then." She winked at Im. "We've plenty of practice at that."

"Too much practice," declared the boy, laughing, before eyeing the horses once more. "I should learn to ride someday."

"But this journey is certainly not the time for it. Is your demon about?" asked the chief wizard of Tesra.

Im shrugged. "Somewhere. It may show itself once we get out of town. Are we waiting for the priestess?"

"She'll join us further up the road. Her goddess' shrine is in the hills above the town." Holos looked up the road toward those hills. "We might as well get moving then. I'll walk with you for now." He gave the signal to proceed along their way, the wide central boulevard of Phamahd that ran from harbor to hills and beyond.

Half a dozen soldiers had joined their party, those Holos had requested of the governor. Apparently some business had been accomplished on their visit yesterday. Half a dozen—these Tesrans, as her people back in Hirstel, employed a sensible system of numbers based on twelve. For some reason the Ildin insisted on using ten, despite its awkwardness.

Na's attention went back to their road. Its smooth gray surface of fitted stones lay as far as she could see ahead. "Is this road paved all the way to Tesra?"

"It is. All the major ways are so."

"At least we won't be eating the dust of your horse," commented Im.

Na could readily agree with the sentiment. "We had enough of that on our previous journeys. All the Ildin roads were dirt, even the ones between the ports."

"We have our share of those, too," the chief wizard assured them, laughing. "But there are two good stone-paved ways between Tesra and the Great Sea, this and the road that runs to Robon. That is a shorter path across the hills but passes over higher and more rugged terrain."

"So trade goes this way," concluded Im.

No doubt, thought Na. The subject did not much interest her at the moment. "That must be Arana ahead."

"Yes. The shrine of Fasenais lies among the hills up that way." Holos gestured somewhat northward.

"We should learn more of your Tesran gods," said Im. "Do they show themselves much?"

"Almost never. If you ignore them they will be likely to ignore you. Hail, Lady Arana!"

A modest entourage accompanied the priestess. Of males there were four who bore her litter and another four who probably alternated at this duty. Another drove an oxcart. The rest were women whom Na assumed to be priestesses of lesser rank. Six of them followed in Arana's wake, in enveloping robes of a dark blue. Or were they more green?

She gave thanks for the warm cloak and hood she had purchased yesterday. It was cold yet this morning and Na doubted it would be better in the heights before them. Arana's party fell into their column and all continued westward.

Despite Xido's warnings, there would be no hurrying on this journey. They shared the way with a fair amount of other traffic, most headed the same direction as they, wagons carrying goods toward Tesra. The creaking of the many wheels, the clopping of hooves on stone, was at first an annoyance but faded after a time.

Im leaned in and whispered, "How soon do you think till the great wizard takes to his horse?"

"Soon," she whispered back. "Before lunch, certainly." Na doubted Holos had the stamina for a long walk. He now ambled along beside the Mec Arana's litter, conversing but probably of nothing of importance. "I wonder how our sailors will hold up."

The two Hirstelites' newly acquired attendants walked close behind them now. Im looked back over his shoulder, asking, "Have either of you been to Tesra?"

Tau shook his head. "Once," answered Zerc. "Musta been, um, seven, eighteen years back. Went along with a cartload of goods." He raised his eyes toward the road ahead. "As I recall, the highest ridges was near the coast. Crossed 'em the first day or so." The old sailor screwed his face up as he strove to retrieve the past. "I remember it all takin' a week maybe."

"I've heard eight days from the other attendants," Tau added to this.

A week. Na had to think for a moment, as the concept of weeks had not existed in Hirstel. They had no use in that city which measured time only by the phases of the moon that stood above the unchanging desert. But a Tesran week was six days. She was pretty sure of that. The Ildin they had lived with the past months used a different count.

Tau broke into her momentary reverie. "I think I spied your

monster over to our left. The sun was reflecting from something red anyway." Unlike Zerc, the young sailor had not yet actually seen Qu'orthseth, save as a statue. It was to be sure he would have heard plenty of tales from the other servants.

Im shrugged at the news. "I assumed it was somewhere near."

Na surveyed the barren hills but could not pick out the demon. "We may need to share our lodging with it tonight," she warned. "Wherever that might be."

"There are caravansaries along the way, my lady," came a voice at her elbow. She turned to see Holos's assistant, Tuthinos. "I suspect my master will wish to stop at one we reach by the mid-afternoon." The man smirked oh so slightly. "Or the Lady Arana will bid him to."

"And he does what the priestess says?"

"Within reason. Lord Holos knows what battles to fight and which to avoid."

As should we all, said Na only to herself. She hoped Im had learned that. He could learn from Tuthinos, maybe. The sorcerer appeared to be somewhere around her own age but she suspected he might be younger. Whatever his years, he must be capable to be in the service of the chief wizard of Tesra.

Whether he was talented was another question. That might not be of much importance to Holos. Hmm, not so hard on the eyes either. Such daydreams were probably as good a way as any to distract her from the boredom of this journey. Yes, boring already and they had not even stopped yet for lunch.

But a lunch came and went, and they walked on across the rounded featureless hills. Trees were few, small and twisted, standing in heather gone brown in this season. Na did hope things looked better on the other side of the range.

And no sign of their demon. Im's demon. She could make no

claims on it and knew it would not so much as look her direction were she in mortal trouble. Cory cared only about keeping Im alive.

Im had managed to do a pretty good job of that himself so far. Yes, and so had she. They had both handled themselves well recently. There was nothing wrong with admitting that. Holos had surely been impressed by Im's knifing of his assailant in the wizard's banquet room, even if both attempted to be casual about it.

And Cory—it was not the demon it had been. Still strong, to be sure, but its powers were somewhat diminished from what they had been in Hirstel, when it guarded the tower and spell-book of Piras Tindeval.

The caravansary in which they stopped—indeed, in the middle of the afternoon—felt familiar at least. Na had slept in places of similar design across the sea, a stockade, its inner walls lined with open sheds, surrounding a central courtyard. She depended on Zerc and Tau to find them a sleeping place. She had been too weary to bother and too weary to go spend any time with Holos or the mec. Maybe tomorrow. Or the day after.

As she slipped toward sleep, she heard a distant yipping, a yipping that turned into a high, piercing howl. More howling joined it.

Na sat up and listened. "Coyotes?" she hazarded.

Tau spoke up. "Jackals, most likely. We have no coyotes on this side of the sea."

"Y' ever seen a coyote, boy?" asked Zerc, who had been standing looking out into the night.

"Well, no, but I heard them howling. And there were skins in our cargo."

Na had no idea what a jackal was and felt no need to learn right then. She pulled her blanket about her and soon fell fully into sleep, on this first night on the road to Tesra.

15

"IT MIGHT HAVE BEEN EASIER to turn back into a statue," said Im.

Qu'orthseth had slipped in sometime during the night and now hovered, horizontal, among the open beams above them. The demon slowly righted itself as it floated down to the floor. "That I shall not do," was its only comment.

"Then, walk with us today or stay out of sight, as yesterday. It's up to you."

"Maybe best if these humans don't see me. Traveling over the hills is not difficult."

"Well, don't let the jackals get you," put in Na. "They were certainly carrying on last night." She joked, of course; no jackals would get near the demon, unless they were much larger beasts than she had been led to believe. And, too, Cory would not smell like prey to them. Maybe to a cow.

"Not jackals. Jackal-men. Ghalun."

That might have been surprising but Na was somewhat past being surprised by anything these days. "Holos should know of this," she said to Im. "Once we get moving again. I need some breakfast now."

They crossed the courtyard, where men busied themselves hitching oxen and otherwise preparing for departure, both members of their own party, and teamsters and traders heading one direction or the other. "A meal can be bought," Tau told them. He pointed across the enclosure. "There's a stall and kitchen over there."

"But Holos'll feed y' for free," added Zerc.

"In that we have no money we must take the second option," said Im, and laughed. "Unless we sell these fine new clothes." He pinched a fold of his long robe holding it out and pretending to examine the material. "High quality, I'm told."

"The best," stated Tau, who seemed uncertain how serious the young wizard might be. "I picked it out myself."

"I shoulda gone," growled Zerc. "Got y' somethin' more practical." He turned and scowled at his comrade. "Remember I'm Master Im's man, youngster."

Tau took this with good nature, having no trouble recognizing the older sailor was not completely serious. He could have pointed out that he also chose the coat Zerc was wearing; Na was pleased he chose not to. After all, Tau was her man and aught he did reflected on her.

"Cory's disappeared," noted Im. For an eight foot tall red demon, Cory was exceptionally good at being unobtrusive. The half-light of dawn probably helped there, as well as a fair amount of fog.

The fog seemed even thicker by the time they took to the road. Holos had taken to his horse from the first this day. Still, he had to hold himself to the pace of those who walked. The wizard appeared nervous, moving back and forth, up and down the column of travelers.

He saluted them once and moved on. Na would catch him later. As she watched him ride to speak to the three soldiers bringing up their rear, Im spoke. "What led you to take on Tau as a retainer?"

Na had rehearsed an answer in her head, knowing Im would bring it up sooner or later. "He proved himself valiant and resourceful at sea. Smart, too, I think, and he feels a certain loyalty toward you."

"That may not be such a good thing," Im observed.

Na had to agree with that, though she wasn't about to say so. "Also, his, ah, preferences might keep him from making some stupid male mistakes about our relationship." Her eyes went to the young man, walking beside Zerc a few yards ahead of them. Having him in her service might make her life simpler but complicate Im's.

She had recognized that from the start—and rather liked the idea.

The sorceress dismissed any second thoughts. Tau was her attendant now and that was that.

Holos came riding back their direction. He reined in as Na raised a hand in greeting. He's a pretty good rider, isn't he? she thought, though she knew little of such things. "Good morning to you, my friends," spoke the sorcerer. "I've been neglecting you, I know, even though you are the reason I left the comforts of Tesra!"

"Then walk with me a few minutes," she said.

He at once dismounted. "Give us some privacy, will you?" she whispered to Im, and then advanced to walk beside Holos. Her companion discreetly dropped back a little.

The wizard led his gray steed. It was not a particularly large horse, Na felt but, again, she knew little of horses. She was not even sure of its gender. At once, she filled him in on what Cory had told them.

"Ghalun," he mused. "Most certainly the work of the Wizard-Lord. The ghalun are not native to this area."

"Nor even this world, I would think."

"No." Holos seemed to be deep in thought for a little while. "I heard he had pulled some here to guard the gates he controls. The gates that lie within his realm."

"I know of only one gate in this world, and that is the one Xido brought us through."

"But you have seen ghalun before?"

"They occasionally would blunder through one of the ways that lead to Hirstel. There was nothing in our world they wanted so they left on their own." Na smirked slightly. "Or with just a bit of prodding. But how did they get here? Is there a gate nearby?"

"None particularly close. Their pack would need have traveled afoot some distance." Holos's voice took on a sudden edge. "I must send couriers to both Tesra and Phamahd immediately to alert them."

He looked ready to mount his horse at once and tend to it, but turned back to Na. "Torut wishes to kill Im, of course," he said. "What his intentions are toward you, I can not guess."

"Nor can I," she admitted. She could imagine all sorts of things but there was no use in indulging such phantasms. "Why destroy Im?"

"Im may be the one wizard in this world able to match, aye, and outstrip the Wizard-Lord. It's not in me, Na, and I doubt it is in even you, powerful as you are."

The sorceress knew the truth of this, as little as she liked to admit it. Im was the greatest talent she had ever known, in this world or their own. Even with his relative lack of training she doubted she could best him in most contests. "And Im has a grudge against Torut for what he did to Atima," she said. "I think that, more than aught else, decided him to make the journey to Tesra."

"To protect her?"

Na nodded. "He will surely return to her in time. I can not see Im remaining in your city."

"But perhaps you?"

She could only shrug. "Perhaps."

16.

"This gap is the highest point on our road," one of the teamsters assured them. No more than a couple hours past the noon it was. The hills stretched before them, as far as eye could see, blue and hazy. They were not really far up at all, Na realized. Perhaps not as high as the shrine of Banat nestled in the hills above the River Lantabee.

Soon they were noticeably descending into a valley that widened as they went. Trees grew more thickly than before though it would be a stretch to call the drab slopes forested. In this season, a few brown leaves yet hung on the branches. The road remained the same, wide, smooth, gray. Another caravansary lay not too far down that road.

"It looks like we're going to halt here," remarked Im.

"Fine with me," Na replied. "The sun seems to set early."

"Something to do with seasons. I don't completely understand it."

Neither did she but she didn't mind how the days varied constantly in this world. It reminded her that things happened here. Had she really been alive in Hirstel, with the languid unchanging days following one upon the other?

Cory slipped into their sleeping space early that evening. Walls stood between those spaces, affording them some privacy, so it need keep its distance only from the side open to the courtyard. In the darkness, the demon was unlikely to be glimpsed.

Zerc and Tau kept their distance, as well, and their silence. "The ghalun remain close," it reported. "They mean harm?"

"Harm to me," said Im.

"It does seem," Na added, "they were sent to kill him."

The great red creature stood quietly for a moment or two. With its lack of features—and little in the way of body language—it was impossible to say what it might be thinking. At last, "The police sent them?"

Im and Na looked at each other. They hadn't thought that through.

"Maybe," the sorceress allowed. "We think this Wizard-Lord, this Torut, called them here, but he could be working with your demon authorities."

"As he did before," said Im.

"Hmmm." It came as an almost impossibly low drone. "I could go hunt them but they are tricky little beasties. Best I stay close from now on, Master Im." A deep chuckle, like rocks grinding together. "I shall try not to scare the humans."

"Good luck with that," muttered Zerc.

Cory, however, did not join their party in the morning. It had already disappeared when Na awoke. "I can only guess that it plans to remain close, but hidden if possible," said Im. "Scouting, maybe."

That seemed logical enough. It might even be right. But hiding was surely becoming more difficult, for the countryside here was not so deserted as that they had passed before. Farms and villages lay along the road, inns and taverns. Places with four walls in addition to their roof.

It would be as difficult, Na realized, for the ghalun to hide here as the demon. An ambush seemed unlikely. An attack at night? She couldn't guess, but there were soldiers and caravansary walls, and Cory would certainly be close.

"We should be about halfway there, right?" she asked, addressing no one in particular.

She got a mumbled 'reckon so' from Zerc and a shrug from Im.

"I'll go ask around," volunteered Tau, who disappeared into the pre-dawn grayness. By the time they were ready to breakfast, he reappeared saying the consensus was a four day journey yet.

"You can perch on the back of one of the carts, if you want," he announced. "Now and again, to rest up a little. The drivers don't mind now that we're on an easier stretch of the road."

Na doubted she would. If those priestesses who attended Arana could walk all the way to Tesra, so could she. Though it could be noted that the mec's off-duty litter-bearers were not averse to hitching a ride! "Better take advantage of that yourselves, you and Zerc," she said. "I know you sailors aren't so used to walking."

"We should stay close to you," Zerc responded at once.

"Right," said Tau. "You're our responsibility."

Na could believe they did feel that way. They probably also saw Im and Na as their ticket to a better life; that was all right. A mix of self-interest and duty was more potent than either on its own.

That day and the next were without incident. Since crossing the highest hills their path carried them almost due west, though it wound about the hillsides. Farms lay here and there but for long stretches they saw only animals grazing on either side of the road. Some Na recognized, some she did not. Sheep, yes, those she knew, and the cattle. But long-necked creatures unlike any she had ever seen, with wooly coats, stared at them from some of the fields. Shepherds sometimes waved as they passed. Their dogs eyed them vigilantly.

"I think I want a dog," remarked Im as they passed another pair of black and white canines, expertly moving their flock.

"Cory would be jealous." Maybe Tau too. That she had best not say. "I'd rather have a cat." Several roamed the shrine of Banat. She'd become accustomed to their company.

"Too bad neither can talk in this world."

"The old books in Hirstel say they did not develop the capability until men took them there."

"Oh?" Im seemed surprised by this.

So there were things the boy didn't know. He hadn't had the opportunity to study deeply before they left their home. To study at all, really. She'd had many decades.

"Then it was another instance of magic coming too easily in

Hirstel. Maybe I should go roundabout through another world and see if I can look into the brains of one of those dogs."

"Dangerous," felt Na. "If you could do it at all." Sending a part of one through multiple worlds was perhaps the most difficult of all acts of sorcery. Most never mastered the skill. No, most never even attempted it.

"True enough." Im giggled. "It would help if the dog were also a wizard."

"Indeed! You know, we should practice such things more."

"How do you know I'm not?" The boy only snickered when she gave him a suspicious sidelong look.

Ah, there would be time to practice in Tesra and time to learn much more. Despite being one of the greatest sorcerers of Hirstel, Na had needed to relearn much in this world, a world where magic did not come so readily, where one could not call up a demon at any time to fulfill ones whims.

Calling a demon was more trouble than it was worth here. It was also quite unlikely to obey ones wishes. But Xido had taught them new ways of wizardry, the reaching into other worlds, the speaking from afar. As he was teaching Atima, prophetess and priestess of Banat, even now. Or would be. The god said he had somewhere to go first. She knew better than to pry into his business.

That evening, as they halted at yet another of the caravansaries—why did they all look identical?—they were told they would be climbing again tomorrow, crossing the last high ridge before descending toward the Sea of Sanctuary.

17

"Mines," Holos told them. "Silver and lead, mostly."

A torn and desolate land lay beside their road, pits here and there, some with men delving in them, others abandoned. "What sort of men do such work?" asked Na. She was wondering aloud as much as posing a question.

"Not slaves nor prisoners, if that is what you are thinking," replied the wizard. "Miners are wage-earners. Some have a stake in their operations."

Holos had remained surprisingly distant throughout this journey, occasionally walking and gossiping with them but saying little of importance. Na realized he had learned much more of the Hirstelites than they had learned of him.

He was skillful and subtle in this. She reminded herself that the chief wizard of Tesra was as much a politician as a sorcerer. But Holos seemed an excellent sorcerer as well, on the few occasion he had revealed his powers.

Again, his similarities to the ruler of Hirstel, the Prince-Sorcerer Piras Tindeval, came to mind. Both were potent wizards, both smooth politicians, both somewhat self-indulgent, but Piras was content in his power and disinclined to exert himself more than necessary, whereas it was clear Holos took seriously the task of defending his people and worked hard at it. Though he hid that beneath his urbane manner, Na could see it.

Perhaps that was what took up his time on this trip, for couriers came and went. Too, she suspected he spoke from afar with someone in the evenings, other wizards in Tesra perhaps.

They had seen even less of the priestess Arana, who kept to herself through most of the trip. More often than not the curtains of her palanquin remained closed. Na sometimes noted one or another of the lesser priestesses—she could not distinguish one from another—walking beside the litter, conversing or reading to her mistress.

A soldier hurried toward them, saluted the chief wizard and after a moment's hesitation, reported, "There are reports of wild animals, Lord Holos. In the area near the road, that is. Sheep and cattle killed by something. Wolves, some say, but there haven't been wolves here in generations." He paused abruptly, out of rehearsed words. Then, "Thought you should know, sir."

"I thank you for it. You may return to your place." As the man left, Holos turned to his companions. "Our ghalun, perhaps?"

"If Cory showed himself I would ask," said Im.

"I trust he remains near." The wizard looked about. "The stretch of highway ahead of us is better suited to an ambush than that we have already traveled. If they intend to attack, we should expect it soon."

And we'll soon be across the hills and approaching the city, thought Na. The ghalun would not have much more time to act. "Then we must be vigilant."

"That is certain. I will have the word passed among our party." Holos turned to the attendant following a short distance behind with his horse. "Ho, bring up Tira."

The name meant something like Moon-Girl so at least Na could assume the steed's gender now. For a stout, middle-aged man, Holos mounted to the saddle with surprising grace. A nod and he was off to spread a warning to the rest of the travelers.

Shortly after noon, there came a loud crack, followed by the screech of wood grating on stone. Something round rolled some distance down the road toward where Na and Im walked, before falling onto its side. A wheel had parted ways with one of the carts. It would not do to leave wagon and driver behind, so all must halt while it was

81

repaired. "A broken pin," Tau reported to them. "It shouldn't take long to replace."

But it did take time. The wagon was heavy and need be unloaded, in part, before one side could be lifted by several burly cursing teamsters and the wheel slipped back onto its axle and securely pinned. An hour further along the road, one of Arana's attendant priestesses fainted. Again, some time was spent in reviving the woman and getting her into one of the wagons. Not a great deal of time, but some.

The countryside grew wilder and less settled as they climbed higher into the hills. Conifers grew thicker here, dark and dense in the valleys. "It is growing late," spoke Im. "I think we were supposed to reach another caravansary before dark."

Na thought so as well. Dusk approached, the long twilight to which they had now become accustomed. "I fear trouble," she said.

"As do I" came a cavernous voice at her elbow. "The ghalun do not like the light of day and they are too timid to enter a secure compound at night." It looked about. "This suits them."

"Well, Cory, you've joined us at last," said Im. "Things must seem pretty grim for that to happen."

Some of the other travelers had spied the huge red demon now. Some gasped. Most backed away. Tau at once called out, "Don't fear! He's friendly!"

Na thought to correct him as to Qu'orthseth's gender but decided that could wait. Especially when crouching forms came bounding over a ridge toward them. The fading light hid details but they seemed to have blotchy white or gray skins and sharp teeth in their protruding muzzles. The creatures at some times leaped forward on all fours, at others shambled in a semi-upright posture.

Holos galloped up to them, reined in Tira. "More than I expected. Ho, soldiers, to us!"

The soldiers, however, did not head toward Im and Na and Holos but hastened to surround Arana's litter.

"Shadow won't help here," remarked Im. "I suspect yon hunters have good noses. Hey, Cory, don't have any thoughts of carrying me away to safety, now."

The demon only grunted. It would have certainly considered doing just that. Only Im's life mattered to it and if things got too dodgy it could be counted on tucking the young wizard under its arm and taking off.

Yipping and howling, the ghalun rushed forward, seemingly with no particular target. They might not know which is Im, thought Na, nor even care. Her thoughts then turned to the practical matter of defense. No swords! That hadn't worked so well the last time.

Im was already reaching for something, somewhere. Fire, as she had thrown at the pirates. That's what she would look for. What was that wind? From the corner of her eye she glimpsed Im directing a—a sand-storm! Straight from their one-time desert home. The blinding sand engulfed the charging ghalun.

That wouldn't stop them though, not for long. There was the fire she wanted, the volcanic ash she had used before. Not as thick this time, was it? Enough to singe those dog-things. Ah, it was good to hear them howl as she rained it on them. But now they were among the travelers and she could no longer safely attack that way.

Holos and others rode here and there, not using magic but striking with whatever weapon they had at hand. The chief wizard's heavy staff hit home again and again, sending ghalun limping away, whimpering. Yet it could not be said one side or the other had the upper hand. The increasing dark could only be to the attacking ghalun's advantage.

The creatures darted about, yapping and snapping, but rarely closing with anyone yet. They stood perhaps four feet of height, when erect, but mostly they ran about crouching or on all fours, their muzzles turning back and forth, seeking.

Cory drove into the turmoil, a red storm wind. The demon had surely waited until it felt it safe to leave Im. Maybe Zerc and Tau standing guard over their mistress and master, knives drawn, convinced it. But the ghalun proved elusive, difficult even for the surprisingly nimble monster to catch in its thick, powerful, claret-colored fingers.

Not unexpectedly, some of the attacking creatures did turn their attention to Arana's palanquin and her undoubtedly tasty attendants. There, though, the soldiers quickly threw them back, yelping in pain and disappointment. Yet the men seemed unwilling to advance, to carry the battle to the ghalun.

A whirring sound. What? Where? Oh, atop the hill the ghalun had charged across stood a handful of men, no more than silhouettes, swinging their arms about in an odd manner. Then those arms straightened and a rain of rocks came flying down, finding targets among the ghalun with astonishing accuracy. Astonishing to Na, at any rate; she had never seen such weapons used before.

Yes, slings. I am sure someone will explain their use to our sorceress in time. But maybe not in this story.

That seemed to be enough. One long loud howl was the signal for all the ghalun to turn and run, escaping into the impending night. The men descended the slope to the chaos left in the wake of battle.

"Who be in charge here?" asked the foremost of them. It was hard to say where his beard ended and his sheepskin mantle began.

"That is I, sir," responded Holos, now dismounted and leading Tira. She stamped in excitement but seemed none the worse for her adventure. "And I give you thanks for your assistance. Shepherds you are?"

"So we be. We have tracked those beasts for days since they ravaged our flocks." He looked about. "We did not know they hunted men as well."

"They are ghalun. They will hunt anything." Holos gave him a half-smile. "As long as they think the odds are very much in their favor."

There were murmurs among the shepherds. They had heard of ghalun, surely, but they would have been little more than myth to them. "It's good we changed the odds, by Kerais," stated one of them.

"That is so," agreed their leader, nodding solemnly.

The sergeant of their little band of soldiers approached. Na would have liked to have words with him! Maybe later she could acquaint him with her opinion of his ancestry and intelligence. She'd leave that to Holos for the moment.

And make sure Zerc didn't use his knife on the fellow. From the look in his eye she was sure he was considering such an action.

"None are dead, Lord Holos," the man reported, "nor seem likely to be anytime soon. More than a few wounded in some manner. Bites mostly."

Holos gave the man a long look, a most unfriendly look. "Why were your men not in the fighting?"

"It's what Governor Azil ordered, sir. He said protect the priestess before all else."

Holos stared at him, his face impassive, for a moment, then nodded in understanding. "Ah. Very well. Tuthinos! You and the sergeant get things in order." He turned back to them. "It seems my quarrel must be with Azil. Will you accompany us to our night's lodging?" he asked the shepherds. "We owe you at least a meal and bed."

The leader shook his head. "Best be back to our flocks," he replied. A minute later he and the rest of the band had melted into the night.

Torches were lit, wounds were bound, some semblance of normalcy restored. Three ghalun had been left behind, all dead. At least now. These travelers would not have been well disposed toward any wounded ghalun. That was too bad, felt Na. She would have liked to learn more of them.

She had thought they were hairless when they came bounding out of the dusk but saw now they were completely covered with short fur. Their smell was—odd, pungent. Not terribly unpleasant but she wouldn't want to live with a pack of ghalun. As she pondered the bodies, Holos came up, saying, "The ghalun had grown desperate, I think. This was their last opportunity to attack."

"Could someone have been responsible for creating this opportunity?"

"It is possible. Better to sort that out later."

Im and his demon joined them. Holos glanced at them and continued. "I did not expect such a large pack. There could have been as many as thirty of them."

"Twenty-eight," said Cory.

18.

"I'M NOT SO CERTAIN I want a dog now," Im told his companions. They were not getting off at all early today, after arriving at the caravansary hours after sunset.

"There be dogs and there be dogs," stated Zerc. Being cryptic, thought Na. The old sailor seemed to enjoy sounding wise when he truly knew nothing. Oh, maybe he really did mean something with his utterance. Or thought he did.

"Cory called the ghalun jackal-men," Na said. "I've yet to see a jackal but I doubt they are much like the dogs we know." She realized as soon as she said this that she was also covering up a lack of knowledge.

Cory stood near, immobile, most likely replenishing its energy, connected to the sun of its home world. It made no attempt to hide itself since their encounter with the ghalun. Holos felt it might be just as well if the demon marched into Tesra at their sides, allowing everyone to know of its existence and presence from the outset.

They went into the crowded courtyard, where Holos himself was overseeing the sorting out of their party. He spoke with those bitten or wounded at the moment. The priestesses had proven themselves more than ornamental when they had tended to the wounds last night, cleaning and dressing them.

"Who could know what poisons might lurk in the bite of a ghalun?" asked the chief wizard.

It was perhaps a rhetorical question but Im answered. "Germs," said he. "Not poisons but tiny living creatures. Xit taught me about them and how I could pull a bit of the blood of another being into myself to protect me from them. Someone who already had been stricken and recovered, and now could resist a disease."

Na nodded. The god had explained this to her as well. She and Im might have become very sick, even died, when they first came to this world and were exposed to new diseases, had not Xido done this to them.

Holos considered this information. "You must write this down when we reach the city. It should certainly be added to the lore of wizardry."

"I'm not sure anyone but a god like Xido actually has the powers needed for it," said Na. "Maybe an extremely able sorcerer." It required all sorts of reaching around through other worlds and merging with other individuals.

The sorcerer nodded. "Understood. None the less, knowledge is useful." He turned back to the jumble of carts and oxen, men and women. "As would be getting on the road again. Mec Arana!" The high priestess huddled conferring with a knot of her followers. "Do you think we should travel today?"

She straightened up, turned to them. "I do not, Lord Holos. A day of rest would do us all good. And are there not more soldiers on the way?"

"There are. I sent for them when I first heard of the animal attacks."

Im leaned in and whispered, "So Holos suspected the ghalun were up to mischief."

"He certainly suspected something," Na replied. And had from the first. There had been plenty enough warning this journey might prove dangerous. "Let's get some breakfast. Or is it time for lunch?"

"If we are stuck here all day it hardly matters. Let's purchase some-thing good and tell them the chief wizard of Tesra is paying."

Which he was. They could have spent Holos's money all along, had they wished. Perhaps it should be called the prince's money. They would surely meet that prince, Huenoziles, ruler of Tesra, soon.

A commotion arose behind them. Qu'orthseth came stalking from their quarters, flanked by Tau and Zerc. The pair of sailors-turned-attendants seemed more than a little satisfied with themselves as they sauntered by the monster's side, the center of all attention. People still gave the demon a wide berth, to be sure, but seemed somewhat well disposed toward it since it came to their defense last night.

Cory might be frightening, with its size, its massive featureless head and smooth, shiny, wine-colored body, but it would not provoke the revulsion something like the ghalun might. It was too alien for that, more like a statue than a living creature.

Holos, too, came toward them. "If we are to remain another night in this caravansary," he said, "no tasks require my immediate attention. Will you eat with me?" The wizard's eyes went to Cory and company. "You, as well."

"I do not eat," the demon reminded him. "I have just filled up on the light of a distant red sun."

Im must need correct. "Not distant. Or no more distant than any other world in the infinite. Each of them is next door to all the others."

"Is that something Xit said?" Na asked him.

The boy grinned. "Banat, actually. He and I had time to talk when we journeyed together to Pas."

Holos squinted at him. "Banat is a god, right? A god of the Ildin."

"That he is." Im seemed to ponder something for a moment. "I think he is my friend, and I his. More so than with Xido."

"Atima may be a factor in that," remarked Na.

Im only nodded and seemed to lose himself somewhere. His thoughts were surely with the priestess of Banat, across the wide sea. "It is good to have a god as a friend," said Holos. "Two is even better. But your Atima—she is Ildin, no?"

"She is." Im spoke flatly, as if unsure of the wizard's intent.

"Then not long-lived. That is always a sorrow to we who have more years than other mortals, yet love them none the less." Holos, too, seemed to lose himself for a moment. "We should get you back to her as soon as we can. You must lose as little time together as is possible."

"When I have done what is needed here."

"Defeating the Wizard-Lord may be beyond any one of us. Or all of us together, for that matter. But never mind that for now. What would you like for lunch?"

Holos ordered them a kind of steamed bread at the food stand. These too seemed identical at all the caravansaries. Na, a bit reluctantly, forewent the soup that accompanied it, when Im turned it down. It contained some sort of fowl and its rich odor was quite intriguing. Tesran cooking was not nearly so spicy as that of the Ildin but it had many subtle flavors.

As they settled to eat, Holos spoke. "Might I ask your age, my lady Na? I know it is not polite."

"Isn't it? I've never heard that." She nibbled a bit from her roll. It was tasty even without the broth. "Ninety-four. I think. I've lost track of the date in this world. My birthday would be forty-three days past the new year in Hirstel."

"We celebrate the changing of the year quite soon in Tesra, at the winter solstice."

"Oh, our new year fell on the anniversary of the city's founding. It had nothing to do with the sun or moon or any of that." She ate a little more, washing it down with tea. They had something called tea in Hirstel, concocted of what came from the vats of slime that fed the city. It did not taste like this. "I'm fairly sure our years were of the same length." Or close to it. "So how old are you, Holos?"

"I've a hundred and twenty-two years," he replied. "I age more quickly than you, I suspect." She saw his eyes go to Im.

"He really is a boy," said Na. "What are you, nineteen?"

"Probably," said Im. "I never knew when my birthday was. I was a poor lad of the streets, without mother nor father." He gave them an exaggerated sniff.

As far as Na knew, this was truth. Largely, truth. The boy was making fun of his origins as a sort of self-defense. "Yet you probably could have ruled in Hirstel, eventually, had you remained and become the Prince-Sorcerer's apprentice."

Im shrugged. "I like it better here."

"Me too," she admitted, and turned her attention back to Holos. "Are many long lived in Tesra? Everyone was in Hirstel, just as everyone had sorcerous power."

"But the two are not connected," he replied. "You knew that, right?" Na nodded. She had never actually heard a word about it before but had noticed some things in this world. "Separate gifts, though both were inherited from the same man."

"Urathu. Or, um, what do you name him?"

"Hurasu."

"Yes, Hurasu. Xido spoke to us of him."

"He brought both wizard powers and longevity with him from whatever world saw his birth, and had thousands upon thousands of children during his very long life here."

"In the Valley of Visions, where he ruled," said Im.

"Yes, and elsewhere, for he was said to be a great traveler. Perhaps everyone in the world can count him as an ancestor. But you asked me of Tesra. Those who founded the city were of the same stock as you two, I am sure, full of sorcery and long of life. Several thousand migrated here, some fourteen-hundred and fifty-five years ago." He peered at the pair. "That is the official date of the city's founding, when Lacoazes and his followers reached its site. I would assume Hirstel has an even longer history as your ancestors went straight there from the Valley whereas mine wandered a few centuries."

Na had to smile. "We had no real history at all. Nothing ever happened."

"Ah. Well, inevitably those first Tesrans mixed with peoples who already dwelt around the Sea of Sanctuary or who later came to the area. Wizardry grew less common, life spans grew shorter." Holos paused, perhaps pondering how far his city had fallen, or maybe just for dramatic effect. "Though it said these gifts also varied in the valley of their origin. We know the wanderers did not all have wizard powers."

Na suddenly remembered something and sat up straight. "Wanderers. That's the word Governor Azil used, wasn't it? Nanem."

Though his voice remained even and conversational, she could sense Holos grew more serious. There was a tension in him. It was there in the way his posture changed, became slightly more erect, how his words came more precisely. The man stiffened; there was no better way to describe it. "It is. Those who believe themselves of the pure blood of the Valley, whether they are or not, call themselves the nanem."

He paused again a little before adding, "I am not."

19.

"I COULD NOT RESUME THIS form and attempt a rescue when you went into the water. The wards Banat and Xido placed on the ship prevented it. I was relieved to see you fished out of the sea, young master. I had expected to return to a cell in my home world at any moment."

So spoke Qu'ortseth as they traveled on, the demon now walking openly beside the sorcerers. Im looked like he might have wanted to laugh but stifled it, smiling only. "It's nice to know you care about me, Cory."

The demon's own laugh came like peals of thunder, echoing from the scrub-covered hills. Some fellow travelers looked to the sky with expressions of concern before recognizing its source. "You jest well! That is good if we must spend our lives in each others company."

"It's warming to me," Im confided, his voice a stage whisper, to Na. She doubted this but said nothing. Cory's only concern would ever be itself. It was thoroughly amoral.

But of course Im joked. Tau stood a bit ahead, waiting for them to catch up after he had visited up the column of travelers. Zerc was not one for that; he trudged stolidly behind them. It was his duty!

"Not much further," proclaimed the boy as they drew even.

"Further to what?" growled Zerc.

"The gap," Tau explained, falling in beside the older sailor. "It will all be downhill from there."

Not all, Na was sure, but they would be across the highest point of this last ridge. They had climbed all the morning since leaving the cara-vansary. A troop of Tesran soldiers had shown late yesterday and now marched along with them.

These wore dark blue tunics that fell beneath their knees, with long sleeves, and vests of quilted armor. Their helmets appeared to be of bronze or brass. Na wasn't sure of the difference. Trousers or maybe leggings were tucked into high, soft boots. Broad-headed spears they carried, and short swords. In these things, they all looked the same.

Otherwise, they varied much. These were not all men of one race. A few looked as she had expected of Tesrans, that is like herself and Im. The greater part of them looked less that way but still appeared to have some common ancestry. There was one man who looked like Xit. Almost certainly a Bazu. Na could not guess why he wore the outfit of a Tesran soldier. A couple had coppery skins and high cheekbones, with dark straight hair protruding from beneath the rims of their conical helmets.

She heard the sudden intake of Im's breath and looked up. Wrapped in her thoughts Na had not been prepared for the scene before her. The land fell away, rather steeply, into a tangled valley and there, far out, lay a great water, a hazy blue extending to the horizon. The Sea of Sanctuary.

A lake, yes, she knew, but from here it looked like a sea indeed. There might be ships out there. It was too far away to be certain. "Tesra lies south now," said Zerc. "The road turns and follows the shoreline."

"Then we'll see the water for the rest of our journey?" asked Im.

"Reckon so. That's how I remembers it."

The road did bend southward and through the afternoon they gradually neared the sea. The land had changed, and those who dwelt there. Farms lay along their way, and well-tended groves. "A vineyard," announced Tau, pointing. "The wines of Tesra are renowned."

"Only t' boobies like you," responded Zerc. "We grow better on the other side of the hills, where the cool wind blows up from the sea."

Na wondered whether cool breezes didn't blow up from this sea too. Right now they seemed to be from the south and pleasantly warm. "We won't get to Tesra today though, will we?" she asked.

"Tomorrow," said both Zerc and Tau.

One last caravansary was entered that afternoon and, yes, it looked like all the others. She at last mentioned this to Holos when they sat together at an evening meal. The chief wizard had invited both Hirstelites, perhaps wishing to speak to them before reaching his city.

"Yes, they are built and operated to a government specification. Tesra has a thriving bureaucracy to deal with such matters."

"Na knows something of bureaucracy," volunteered Im. "She helped keep things running smoothly back home. You oversaw the slime vats, didn't you?"

"For a time," she admitted and wished she could slap the smirk off the boy's face. He was getting worse the closer they drew to Tesra. Maybe because they drew closer to Tesra. Im could just be trying to take his mind off his doubts and regrets about the whole affair.

Be that as it may. She had her own doubts to deal with. "It should be a couple days before the prince asks to see you," said Holos. "That too may depend on bureaucrats. Even I must deal with them." He smiled toward the high priestess Arana, who had added little to their conversation thus far. "The Mec Arana might be more successful in these matters than I."

She looked up at the wizard, a faint smile returning his. "That is because you work for the prince, Holos, even if your position is second only to his. I work for Fasenais."

"I know little of Tesran gods," said Na. A change of topic might be a good idea. "Is Fasenais your greatest god?"

Arana laughed aloud. "I like to think so! Perhaps Fasenais does too."

"There are four gods of equal power," Im broke in. "I've been learning about them. Each is, um, symbolic of one of the elements, right?"

"That they are. Our gods are quite symbolic, their natures arising from the philosophies we acquired in the Valley of Visions."

Na thought on this a moment. "Then you created the gods?"

It was Holos who answered. "No, we only found them. They already existed somewhere, at least in potential."

She saw Im nodding. Xido had said similar things to them about gods. "The Ildin gods are quite abstract too. So, what is Fasenais like?"

"She is our Great Mother," said her high priestess, "the epitome of all women and the most beautiful. Her element is water. Lady Fasenais is wed to Kerais, Lord Earth."

Im spoke again. Or butted in, maybe, felt Na. "And Lady Trepais is air and all about intellect, and Lord Zilais is fire and passion." He hesitated a few seconds before adding, a tad sheepishly, "I've been interested in the elements lately, you know."

"We do know," said Arana. "I have heard some of your tale but would like to hear more. Will you walk with me a while and speak of it?"

Holos made no sign of even hearing this so Na gave the young man a quick nod. That was all the encouragement he seemed to need. "I shall, my lady," he said. Holos looked after the two for a while as they wandered into the dusk.

Then, rather abruptly, he stated, "It might be better were Im back at his shrine, protecting she whom he loves, as well as the gems they guard there. Torut greatly desires to get his hands on them."

"The Jewels of the Elements."

"Yes. We know them better here as the Eyes of the Wind. It was our ancestors who discovered them, not far from the Valley of Visions. Indeed, near the gate through which your people escaped to another world. I have looked at old records and think I know where that was. The gems were lost to us when Hurasu died and the valley fell into turmoil." Holos frowned momentarily. "Or so it is believed."

Na sighed. "I know next to nothing of that valley. There were old records, old stories, in Hirstel too, but they made sense to no one. Even a map would be good."

"I fear the histories we have are not much more satisfying, but all we have will be open to you, Na. You may spend your life in our libraries, should you wish."

Na had to laugh. "I do hope there are other things to do in Tesra."

20.

THE GREATNESS OF TESRA, CITY of Wizardry, is only legend now. At its height, it was the largest and richest metropolis the world had ever known, the center of a great empire. There is yet a city by its name, but it is not truly Tesra. That city died long ago and only its ruins, its broken bones, lie beside the inland sea, haunted by a sparse impoverished population. Little of the blood of the city's founders flows in their veins.

But when Na and Im first spied it from the hills, with the sea sparkling beyond, it was not far fallen from its days of greatest glory. Ships laden with the riches of an empire plied the waters, bringing wealth to the harbors of Tesra, and luxury to its people. A golden age it seemed yet. Few noted its fading.

"We were not lied to," said Na. "It really is the largest city we've ever seen."

"I'll even believe it's the largest in the world." Im surveyed a sprawling Tesra, from the villas in the hills above the city to the bustling crowded docks where its streets met the Sea of Sanctuary.

Until now, Hirstel was the greatest city either had known. Not Pas, not Phamahd, had truly rivaled it. Hirstel would be swallowed up here; the difference of scale was so great it was difficult of belief.

Tau was awed as well and could only stare.

Holos reined in his mount beside them. "It will take us a couple hours more to get into the city," he announced, not descending from the saddle, "and then some time to reach my palace. You are to be my guests, at least this night." The wizard glanced at the sun, past its zenith. "We'd best get along or it will be dark when we arrive there."

So they descended toward great Tesra. Na could not tell the size of the largest buildings from this far but some might rival the towers of Hirstel—and these, she assumed, were raised by men without the least help from demons. To her left, she made out what seemed a high wall, angling down from the hills. It and the road ran parallel for a distance.

Then the wall turned toward them and grew even higher, supported on wide semicircular stone arches, high enough that the road's traffic passed easily beneath it ahead. She tried to figure out what it might be on her own for some time but finally gave up. When Holos approached again, as he rode up and down the column of travelers, she made her query.

The wizard chose to alight and walk beside them as he answered. "An aqueduct, bringing water from the hills. The springs and wells of Tesra are not nearly adequate to serve all our people now, though they were the reason the city was founded where it is."

"Is there running water?" asked Na, with unabashed eagerness. "That is one thing I miss from Hirstel!"

Im scowled. "In the residences of the powerful," he said. "My sort depended on the pubic fountains."

"As do many folk here," admitted Holos. "Water flows indeed in my own home."

Na looked out toward the Sea of Sanctuary. "You can not use the water of your big lake? Or is it salty?"

"Somewhat salty along this shore, but not nearly so much as the sea you crossed. The water is fresher on the far side, where great rivers feed the sea."

Im nodded knowingly. He might have already heard this from someone. "And no rivers flow from the Sea of Sanctuary, right? The water just sits there and evaporates."

"That is so." They walked under the aqueduct. Na realized it was narrower than she had thought. There was nothing much to see as she peered at the vault above them. Just more of the cut gray stone of which the road was constructed.

That changed not far ahead, in a stretch where the city was momentarily screened by evergreen trees growing along the way.

Beneath their feet the roadway changed from the fitted stones they had trod all the way from the docks of Phamahd to the small regularly-shaped brownish-red ones she had seen used for the port's warehouses.

The new pavement extended as far ahead as Na could see. "Why do the stones change?" she asked at last. She was getting a bit tired of displaying her ignorance, but how else could she find things out? "Are these from a closer quarry?"

It took a moment for Holos to puzzle out to what she was referring. Behind her, Na heard Zerc snicker. "Ah, the bricks." The wizard managed to maintain a serious demeanor and a polite tone. "They are made of baked clay, Lady Na. Construction from brick was common in the Valley of Visions and we brought the custom here with us. Was it not so in Hirstel?"

A slow shake of the head. Brick. Why hadn't she thought of that? Na had certainly read of it. "We used only stone," she replied, rather shortly. "There was no clay, just sand and rock."

"And brawny demons to cut great blocks of stone and move them into place," added Im.

Na had to laugh at that. "Yes, that did make building easier."

"So I would think," came Holos's dry remark.

If you could have demons raise high towers and dig deep wells for you, you would not waste much thought on the making of bricks nor the building of aqueducts, would you? Im and Na were learning. Give them time, my friends; they have surprised us before and it is likely they will again. What? Well, yes, of course I know the story! You must allow me my storyteller's art.

And, no, I haven't forgotten Im's pet demon is still with them. Now hush and let me go on with the tale.

"I also think," said Holos, glancing back over his shoulder at the tall crimson figure stalking behind them, "it is time to consider how best to have Akorzef enter my city. I am not certain now about it walking in openly, especially so late in the day."

"I could cast shadow about it," suggested Im.

Na shook her head at this. "Neither of us is capable of holding it here long enough, even taking turns. Why not just put Cory in one of the carts where it isn't so conspicuous?"

"As long as I needn't diminish myself," rumbled the demon. It had not spoken for hours but Na had no doubt Cory was fully aware of and taking in everything around them.

"See if you can snuggle down amid the chief wizard's luggage," said Im. "There is certainly enough of it to conceal you."

Holos chuckled at this. "Despite the young master's snide remark, it seems a good idea. Come along with me and I'll see to it you can ride." He mounted his mare and set off toward the rear of their column, where the baggage carts lumbered along, pulled by patient rust-colored oxen.

Cory hesitated but a second or two before following the wizard. Concerned about leaving Im's side but seeing the wisdom of hiding itself, Na thought. It will have many such decisions to make if it remains with the boy.

And how long might that last? Years, even centuries? There might never be a solution to the problem that bound human and demon together.

Houses were becoming more common along the way, one or two stories, and inns and other places of business. Villas could be spied further back, away from the road, not too different in appearance from the one Holos maintained in Phamahd. This was still mostly farmland, however, and many groves lay on either side of their way. Na did not know enough of trees to recognize what these were and, moreover, they were largely leafless at this time of year.

Na did know this was a colder land than the one they had left across the Greater Sea. Drier, too. It was dry this day, at any rate, and only a little cool, the sky still a clear blue, the sea still shimmering beneath a sinking sun.

That sun was almost gone when they entered the massive gates of what Holos named the Inner City. Sometime before that, the Mec Arana had turned aside with her own entourage. Too, various merchants and other travelers who had crossed the hills with them fell away, their destinations not those of Im and Na and the chief wizard. Ahead of them, men on stilts were lighting lamps of multicolored pleated cloth, strung above the wide street, a street still paved with bricks.

The illumination of the lamps was slight but they were many. Holos, now walking again beside them, noted her interest. "These men are employed by the city to light the thousands of lamps each evening, to make certain the candles are replaced. It takes many men and women to keep Tesra operating, not only lamplighters but street cleaners, men to direct traffic and fight fires, those who bury the dead. All work for the city and for the prince."

A weary Na but nodded. She knew of such things; Hirstel, too, had its public employees though much was done through magic or by demons. Hadn't Im's father been a garbage collector before his death? She remembered something about the man losing his position due to a gambling habit, a misfortune that threw him and his family back into the mass of Hirstelites without any real employment, who idled in the city's streets, subsisting on the synthetic food doled out to them, dreaming through the days.

Were there such here? It would be good to know, if she remained in Tesra. They turned from the wide way they had traveled, to the right, on a street nearly as broad. The featureless facades of tall, squarish buildings rose on either side. They were not so different from those of Hirstel, though somewhat less varied in size, and windows and doors lay within the ubiquitous arches of Tesran architecture. Openings tended to right angles in Hirstel.

She almost didn't notice when they stopped before one of those structures."My home," announced Holos, passing in through its arched entry.

Na looked up at the massive stuccoed building and resisted the urge to say, "At last."

21.

Who was that? Someone moved in the near-darkness. "Tau?"

"Yes, mistress," responded the boy. "I just came in to see if you were awake. It's past the dawn."

Na had been given a room on the west side of the chief wizard's palace where she could see the sea—and the street below—but not the rising sun. A heavy curtain and shutters further blocked the light of morning, as well as, it must be admitted, the chill of night.

"You slept here?" she asked. Much of the previous evening was not clear in her mind right then. Maybe it never would be.

"In the antechamber. They didn't much like the idea of me remaining here, mistress. Instead of a woman." A self-conscious giggle slipped out. "One asked me if I was a eunuch."

Eunuch? Na didn't know the word and thought maybe it would be best not to ask. She did understand Holos's staff being a bit uncertain, if not outright scandalized. "Inform them you're my bodyguard," she told him.

"Then I guess I shouldn't have brought water for you to wash up," Tau said, slightly lifting the earthenware basin he bore in both hands. "Beneath the dignity of a bodyguard, I am sure!"

Na barely noticed the quip. Water. Holos said his house had running water. "Put it down somewhere," she ordered, "and see about getting that window open." Too damned dark in here. Were there more candles somewhere?

Tau set his basin on a table, its top of some polished green stone, and went to draw back the heavy dark curtain. When he threw open the shutter, a breeze, strong and surprisingly warm, blew into the room. Na splashed some water on herself and turned to it.

"Westerlies," announced the former sailor. "That means winter storms moving our way, my lady."

Na had learned about weather. Enough, she had learned. She looked out over the sprawling city of Tesra. The skies had gone from clear to slate gray as slabs of cloud moved in from across the sea.

She must be on the second story of this house of Holos. Na recalled climbing flights of stairs but not how many! The street below was brick. She couldn't tell that from this distance but she did remember from last night. The buildings also seemed to be brick, mostly, but many were stuccoed, white predominantly, with some pastels, yellows, golds.

They had the massive, monolithic appearance she remembered from Hirstel, but, again, with the typical Tesran arches. Those arches were wide, sometimes with little or nothing in the way of vertical sides. Roofs were low of pitch, and of tile, reddish-brown most commonly, some a sandy tan. Buildings in Hirstel had flat roofs, when they had roofs at all. It never rained in its desert setting but wind-blown sand could be a nuisance.

It did rain here and it would blow in this window when it came. She turned back to her basin but then thought to ask Tau something. "Um, do your people, the women that is, remain covered up? Their bosoms. It was not the custom in Hirstel and we are a related people."

Tau arched an eyebrow. "You mean you went about with your breasts uncovered, like barbarians?" The boy recognized that as a gaffe as soon as it left his mouth and hurried to stammer out, "No, no, my lady. It would surely lead to chills, would it not?"

"Maybe so. But your ancestors went so."

The young man considered this idea rather soberly, then brightened. "I'll ask Master Tuthinos of it. He would know. Which robe do you wish?"

"I only have the two. Is either clean?"

"Both. I saw to it everything but that under-tunic you're wearing was washed last night." He gave her a looking-over. "As long as Lord Holos is footing the bill, we should buy you more clothes."

Prince Huenoziles, she said to herself. The ruler of Tesra was her benefactor, and Holos but his agent. What repayment might he expect? "I'll wear the old one," she said. "The black." The one that crossed a wide sea with her.

It wasn't really black, was it? Not anymore. The garment had faded to a charcoal tone and there were, it was to be admitted, noticeable stains. Nor was it in the Tesran style, but it was comfortable and made of good Ildin silk. She pulled it on over the sleeveless garment in which she had slept—no point in changing that right now—belted it around her and wished there were decent mirrors here. Na had not had a good look at herself since leaving Hirstel.

Not that there was much to look at in a mirror. Instead, she returned to the window and again gazed out upon the greatest city in the world, revealed by the growing light of dawn. All the structures along this street rose to two, three, four stories; all were of much the same blocky, monumental appearance. The land sloped gradually toward the lake and further off taller structures could be spied. They might be the palace of the prince, or warehouses. Na had no way of knowing.

"There certainly are a lot of buildings," she mused, mostly to herself. "Hmm, the roofs look odd on some of them." Flattened off? It was hard to tell from her vantage.

"Zerc tells me a lot of the city folk live in these apartment buildings," offered Tau. "He and Master Im have the rooms next door."

"Then lets go see them," said Na, turning again from the window. Should it be closed? No, leave it for now. She liked having fresh air in here.

The antechamber, as her bedchamber, was somewhat long and narrow. Tau's pallet lay along one wall, her own meager belongings stacked or hung on the other side. The sailor followed her into what she thought would be a hallway. She remembered a dark hall last night.

But no—it was a gallery, open to a central courtyard. What she had assumed was a massive structure was only a shell. Many of the buildings must be on this plan-shape. That explained the shapes of the roofs. She looked out into the open space for only a moment. "Which way?"

"To the left, mistress."

The door stood open; voices sounded. The old sailor Zerc, leaning in the doorway between the two chambers—identical to those in Na's suite—turned to them as they entered. He gave Na a rather deep bow, at which Tau snickered. "Go right in, mistress. You're expected." She gave only a glance to Cory, standing inert in a corner, and entered the room.

Na hoped they had expected her enough to have some breakfast ready. Holos and Im sat talking, filling the two simple wooden chairs, the only chairs in the room. She raised a palm when Im started to rise from his seat, and went to perch beside Tuthinos on the bed.

It was a very high bed, as had been the one in her room. She had never slept so far from the floor as in these Tesran abodes. There was no breakfast in evidence.

"As I was telling Im, Huenoziles is unlikely to call for you until after the Yule Feast." Holos shook his head, clearly disapproving of this delay.

"That is soon, isn't it?" asked Im.

"Four days. There will be many celebrations to entertain you, at least."

That didn't bother Na. She was in no hurry and wouldn't mind sampling Tesra's diversions. Im might feel differently. "This Prince Huenoziles," she asked, "is he a wizard?"

"He is not," said Holos. "The ruling princes have, for the most part, not been sorcerers, though that blood has shown now and then. Our greatest ruler, Araziles, was a wizard as well as a warrior."

Tuthinos added to this, "And Lacoazes, the first prince, had visions telling him to lead his people here."

That caught Im's attention. "A prophet?"

Holos shrugged. "Possibly. The old annals are rather ambiguous. He might have meant only that he dreamed of a homeland for his people."

Tuthinos accepted that with something of a sour expression. The younger wizard must like to think the best of his historical figures. "He was the grandfather of Araziles," he told them.

Then wizardry ran in the family. Araziles—Man of Light the name meant in Zikem. Ancient Zikem, as the Tesrans called it. "So this Araziles reigned a long time ago?" asked Na.

"Yes, quite a while. He was the third to rule over Tesra, and the longest lived of all our princes."

To this Tuthinos added, "Taganides, his grandson, was the last powerful wizard to mount the throne. It is said he tried to strive against the Wizard-Lord of his time and it drove him mad."

"It is possible," agreed Holos. "It is an occupational hazard for wizards anyway."

Na's mind at once went to Torut, the maddest of mad wizards, their foe, the current Wizard-Lord. "You say the Wizard-Lord of his time. Other men have claimed that title?"

"And women too."

She might have asked more about that but Im at once posed another question. "These Wizard-Lords have always been in opposition to Tesra?"

"Some have been willing to coexist," replied Holos, rising. "Some haven't. I think it is time for some breakfast."

"And I think," stated Im, "it is about time we had that long conversation with Xido."

22.

"MANY OF THE STRUCTURES OF Tesra are on this plan but the ordinary apartment buildings do not have so large a courtyard." Holos allowed his gaze to wander about that courtyard, where they were finishing an ample breakfast.

"So they can fit in more people, I would guess?" asked Im.

"Exactly. Two rows of apartments on each side, or even more, and no gallery."

Cory stood nearby, seemingly engrossed with the fountain standing central to the area. Proof of that running water, thought Na. It might have been carried here by the very aqueduct they had passed beneath. Aside from a few spindly evergreens, there was not much else in this courtyard space. At the far end, servants busied themselves hanging laundry on several lines.

That's likely to be rained on, she thought. It would surely storm before day's end.

Im was also looking about, somewhat more intently. "This place is decidedly well-protected," he announced after a while. "It must have been inconvenient to lower the wards to let Cory in."

Holos chuckled. Though he hid it well, Na could detect a certain pride in his expression. "And then raise them again. No demon policemen will be coming to visit," the chief wizard declared. "Human assassins—well, the bindings won't keep them out but we should have ample warning of any intruders." A sudden frown came to his face; as suddenly, it left.

He remembered how they got past his wards without alerting him in Phamahd, she thought. He hadn't figured it out. Na looked about casually, noting several wardings. They should do. She should learn more of that craft. Xido had skimped on their education there.

Xido. "Are we ready to speak?"

"I am," responded Holos. "Is Xido still at that shrine?"

It did not matter where the god might be but Im replied. "I doubt it. He had errands elsewhere, or so he claimed. Just we three?"

"Or will Tuthinos join us?" asked Na. The assistant wizard had bustled off as soon as their breakfast had been served.

"Tuthinos is putting his ability to speak from afar to other purposes this morning. One of his duties is to receive reports from wizards around the realm." Holos seemed to be debating whether to say more. "The man is able enough but he will never be a great sorcerer. Nor my successor. It is perhaps best he not become involved too closely in what we do."

Neither Na nor Im had anything to say to that. What Im did say was, "Follow me." The briefest of moments later all three were in another world, a meeting place. A part of them was there.

Another brief moment after, Xido appeared. The god had been anticipating this meeting, certainly, leaving a tiny part of his essence here to watch for them.

I greet you, Lord Xido, came Holos's solemn voice.

Na laughed. *Our chief wizard was wondering where you are these days.*

Why, I am here with you, my dear. Xido gave her an exaggeratedly lascivious wink. *But alas, not enough of me to do either of us any good. Most of that which is me in my own world, a world of gods. I hadn't been back since Im drew me to Hirstel. Attempted to draw me.*

Attempted? wondered Holos.

Yes, he mistook me for an ordinary demon. I answered his summons out of curiosity.

Im's brief smile changed to thoughtfulness, perhaps even puzzlement. *I have—I see some sort of picture of your world.*

Remember you have been in my mind, as well as that of Torut. Much of the knowledge should still be muddled and inaccessible but you will be slowly sorting it out. Some of it. The dark god grimaced. *Maybe not Torut's thoughts. I'm having trouble getting through those myself.*

I would fear such thoughts, remarked Holos.

Well you should. They would destroy you. So, tell me all that has occurred.

This they did, in some detail. Absorbed in giving the story, Na did not at first notice that another had joined them, an invisible listener. Startled by the sudden realization, she looked about. Had the others noticed the intruder? Xido gave her the slightest of smiles and shook his head.

Im glanced her way too. Both had noted the presence. Holos seemed unaware. The telling of their tale went on but knowing that shadow was there nagged at Na. Could it be Torut?

Surely it was Torut.

And so we're waiting on the prince and plan to do some sightseeing, concluded Im.

Xido stood silent, contemplative, for a few seconds. *There is much to think on in this account,* he said. *And I shall do just that. Ho, Torut, do you wish to join us now? You can harm none of us, you know.*

The Wizard-Lord appeared, gaunt, naked, with beard and hair long unshorn and uncombed. *I knew most of this story,* he said, his voice smooth, cultured, speaking Zikem, but oddly accented to Na's ears. A shriek of crazed laughter erupted; harshly vehement words followed. *A story of my failures to remove you, Wizard Im! Never doubt I shall try again. You are far too dangerous to allow to live.* His eyes, a deep golden-brown set beneath heavy brows, swept past Holos to fix themselves on Na. The voice again became soft, persuasive. *And I would rather not end you, my lady, but have you at my side.*

Na sniffed. *Is sending kidnappers your idea of courtship?*

Torut cackled. *I did not think you would accept an invitation! But know there is one. You could be mighty, Na, a queen of the world, ruling by my side!*

Holos scowled. *Your queens have not been noted for their longevity, Torut.*

Torut snarled in reply, *They proved unable. As will you, one of these days, my little wizardling.*

I know your mind, Torut, came Xido's even voice. *You wish not to rule but to destroy.* The Wizard-Lord glared at him a moment and abruptly disappeared.

The momentary silence was broken by Im. *I felt another, briefly. A woman.*

Yes, but who she was I could not discover. Unless she was an extremely accomplished sorceress I do not think she would have found us on her own.

Then Torut brought her?

Perhaps not purposely. She might have followed him.

And he sent her away lest her identity be discovered, spoke Holos. *We know well he has spies and allies in the city.*

Against which you must remain vigilant. These two will be a potent force for your side, said Xido, nodding toward Na and Im, *but that does not mean you can expect to throw down your Wizard-Lord anytime soon.*

Can we ever? asked Im. He sounded uncertain about everything at the moment. Na felt rather uncertain herself. And Torut's words had— upset her. No, that was not an adequate word. They had chilled her even as they intrigued her.

Xido's shrug and nonchalant tone did not completely hide his own uncertainties. *In some one of the infinite worlds, Torut destroys Tesra; in another, Tesra overthrows Torut. Ha, in some world, Torut is chief wizard of Tesra and Holos is Wizard-Lord.* He grinned at the chief wizard of Tesra before continuing, his voice but slightly more serious. *But none can say what will come in this world. Not even Atima, I suspect.*

I'd like to go and ask her, murmured Im.

As we are all aware. I fear you will have to deal with Torut first. Your innate power alarmed him as soon as he became aware of your presence in this world, and you stand between him and the Jewels of the Elements. Which you should return to and guard, by the way.

I would consider that a pleasant duty.

I'm sure you would. I'll be returning to Banat's shrine soon, to teach Atima even as I promised, but I must depart eventually and leave things to you.

The god turned back to the others. *We shall speak again, I am sure. Call on me if I am needed, Na. And you, Holos—you can call on Na!* With that, Xido left. There was no reason for them not to return to the garden in the house of Holos.

23.

IT WAS NEAR NOON. NA had never before spent such an extended time in another world. It was wearying, holding a substantial part of oneself there, though she hadn't noticed it till now.

"I believe we shall all want naps," declared Holos. "After some lunch." He looked to the dark sky. "'Tis not a good afternoon to go out and about anyway."

"And you will not need to lower your wardings," rumbled Cory.

"Have you been standing there keeping an eye on us the whole time?" asked Im.

"I have. Your lackey came and looked at you a couple times." This the demon addressed to Holos. Or so it was assumed; it did turn toward the wizard. "I think he was afraid you would be rained on." Cory's chuckle sounded like rumbles of thunder. It was echoed by the real thing.

"Indeed, demon. Had I known how long we would be I would have done this indoors." Holos looked to the dark roiling sky. "And we'd best go in now for our noon meal."

Someone human had also been watching them. Servants at once came forward. "We shall eat in my private chambers," Holos told them. "Inform the cooks." A pair scurried off. Two more threw open an ornately carved wooden double door, lacquered red. The writhing creatures portrayed were none Na recognized. She could see the laundry being hurriedly taken down as they entered the room.

"My staff has already been informed you eat no meat," said Holos, over his shoulder. "Something should be on its way to us shortly." He led them into a nearly square space lined with shelves full of books and scrolls. Between them, narrow, paper-paned windows allowed dim, diffused light to filter in from the courtyard. Coals glowed in a small brick fireplace.

Cory wordlessly found a corner in which to stand.

"Your library?" asked Na.

"It is. I do much of my work here." The wizard pushed aside a pile of papers on the one large dark wooden table central to the room. "Most of my eating too."

"By yourself? Is there a wife?" Im asked him. "If you don't mind my asking." Na wondered about that as well and had since first speaking to the sorcerer from afar. There had never been any mention.

She would not have asked but she was glad Im did.

"I have been a widower for some time. My wife was not so long-lived as I." Holos gave Im a long look then. His Atima would be the same, would leave Im while he was yet a young man as their people reckoned lifespans. "Our children are grown and elsewhere now." A half-smile. "None had wizardry in them. Ah, Tuthinos."

The younger wizard entered, and lunch came behind him. Tuthinos ate with them and spent some time filling his master in on what was transpiring about the Tesran realm. Most of it seemed exceedingly uninteresting to Na.

Until they turned to a discussion of upcoming holiday events. "You may attend any of them," Holos told the pair of wizards, "whether you have been formally invited or not. Even as I." Na could not read his brief smile. It was all in the lips and his beard hid much of it. "Though politeness and politics are my main reasons for being at such affairs."

Na had a suspicion Holos might just enjoy himself too. "Tau thinks I need more clothes," she announced.

"And he is undoubtedly correct. I shall send for tailors to fit you both for new wardrobes. Livery for your attendants, too. They are a reflection of those they serve."

Im chortled at a sudden thought "Should we make Zerc and Tau match?"

"Only if we wish to lose both of them." She turned back to the chief wizard. "How soon?"

"As soon as you wish. Ho, Catha." A diminutive, somewhat young woman entered, in a patterned red robe. It seemed too large for her. "My secretary," he explained. "Arrange for my tailors to come this afternoon. After a nap, perhaps?" Na nodded. "Mid-afternoon, then." The woman bowed and left, but not without a furtive glance at the monstrous form lurking in a dim corner of the room. Na had almost forgotten Cory was there.

"By the way, Mursoazes is coming for the Yule. We should see him if his wife doesn't claim too much of his time."

"She doesn't live with him in Robon?" asked Im.

"That would inconvenience his mistress there." Na was unsure whether to laugh at this. Im had definitely decided not to, his face remaining expressionless. This did not surprise her; she already knew how surprisingly principled the boy could be. "Murso is one of the few men I trust completely," continued Holos. "We will have to speak with him of the situation here."

"Of Torut," spoke Im.

"And other matters. It is more complicated than just Tesra pitted against the Wizard-Lord's realm." Holos sighed. The wizard could not hide that he, too, was weary. "Far more complicated. But Torut, most of all. I think he fears you will use the jewels against him, not just that you keep him from them. Torut might not have even paid them any attention until you became attuned to them. Now, he is aware of them and their power."

"I should learn then to use them," stated Im. "But not while Atima lives and uses them for prophecy. She too is attuned."

Damn, he's a good kid, thought Na, and completely right. It was no wonder he got along with that paragon of godly virtue, Banat. She

117

should feel more guilty about resenting him from time to time. "I believe it is time for that nap," she announced.

"And then come back and explore these books, if I might," said Im.

"You both are welcome to use my library. Know there are far greater ones in the city."

"We have to start somewhere," Im replied. "Ready to go, Cory?"

The demon had already abandoned its corner, anticipating their departure. They might forget its presence momentarily but it paid attention to them. Na paused to examine the carvings on the door as they passed out of the room.

"Dragons," rumbled Cory.

"Oh. I've never seen a dragon."

"Me neither," added Im.

"Some serve the city," said Holos. "Some serve Torut, but I am assured they all dislike him. Mostly they live in the mountains beyond the sea and have little to do with any of us."

"Never trust a dragon," was all Cory had to say.

24.

"WE SOMETIMES HAVE A LITTLE snow here along the shore. It does not last long."

A thin layer of white covered the courtyard they crossed. "Until now we have only seen it from afar, atop mountains," said Na.

"And I wish this had stayed there," grumbled Im. The boy apparently did not like snow at all. Cory seemed to agree. It was not deigning to set foot in it, floating along a few inches above the ground.

And well might you, had you the ability, my friends. Remember poor Qu'orthseth came from a climate where metal ran liquid in rivers.

Na didn't think it was that bad.

Tuthinos went on as they hurried into the library. "We have much heavier snowfalls in the regions beyond our little sea."

"How far does your, um, nation extend?" asked Im. "Or is it what they call an empire?"

Holos looked up from where he sat writing at the table. "Our empire, as you name it, is based on commerce, not conquest. We call it the Unem, the Streams, in reference to the riches flowing down the rivers to the Sea of Sanctuary."

"There are maps," offered Tuthinos.

"So there are. Why don't you show them?" The chief wizard inked his stylus and considered the page before him, before looking up again and giving them a smile. "My aide loves maps and histories. He will go on about them all day if you permit him."

Tuthinos gave his master a little bow. "But we haven't all day, sir. Breakfast is on its way and then we go out into the city."

"Yes, of course. This can wait." Holos shoved his work aside. "Bring the map of the Unem. You know the one I mean."

Shortly, a large chart was unrolled on the table. "Here is where we are," said Tuthinos, pointing.

No need, thought Na. The name is written plainly. Ah, but there were always those who needed to explain things. She would not judge the wizard harshly.

Two great rivers flowed into the western end of the Sea of Sanctuary, and a smaller one further up the coast from where Tesra lay, to the northeast. Several isles lay in the big lake.

"Thinev Tenac?" spoke Im, reading the name from the chart. "The Great Water of Sanctuary?"

"That is the official name but commonly we call it Lan Tenac, Sea of Sanctuary. We had no word for sea when we came here and borrowed one from the Bazu."

As they had for the Greater Sea. That lay on the right edge of the map. And there was where they had crossed the hills—such a small distance within the expanse of this wide Tesran realm. "All of this is your Unem?" she asked.

"No, my lady," said Holos. "This area down here is desert waste, and Bazu cities lie along the coast. We have outposts in the far north, even some on these islands here in the Greater Sea." He pointed to them. "But can not claim to rule there. And here—" His hand swept along the left side of the chart. "Here lie our uncertain borders with the Wizard-Lord's domain, borders that shift back and forth.

"Our Tesran realm lies about the Sea of Sanctuary and on up through the region of Lades Rusac, Golden Lake. Above it are found two great inland seas where our control is challenged by that of the Rift. Especially in the more westerly one. Mursoazes could tell tales of the naval battles there."

Im scrutinized the chart. "The Rift. That's not on this map."

"It lies beyond," said Tuthinos. "In truth, that part of the world has never been accurately charted."

"Of old, we named it Tul Sunac, the Broken Place," Holos told them. "It is a place of power. Even before the death of Hurasu it was said to be a stronghold of powerful sorcerers."

"It is also said they harassed those who followed Lacoazes here," added Tuthinos. "Ah, breakfast. Bring that over here. We're all famished, I'm sure." He rolled up the chart to make room for the laying out of an ample meal.

"I must leave you to my able aide this morning," announced Holos. "I've duties to which I must attend. He can show you something of the city, should you desire."

"Or you can wait until your new clothes are ready," Tuthinos added to this. "The tailors have promised to return on the morrow for a final fitting, though they are quite busy this near the holiday."

Holos chuckled at this. "One of the advantages of being a guest of the chief wizard. But I do not think our guests are overly vain about their apparel, Tuth."

Im certainly was not at all self-conscious about such things. He would probably parade through Tesra in a loincloth without another thought. Na did not consider herself vain, to be sure, but she did know her clothes were not likely to make an impression. Not a good one, anyway! Today she wore the robe she had purchased in Phamahd, of wool, and of a dark ivory color with red facings.

She disliked its cut. Too enveloping. The black Ildin robe was more comfortable but quite out of style here. As was her long hair, which tumbled in sun-colored curls to the small of her back. The dressmaker had said something of this yesterday.

Im had trimmed his hair quite short while they were still among the Ildin, and his beard as well. It was the fashion there, and Xit's way too. It was practical. Perhaps she should be more practical.

The practical thing right now was to get some of this breakfast into her. There was more of the fragrant Tesran tea, to which she was becoming completely addicted. It was certainly an inducement to remaining here!

But she would need more than that. She would need to know this was the place she belonged in this world. Na was not certain of that, not yet. Im seemed to have found his place, on the far side of the Greater Sea.

And that was good. She liked the boy but not playing second best to him. In Tesra, she might well be the most powerful of all magicians. Holos had certainly hinted so. Only Torut would be able to outstrip her and he, as Im, would be far away. Yes, these Tesrans intended to use her and her powers. She could see that. It only meant that she was needed and that was a good thing. She could belong here. She could find stability, after feeling rootless and lost. Na had never seemed completely in place even in Hirstel.

What were they talking about? She should have paid attention.

"What of Cory?" Im was asking.

The demon spoke for the first time. "I will accompany the young wizard."

Holos regarded the great crimson form for a few moments, looking as sincerely thoughtful as ever. Perhaps it was no pose this time. "Yes, yes, I am sure you will. The people of Tesra are sophisticated about the ways of magic yet a huge red demon stalking their streets might be a bit much."

"It could fit in your coach, sir," offered Tuthinos.

"And still be seen. That will be as it is. We can't hide it forever, and those in authority have been informed of its presence. Hmm, I'll have to lower some wards. Later." The chief wizard of Tesra helped himself to another fruit-filled pastry.

25.

THE COACH SLUGGISHLY TRUNDLED INTO the street through an arched gateway. The two silvery-gray horses pulling it were the largest Na had ever seen. She stood no higher than their withers. The carriage itself was not as impressive; it resembled nothing so much as the carts that traveled with them across the hills. Lattice sides enclosed it and supported a curved roof. Entry and exit was through a single half-door at the rear, as the two tall wheels prevented any opening on the sides.

Qu'orthseth had entered behind them, barely fitting through the doorway. "Tight," it said, surveying the cabin. There was room for it, though not enough to stand, nor did it fit the human-sized seats. The inconvenience of crouching did not seem to trouble the demon in the least. "It will be interesting to see this city," it commented, and no more.

"It will," agreed Im. "It's big."

"There are over a hundred thousand souls living in Tesra," Tuthinos informed them. "It is assuredly the largest city in the world. Perhaps the largest there every has been." He paused but a moment before expounding further. "Our ancestors named it Tesra, the Place of the Way, when they found the streams and springs here and chose to build their town. Now we depend on our aqueducts and on deep cisterns to provide water for all our people."

Tez was the word in Zikem. The Way. So had been named the great river that flowed through the legendary Valley of Visions. Legendary to Na and the people of Hirstel, and probably to those of Tesra as well.

"The Place of the Way," repeated Im. "That has a connotation of the end of a journey, doesn't it?"

"That it does. Our way led us here." He gave them an uncertain smile before adding, "As it has you."

"It's not the end of my way," Im replied and turned his eyes to the streets.

The boy's rudeness was not intentional, Na was sure. "Are these shops?" she asked, to break the awkward silence that followed.

"That they are," answered Tuthinos at once. "We are in the Street of Jewelers. Would you, ah, care to see their offerings?"

"Ho, Tau," she called to her attendant, seated beside the driver. "Do you think I need some ornaments?"

"Certainly not, my lady," came the cheerful response, "but you might pick something out for Master Im."

She could hear the harrumph from behind her where Zerc rode with one of Holos's household guards, perched on seats on either side of the door. "We could always get Cory a pair of earrings," quipped Im.

Na wasn't sure how the demon would react to that. It could be annoyingly literal minded at times. But no, a rumbling chuckle came from it. "Maybe rings for my fingers? Could we find any that fit?" It held forth a hand with digits as thick as Na's wrists.

Tuthinos sat gazing at Cory for some time. "This is as good a time as any to let you be seen in public," he decided. "Let's go find your ring, demon."

"We need some serviceable clothes too," Na told him as they stepped down from the coach. "Those robes we're having made are fine but we need everyday things."

"Of course. Ha, Cory is being noticed." Tuthinos called out, "Fear not! The demon is under our control!"

"And I won't eat you if you behave," announced Cory. It turned to Tuthinos, adding in a lower voice—still a rather loud rumble—"Know, wizard, I am under no one's control but my own."

The wizard answered cooly, "I do know but it is better if they don't."

Cory shook its massive head. "Humans," it muttered.

As they strolled along the way, peering into one shop after another,

Na could observe the citizens of Tesra, the ordinary people, as they went about their lives. Many looked somewhat like Im and herself, their Tezian blood predominant, but there was considerable variety. The blond hair universal in Hirstel was only occasionally seen here.

These were well to do men and women, she suspected, or reasonably so, but few wore the sort of robe she was wrapped in, enveloping with long sleeves. Their garments, both those of women and men, more resembled what she had brought across the sea. They wore mostly shorter, calf-length robes over trousers. The women pulled their pants in tight and tied them at the ankles, while many of the men tucked theirs into boots. Na had seen such trousers on some of the sailors with whom she had journeyed, but they left them loose and untied.

She mustn't forget to outfit their own sailors. "Holos does business with this jeweler," spoke Tuthinos, halting before a shop that looked like all the others. "Or did when his wife lived." They followed him in.

An older woman was busy behind the counter. An armed man, a rather large one, stood in a corner. He became at once alert and looked Cory up and down with definite concern. "Greetings, Lord Tuthinos. So this is the demon I've heard of?" asked the proprietress. "Rumors have been flying. It's all right, Kyram," she assured her guard.

"These are guests of Lord Holos and the prince," Tuthinos informed her. "The sorcerers Na and Im. I am but showing them the sights of Tesra today, madame, and what sight better than your wares?"

Laying it on too thick, thought Na, a parody of a subtle man such as Holos. But some fell for that.

"What is this?" asked Im, his nose close to several lustrous golden stones.

"That is amber, lad, from the far north," the jeweler told him. "It is found along the shores of Lan Sejadedac."

"The Amber Sea, the northernmost of our great lakes, our inland seas. The name is from the language of those who dwelt near it centuries past and is no doubt corrupted, but supposedly means 'god-stone.'"

The jeweler laughed. "I remember well how you like to lecture, Tuthinos."

Tuthinos chuckled as well, perhaps covering a bit of embarrassment. "I do, don't I? But our guests need to learn!"

The woman gave Na and Im a somewhat sharp look. She had been uncertain whether or not we were Tesran till now, hadn't she? thought Na. Maybe there were rumors about that too, floating about this city.

Unexpectedly, Cory, also gazing at the amber, rumbled, "I could shine like that." The demon sounded almost wistful.

The jeweler looked Cory up and down. "That would take quite a bit of polish. And several buffing cloths." She broke into a wide and sudden smile. "A living jewel!"

"Have some sent to the house of Holos, will you?" asked Tuthinos. "We owe you Cory." He casually looked over the selection of jewelry. "And that little pendant there."

"Certainly, my lord."

Tuthinos nodded a farewell and led them back into the open street. Zerc and Tau waited at the curb, attempting to look their parts as servants of important persons. The other two attendants slouched in their seats.

"Penzo," said the wizard as they climbed into the coach, "take us someplace to purchase clothing."

"The Street of Tailors, sir?" asked the driver.

"No, ready-made garments. Know you the establishment of Nuthinides?"

"I do." Penzo clucked to his horses, shook the reins, and they started up the brick-paved way.

"Nuth's is where I buy many of my own garments," Tuthinos confided. "His selection is wide and of good quality. Generally of good quality."

"What sort of shop is that?" queried Im, his head half outside the tiny, round left window. It was a squat, flat-roofed affair, set among the two and three story buildings that lined the street. These were placed close together but there was a space about this smaller structure, where cedars grew.

"That is a shrine. Small temples are scattered through the city and the countryside, dedicated to some minor deity or aspect of the Tetrad. We call them *phons*."

Na craned her neck to get a look at it through the lattice. The only temples she had seen previously in this world were the small open-air structures the Ildin placed atop mounds or hills. The shrine to Banat where she had lived a short while consisted mostly of monastery grounds. There had been a shrine of sorts to Urathu in Hirstel, at the site of the now blocked-up gate through which her ancestors had arrived. No one worshiped in it nor, truly, anywhere. "It's not very impressive," she commented.

"We shall visit the great temple soon," promised Tuthinos. "There will be much going on there with the Yule celebrations. But not today."

"Cory too?" asked Im.

It seemed Tuthinos had not considered this. "I suspect not. The priests would surely object," he answered after a few moments hesitation and a quick glance at the demon. Cory had no comment.

Penzo cried out some word of command—apparently to the horses —Na had never before heard and the coach lurched to a halt. "Ah, here we are," spoke their chaperon. There was another arched colonnade at the ground level of another apartment building. It looked much like all those they had passed that morning.

"Let us outfit your attendants as long as we are here," Tuthinos went on. "Come along, you two."

Zerc and Tau fell in behind Cory. "We should have weapons, too," spoke the older sailor. "Like your guardsmen."

"There are strict laws about who may carry weapons in the city, and of what sort," Tuthinos told him. "Your knives may not be quite legal. The rule is no blade of length greater than a span without a dispensation."

Tau snickered. "We could use Cory's hand to measure our span."

"That would be more a short sword," observed the wizard. "I shall see about having you two licensed."

An hour later—a Tesran hour, that is—they left the shop of Nuthinides fully equipped with undergarments and sensible coats and much more. Some few items they chose to carry back to the house of Holos with them; most would be sent along by the more than pleased and quite agreeable merchant.

A Tesran hour? Let me see. Hmm, they divided the day into twelve hours as do we, but that includes the night. So it is twice the length of the hours you know. And if we have any more interruptions there may not be enough hours in this day to finish my tale! Now where were we? Ah, yes, in the coach, headed back to their lodging.

"We could have stopped for a lunch," offered Tuthinos as the carriage trundled on along one brick street after another.

"I'd rather try out our new clothes. Your friend Nuth was sending them at once, right?" asked Na.

"So he promised." Shortly, they were slowing to a halt.

"This must be home," said Im. "They all look the same to me."

To Na as well. The tall building, stuccoed and painted white, did not have the typical colonnade on the ground floor, only one wide arched entry. Its heavy wooden doors hung open. Penzo turned his horses into the opening.

"What?" They had been stopped short, a jolting, jarring halt. The horses bucked and reared. Penzo cursed. Tuthinos looked chagrined. "My master must have raised the wards again and the demon can not pass through. I'll call to him."

Im stepped down to the pavement and gave the gateway a cursory look. "Pretty simple," said he. "Either of us could undo these, Na."

She followed him out of the coach. Yes, the boy was right. It probably was not a good idea, however, to criticize the chief wizard nor to tinker with his work.

A voice thundered from behind her. "I can not move! There is more than your wizard's bindings at work here." She turned to see the Cory struggling to move its limbs. The great red creature was enmeshed in a web of bindings, both more subtle and intricate than those that kept it from Holos's house.

Such work, the preparation of a snare for the demon, would take thought. Planning. This was part of a plot. At once Na took in their surroundings. Surely there was danger.

Two men approached, casually, until they realized the sorceress was staring at them. Then they dropped any pretense. Then the knives came out.

"Watch out!" cried Na. Where was her own knife in this bulky robe? Someone brushed past her, Zerc, with his long, perhaps not quite legal, blade in his hand. His left hand. Why hadn't she noticed that of the old sailor before?

Ha, old! Na had no idea of his actual age. There was the scabbard. She put her back to the carriage and slid the knife out. Im? He would once again be the target. She looked about but did not see him. Could he have escaped into the house? She caught movement, to her right, from the corner of her eye. "Tau?"

The boy popped his head out through the coach's doorway. He too had a knife in his hand, perhaps even longer than Zerc's. "I'm guarding Master Im," he reported. "He's in here trying to get the demon loose. Thuthinos is helping."

Sensible. Maybe she could make a run toward the courtyard herself, get out of this. Those men probably had no orders to kill her. But the horses were still stamping and snorting ferociously in the passageway, tangled in their harness. Their driver was too busy dealing with them to have do with aught else.

She certainly wouldn't try to get by them! Maybe the commotion would bring someone out. Na turned back to see Holos's guardsman lying face-down on the bricks. Zerc battled one assailant while the other deliberately stalked her, blooded blade in hand. For the briefest of moments, she considered simply running up the street. Instead she gripped her knife more tightly and waited.

Yes, I know I am dragging this out. All this was happening much more quickly than I am telling it! Mere seconds, my friends, but you would feel cheated if I didn't give you all the details, now wouldn't you? And they do say time slows down in a crisis. Don't give me that look, young fellow. When have you ever faced any more of a crisis than your mother giving you a well-deserved whipping? Now—settle down, good people, and we'll get back to our story.

"Stand aside, woman," ordered the assassin. "It's the boy I'm after." He frowned at the young sailor standing in the door-frame. "I was told you had a bit of a beard."

He's mistaken Tau for Im, thought Na. She stepped back, still holding her knife before her. Tau wouldn't desert his post and this man would have to deal with having her on his flank. Had he any sense he would have tried to slay her at once. Unless he had orders not to.

Could Tau handle a knife? She doubted he had the skills of Im; Xido had taught the boy a few things while they were together. Aye, he'd taught her more than a few things as well, and some of them even had to do with a blade.

"Look out, my lady!" Na turned to see the second assassin rushing toward them. Zerc was kneeling, holding his hand to a profusely bleeding arm. The sailor stumbled to his feet, weaponless, and doggedly pursued the man who had wounded him.

The other now slashed at Tau's legs, the obvious target for a man standing above one. Tau himself was not at a good angle to strike back, but could only wave his knife back and forth, attempting to hold his assailant at bay. Was Im having any success unraveling Cory's bonds?

Scarcely thinking about it, Na reached out into another world and grabbed the first thing that seemed at all useful—a torch. She immediately thrust it into the face of the new attacker. His eyes had been on the dagger in her other hand. The fire was a surprise. The man stumbled back, cursing. He stumbled back into Zerc, who gave him a great clout with his good arm, knocking him to the pavement.

Of a sudden, Tau launched himself from his platform, full atop the man he had been holding back. Na heard a sickening crack as the assassin's head struck the bricks. "Ouch," said Tau. A knife protruded from his ribs. The sailor tried to rise and then slumped across the other man's body.

26.

"A POWERFUL SORCERER COULD HAVE accomplished this from a great distance," said Holos, "as you are aware."

"But it seems doubtful," Im replied at once.

Na nodded her agreement. "There were too many things to go wrong without someone close at hand to keep an eye on it all."

"Someone not only had to bind the demon but also throw up a makeshift ward on the gate after I had taken it down, to halt you for a moment." Holos gave them the faintest of smiles, mostly visible around his eyes. "It was most flimsy and could have been taken down quickly."

There was no need to let Holos know they had thought it his work. "If we'd any sense we'd have gone after it instead of the bonds on Cory," said Im.

Na doubted it made any difference. It would have taken too long to get the horses settled down. Tuthinos slipped noiselessly into the library, Zerc in his wake. The grizzled sailor's arm was in a sling, his eyes red. "Tau is dead," the sorcerer reported.

Im's mouth hardened. "I owe Torut once again."

And I too, said Na only to herself. Aloud, she asked, "What of the wounded man? The would-be assassin, I mean." Holos's guard had survived, as well, with little actual harm.

"Alive enough to be questioned," reported Tuthinos.

"But unlikely to know much," Holos said. "Perhaps he can give the name of someone who hired him. Not the sorcerer who planned this." The chief wizard shook his head. "Never has such happened before in Tesra. No one on the streets knew how to react."

"Indeed something new," agreed Tuthinos. "Spies are common but assassins are not a part of life here."

"They weren't a part of life," said Na. "Now they are."

"I fear that is true, my lady. Lord Holos—what wizard might have such power? Could it be someone who lives in the city?"

"Who can say? Had I examined the bindings I might have been able to make out someone's handiwork, but there remain many sorcerers unknown to me."

"I saw them but they were beyond my abilities," admitted Tuthinos. "They baffled Im for some time."

"They were well done," Im agreed. "Complex in design but not so much in their application. I would think there was not enough time for that."

"They would have unraveled on their own in a short while," stated Cory, standing quietly aside, as usual. "That even I could see."

Im nodded and sat wordless for some little time. "What are the funeral customs here?"

I should have thought of that, Na told herself. Tau was my man. "We would want Tau to have all that is proper," she said aloud.

"And I shall see to it," replied Tuthinos. "Our dead assassin will go to an unmarked pauper's grave."

"You bury your dead, then?" asked Im.

"We do," came from Holos. "The custom is not so in your home?"

Im looked uncertain. He doesn't know what becomes of the dead in Hirstel, thought Na. "We do not," she said. "The bodies are sent to the farms beneath the city." Farms was a polite term for the vats of slime and beds of fungus, tended by demons. "A few would wander into the desert when they felt their time was near, and allow themselves to become mummified."

Or if they simply wanted to end their existence. It was more than a few, truly. Im probably did not know that either.

An uneasy silence ensued. Holos and Tuthinos each seemed to be waiting on the other to break it. "A priest can speak the rites here," said the assistant wizard, at last. "Or you can accompany him to the cemetery and it will be done there."

"Here would be fine," said Im.

"Yes," agreed Na. She didn't need to see the boy go into the dirt. The boy's body. Where Tau himself had gone she could not say nor whether he had gone anywhere at all. Xido had told her not even the gods had seen what might follow death.

She felt very weary, all at once, and rose slowly to her feet. "I think I would like to go to my room for a while," she announced.

"Me too," said Im. "Will you come with us, my friend?" This he addressed to Zerc.

"I would sit with Tau a while, if it's all right with you. Um, maybe later, sir."

"Of course," said Im at once. For just a second he seemed hesitant, perhaps feeling he should join the sailor, but he said nothing more.

Tuthinos did speak. "I'll assign you two attendants for now. And have some food sent up if you'd like."

"That would be fine. Thank you." Na gave Holos a polite nod farewell and turned at once to the doorway. Im followed her as she walked swiftly into the courtyard, Cory stalking behind.

The boy caught up, entered the arched way opposite beside her. Neither spoke till they stepped onto the stairs. "If you will have him, I would pass Zerc on to you," said the young wizard. "I shall not remain, after all."

"And Zerc needs someone to look after him? Very well. If I remain in Tesra, I would gladly have him in my service. For now, though, I probably should have a woman."

Im nodded an absent-minded agreement to this. "It was foolish of him."

"It was." Also courageous.

Her new clothes were in her room, both those she had brought back in the coach and those delivered since. "Any of mine mixed in?" asked Im.

"It doesn't seem so. Ah, but these are the ones I chose for Tau." Or Tau had chosen for himself might be more truthful. "They would probably fit you well enough. But this robe—" She held up one of green silk. "This should be his burial garb."

Im held out his hands. "I'll take it down later."

A young woman appeared at the door, bearing a wooden tray. "There's food for you, master, in your quarters," she said. Im mumbled a thanks and slipped past her as she placed her burden on the table. "I'm to be your maid, if you've no objections, mistress."

"Very well." She wasn't really hungry nor did she wish to engage with this woman right then. Na went to the window and opened it to the cool air. The skies were cloudless; the Sea of Sanctuary sparkled as the northerly breeze played across its surface. White sails appeared and disappeared in the glare.

A cart was stopping in front of Holos's house. No, not a cart, she was fairly sure. It was hard to say from this angle. She could tell a pair of dark horses pulled it.

The maid came over to give a casual look. "I would guess that to be the admiral in his chariot," she said. "He was 'spected this afternoon."

The vehicle had pulled off the street and was no longer visible. "Mursoazes?"

"Yes, ma'am. Him and Lord Holos are old friends."

The wizard had mentioned the man was coming. She could greet him later. Perhaps she should eat something—

Na sat down on the bed. A moment later she was asleep.

27.

"I AM AFRAID I SENT your lunch away, mistress. Would you like me to bring something else?"

Na sat up and looked at the woman. It took a moment to brush away every cobweb of sleep and place her. A young woman. Fairly young, at least in appearance. "What do I name you?"

"Cuna, mistress."

"Very well." Na was feeling hungry. She glanced toward the window. The woman had pulled the drapes and probably closed the shutters. Na had no idea how late it might be. "I suspect if I went down to greet Admiral Mursoazes, Holos would feed me."

Cuna gave her a slightly tenuous smile. "Most likely, mistress. Shall we pick out something to wear?"

"We'd best. It wouldn't do to greet him nude."

The smile was much broader this time. "I daresay the admiral might appreciate it, from all what I've heard of him. Not that I'm one for gossip, you understand."

"Of course not, Cuna." Na stifled a snicker. Cuna might have done the same. "I see you have been getting all the clothes in order."

"Yes, mistress. What of those meant for that poor boy?" The maid gestured toward a neatly folded stack.

"Have them taken to Master Im's room. He might find them of use."

Cuna nodded. "He might not wear the leather, you know. Or so I've been told." Her voice rose on the last of this, coming out almost as a question.

"Oh. That is so." Na hadn't thought of it, but it went along with Im's rejection of eating meat. She was definitely not willing to go that far herself. "Well, if he doesn't want them, it will become his responsibility to hand them on to someone else. Now, I need a fresh under-tunic." She shucked the drab and bulky wool robe she had worn all this day and began unbuckling the belt around the sleeveless silk garment beneath it.

Cuna's eyes went to the knife dangling from that belt. "Mistress," she spoke, "it is customary to keep ones belongings, knives included, within ones sleeves."

Na but raised her eyebrows at this bit of information. It might have been nice to know it sooner! That would certainly be one use of those voluminous sleeves. She still disliked them. "I should wash," she said.

Im was already in the library when a refreshed and newly garbed—and ravenous—Na arrived. Mursoazes and Holos sat speaking with him but of Tuthinos or the secretary there was no sign. The admiral hadn't met Im before this day, had he?

"You look a true Tesran, Lady Na," said Holos, rising from his chair and giving her a bow. Mursoazes seemingly concurred, lifting his cup to her but making no effort to leave his seat.

Na hoped Holos was not being merely polite and she had committed no fashion gaffes. Her robe was for everyday wear, one of those purchased that morning, dark blue and falling to mid-calf. Cuna had coerced her into wearing trousers beneath it, and slippers. Im was garbed not much differently. A pair of comfortable looking felt boots protruded from his patterned robe. Maybe she should have had some like those.

Did women wear them here? No matter. She would! Was there any food about?

As if reading her mind, Holos said, "I think we shall have a bite to eat right here. There's to be a formal dinner tomorrow night but there's no need for any of that now."

"But first a toast to your Tau," spoke Mursoazes. "He was a fellow man of the sea and must be sent off properly. And then I must be sent off home."

Na had enough life behind her to know it was not good to drink on an empty stomach. Just one though—

"He liked Peran wine," she offered.

Im gave them a halfhearted smile. "Zerc didn't think much of his taste."

"Yet a good seafarer's drink," felt Mursoazes, "which I've imbibed in many a tavern."

"And a few lady's bedchambers, I've no doubt," Holos said. "There's some about." He clapped a pair of flattened pieces of wood together and a servant at once appeared. "A pitcher of Peran. The red."

The man bowed and hurried away. "Had you wine in Hirstel, Lady Na?" asked the wizard.

"We had what we named wine. Beer too. They did not match up to any I have tried in this world."

"The beer was made of fungus, right?" asked Im.

"It was. I trust you do not use that here!"

Mursoazes laughed outright. "No, my lady, no mushroom beer! We grow plenty of good barley on the slopes north of here. This wine, however—" The servant returned at that moment with a clay pitcher. "Comes from the sunny coasts to our south, the Peran Marches."

"Perhaps too sunny," said Holos. He poured the somewhat pale red liquid into four goblets.

Im raised his cup. "Twice Tau leaped into danger for my sake. I drink to his memory."

Na was surprised the boy took charge so readily, leading the toast. Ah, Im would probably keep surprising her. He was growing.

The wine was decent. Not very flavorful and rather sweet. Possibly higher in potency than she was used to in this world. There had been a process in Hirstel, involving heat and magic, that increased that potency. It helped make life bearable there.

She drained her goblet. That was strong, wasn't it? Na felt a tad unsteady for a fleeting moment. She wisely sat down and the moment passed.

Na.

Someone was there, whispering from the darkness. The sorceress had let her barriers down for one dizzy moment and Torut had reached out. *No*, she said, possibly aloud, slamming up her guards.

Na looked up to see both Holos and Im staring at her. The admiral seemed oblivious. "The Wizard-Lord. He sensed a moment of vulnerability."

Mursoazes deliberately placed his empty cup on the table. "The enemy grows ever bolder," he stated. "Today was more evidence of this."

"He has allies in the city. We can not deny this."

"Not with the open unrest. There are those who fear the Wizard-Lord and those who would welcome his advent. I understand there was more rioting this past summer."

Holos slowly nodded. "Which you missed, being with your ships. There are also those who foment trouble, and networks of spies serving many masters."

Mursoazes's laugh was curt. "It seems we're all spies for one master or another. At least we two are on the same payroll."

"Indeed. And our wizards and those of the Wizard-Lord are forever attempting to spy on each other's communications."

"Wizards seem to have been involved in much of what has happened lately. Magic was used both today and at your house in Phamahd."

"And elsewhere, though not so openly. What powerful sorcerer—or sorcerers—might be aiding Torut, I've no clue." Holos hesitated a moment, swallowed the last of his wine before saying, "I suspect Azil of being involved but have no proof. Moreover, he has powerful friends so it would not do to make any accusations."

"The governor is no wizard."

"He is not," agreed Holos. "You won't stay for some supper?"

"I'd best not. I may neglect my wife when I am across the hills but that does not do in Tesra."

Im said, "I think I shall go sit with Zerc a while."

"An admirable thought, young wizard," said the admiral. "I'll go with you and then let myself out. Good evening to you, Lady Na, and to you my friend."

With that, the two went out into the darkening courtyard. Cory followed.

"It seems only the two of us will dine," Holos told Na. "Unless Tuthinos finds his way back. I'm not sure where he is but I do know there is much for him to deal with."

"The prisoner?"

"Already on his way to the cells of Prince Huenoziles. I am quite willing to leave his questioning to others less, um, squeamish than me."

A meal appeared almost at once. Na assumed the servants of the house had been waiting, ready to bring it forth. "No wine," Holos told them when another pitcher was brought to the table. "Some hot hutnee."

Hutnee proved to be a brown sweet liquid, flavored with spices, and pleasant enough. Na was entirely willing to wash down the simple meal with it. "You and Admiral Mursoazes are old friends, I understand," said she, once her stomach began to feel comfortably full.

"We grew up together. You would not have guessed we were of an age, would you?"

She would not have. Holos looked a good bit older than the

admiral. "He will assuredly outlive me by quite a few years, if he doesn't drown in the meantime. Centuries even."

"I forget there is so much variation among your people," murmured Na.

"I am one who has outlived those I loved," Holos said, "even as Murso will outlive me. And, you I suspect, will last longer than either of us."

Na thought it best to make no comment on that. Instead she held up her cup. "What is this? Is this like the coffee the Bazu drink?" She had seen Bazu merchants drink their coffee across the sea but never tasted it. This hutnee did not smell at all as she remembered that brew.

"It is not, nor will it keep you awake as coffee might. Or tea, for that matter. It is made from the bean of a tree that grew wild on the arid slopes around here when first we settled the area. The name comes from what the native folk called it."

She sipped some more. "I don't think I like it nearly so well as tea."

"Most would agree, I am sure. It is common and inexpensive, and used in our cuisine as well as to feed animals." Holos chuckled. "We even export it."

Na thought to ask where but decided she could learn about Tesran trade some other day. They must export some of that tea as well. Where was it grown? Time enough for such matters if she remained in this city.

As Holos said, she would probably outlive them all.

28.

"NA! NA! NA!" THE WARRIORS proclaimed, striking the butts of their spears in rhythm against the ground, creating one great throbbing drum. Their ranks extended as far as she could see, illuminated in the night by a vast distant fiery mountain, one among many in a high jagged range.

Black was the sky beyond them, without stars. She sat up abruptly and that black void became the lesser blackness of her bedchamber. Na casually pulled in a little light, a brief light, from another world. She was getting better at that sort of thing. No sign of Cuna. Did she sleep in the antechamber, as had Tau?

Tau. She felt a sudden emptiness. Was the boy's death her fault? She had brought him here for no good reason. Not really. It had been but a caprice, as much a joke on Im as aught else. Na set her feet on the floor. They barely reached.

What sort of dream was that? It faded now but enough remained. She had been a queen, yes, and by her side—she couldn't see but she suspected her king's identity. Had Torut planted something or had it all arisen from her own mind? The floor was cold, even through the carpet. She rose, wrapped a warm robe about her, and stepped into the other room. No sign of her maid.

That was just as well, wasn't it? She didn't need that girl here in the night. Na opened the door, peering out into the colonnaded gallery. Only the light of stars filled the sky but lamps burnt all around the courtyard, on each level of the house. A servant filled them all with oil and lit them each evening. She had glimpsed him on his round. Na found that quite as fascinating as anything else she had seen here.

She had not expected the armed guard. There was one at Im's door, as well. "Good morning, mistress," spoke the man.

Na looked him up and down. The costume seemed familiar; it was like those worn by the soldiers sent to meet them on the road. Soldiers of the prince. Huenoziles must have taken notice of Im and her after yesterday's escapades.

This soldier would know nothing of Cuna. She nodded politely and closed the door behind her. As long as she was up she might as well pop into Im's rooms. The guard there was one of those with coppery complexion, as she had seen before. It might even be the same one. She tapped on the door and, not waiting for an answer, went in.

A light came from the bedchamber, a candle, and voices as well. Im and Tuthinos could be glimpsed, sitting at a table, while Zerc snored on his mat to her right. Cory? She looked up. Yes, there he floated, seemingly oblivious.

"My head hurts," croaked Im.

"I do not think our young friend has ever been drunk before," explained his companion.

"Nor ever again!"

"He and Zerc were sitting with Tau and sharing too many cups of wine." He gave the boy a sidelong look. "Or maybe pitchers of wine."

"And Tuthee here joined us," added Im. "He can drink!"

Tuthinos was a substantial man, though not plump like his master. Na could believe the wizard able to hold his own. Im, of course, was but a slender boy.

Na was rather slender herself. She knew enough not to overdo. She had her limits. "So the three of you got drunk together, in honor of our poor Tau."

Im giggled. "I got drunk, anyway. And then I wrestled with Torut." He at once became deadly serious. "He won't try that again!"

So the Wizard-Lord made an attempt on Im as well?

"I entered as best I could, once I realized what was happening, but caught only glimpses of their struggle," said Tuthinos. "We've but returned from telling all this to Holos."

"And you were able to withstand him, even drunk?" asked Na.

"Had I been sober I might have destroyed him," declared Im. Na somewhat doubted this but was not about to say so. "I was slowed down. I know this. My thinking." The young man tapped his head and paused, gathering himself. "But it also opened some of the doors into Torut's mind and memories, the ones that have been part of me since—since his attack on Atima."

"He'd been blocking them, Holos thinks."

Na nodded to this. It sounded right.

There came a timid knock. Zerc snored on but voices came from the other side of the door, one oddly accented saying 'go on in.' A moment later, Cuna's head appeared, peeping into the room.

"I was wondering where you had gotten to," spoke Na.

"I have a husband, mistress," came the woman's reply. She seemed to think that answer enough.

"Well, if you've satisfied him, come along with me then. These three will be worthless for a while."

Cuna glanced upward. "Him too?"

"It too, you mean, and I'm not sure whether Cory can overindulge at all." She led the way down the gallery and back to her rooms.

There was nothing much planned for this morning, was there? The tailors—yes, they would be coming for delivery and final fittings of the new clothes. "I've brought water," spoke Cuna. A basin rested on the table, towels beside it. Na did not think highly of Tesran towels and their flimsy, quickly saturated fabric. She should ask of what they were made. In Hirstel, towels were fabricated from fungus and discarded after one use.

She opened the window. Cold. That was to be expected this early in the morning, though the wind no longer sat in the north. The snow had all melted by yesterday afternoon. "Does it snow often here?" she asked the maid.

"Maybe a couple or three times a year, and never heavy, mistress." Cuna glanced out the window. "No time soon, I would reckon. 'Tis said that being on the seashore brings the snow here. The winter wind blowing 'cross the water."

Well, this girl was full of knowledge, wasn't she? More perhaps than she realized. Na slipped off her robe—it was the wool one she had worn into town—despite the chill, and splashed some water on herself. At least it was fairly warm. It might have been hot when Cuna brought it.

"You'll be wanting your best formal robe this morning," said Cuna. "'Tis too bad the new ones aren't ready."

"This morning?" What was going on this morning?

"For the funeral, mistress. At dawn. The priest has already arrived, and the cart that will take that poor lad off for the burying." She looked the sorceress up and down. "That's why I came so early, of course, so you could be ready."

"Oh." How had that slipped her mind? "There's but the one choice, isn't there?"

"Yes, ma'am." Cuna proceeded to lay out a deep red—almost brown—robe with gold-yellow facings Na had purchased at the shop of Nuthinides. The only one of formal cut, long and flowing, added to the more utilitarian array of garments they had purchased. As the one she had procured in Phamahd, it was wool. It did fit somewhat better.

And it was warm. Nuthinides had sold it to her on that point.

She could eat when they were done with whatever ceremony was planned. Na belted the robe about her and slid on slippers. It didn't matter how they looked; they were invisible beneath the floor-length wrapper. "Lead on, if you will. I do not know the way."

The woman seemed hesitant. Na at once realized she felt she didn't belong, that she would be intruding in the affairs of those she served. This was not something she might have recognized once. "Master Tuthinos can accompany you, ma'am," Cuna murmured.

"Certainly." Na wouldn't have minded having the woman's support but so be it. Tesrans had their ways of doing things. She hurried out of the door to avoid any further exchange.

The sorceress saw that the sentry at Im's door was gone. "Have they already gone down to, um, the rites?" she asked her own guard.

"They have, my lady. I am to accompany you."

They could have just knocked on her door rather than leave a message with this soldier. Oh well. She followed him along the gallery, to the left. Na had not gone this direction before, not further than Im's rooms. Down a narrow wooden stairway and she found herself standing in an arched brick hall, opening to Holos's main gateway. Both she and the soldier remained silent as he directed her into a small side room. There was Tau, laid out on a byre in his green robe.

Im and Tuthinos were there, and Zerc. Cory too, of course. Three soldiers, a small man all in white, and a fellow in a black robe and long beard whom she guessed to be the priest. One of the stable hands stood to one side, probably attending out of boredom.

They were in the stables, weren't they? Or close by them. Na could smell the horses. It wasn't a bad smell at all, even with the faint whiff of manure that accompanied it.

Of Holos there was no sign. Na hadn't expected the busy chief wizard to attend. Not that she had actually thought about it.

"All here?" asked the priest. There were nods and a few grunts.

Tuthinos said, "You may proceed." He then came to stand beside

Na, and whispered, "You said nothing when you came to Im's room. We were uncertain whether you planned to attend."

She was not about to tell him she just hadn't thought about it. "What god does this priest serve?"

"He is a priest of Kerais. Kerais is the god of Earth, as well as being lord of the underworld in one of his aspects. The man in white is the director. He is actually running things here and will convey Tau's remains to the cemetery."

The priest said a few words in a rather antiquated Tesran. It was, indeed, not far from the Zikem that was Na's native tongue. Then he asked if anyone had words to speak of the deceased. There was shuffling of feet and looking side to side. Na stepped forward. "Farewell, Tau," she said. "I am sorry that I brought you here but you died with courage."

"You did die well," Zerc added to this. "I'll miss you, shipmate."

The priest waited discreetly a moment or two to see if there would be more. When nothing happened, he nodded to the man dressed in white. White trousers, he wore, stuffed into mud-stained boots. A white robe hung to his knees. The man methodically unfolded a white shroud and covered the still form of Tau. "Who's to be the bearers, then?" he asked.

Zerc and Tuthinos immediately stepped forward, followed by Im when he understood what was going on. "Should be a fourth," said the funeral director. "How 'bout you?" he asked the dawdling servant.

"I shall bear the remains of Tau," rumbled Cory, stepping forward. "This I think I owe him." The demon could readily had carried the byre himself but he took one corner, as the others, taking care not to lift it too high. Na followed them all out into the arched entryway to the house of Holos. There waited the cart that would convey what was left of the sailor to his resting place.

The cart, too, was white, painted white all over, even the wheels, and the single horse pulling it was, well, almost white. No, that wasn't a horse, was it? A mule. Na had learned to differentiate some of the beasts of this world.

Tau was slipped into the cart; the director climbed into the driver's seat, clucked at his mule, and set off down the mostly empty street. It was but little past dawn. The priest did not accompany him, his role apparently played.

"Will you breakfast with us, brother?" asked the sorcerer.

"Gladly, Master Tuthinos."

Na turned to see two soldiers—the pair with coppery skin and straight dark hair—elaborately and ostentatiously spit on the brick pavement. She felt immediate anger. "Are they disrespecting Tau?" she hissed to Tuthinos.

"No, my lady. They are barbarians of the northern tribes. It is a ritual with them, a symbolic cleansing of any impurities, when they have seen death." He gave her a bit of smile. "Even of small animals. This I have seen."

That's not a bad idea, Na thought. She might have done it herself, rid herself of this morning, all that happened yesterday, had she been in private. Maybe later, though she suspected the ritual would not feel as rewarding if she waited.

"We'll eat in the kitchens. You boys are about to go off duty, aren't you?" Tuthinos asked the four soldiers.

"We are off duty, sir," said one. "As of the dawn."

"For you our relief look maybe," said one of the barbarians. He laughed. "Think you kidnapped!"

"Not funny, Ogit," said the first soldier, apparently the corporal in charge of this small unit.

The kitchens lay on the other side of the courtyard but Tuthinos chose not to cut across, leading them through stables and storerooms, then turning right and continuing past workshops, the laundry. When the wizard's attention was momentarily unclaimed, Na whispered, "The priest does not go to the burial?"

"His task is done. The director handles the interment. He is an employee of the city, and paid well enough to do the job. It would not be amiss, however, to tip the priest. I shall see to that."

A typical long-winded response from Holos's aide. Na had come to expect such explanations; indeed, she relied on them at least a little. She needed to know more of this city and its ways.

The guards coming on duty were already seated at a plank table in the kitchen. "We guessed you would show up here when we found the rooms deserted," one said.

"You were sent by the prince, were you not?" guessed Na, sliding in beside them.

"That we were. In theory, anyway." There were grins and a snicker or two from the other soldiers. "Twelve of us, four on duty at any time, the rest ready."

"Supposedly ready," someone added. "That's in theory too."

"If they ain't asleep. Anyway, we four will guard you, um, guests till noon, two to accompany you wherever, two to patrol this place."

"Mostly to watch the gate."

"Aye, mostly."

One of the men eyed Cory. "You have a pretty good guard already, I hear."

But the demon had its own vulnerabilities. Yesterday had demonstrated that. "Don't rely on it to do your job," said Tuthinos. "Ho, let's have some bread here. And eggs!"

Cuna was waiting in her rooms when Na returned, accompanied as far as her door by one of the soldiers. The air seemed as chilly inside as out, and definitely more so than in the kitchen. She could have sat longer there. Though it was yet early, the sorceress felt tired. Maybe a short nap?

Come.

Xido. She didn't really want to speak with him right then. With a sigh, Na sent a part of herself to their meeting place. *What's up?*

Quite a lot, according to your friends. We all spoke earlier, while you slept.

Oh, Tuthinos had said something of a meeting. But not of Xido. *Holos, too?*

Yes. He has some interesting thoughts. But what of you, Na? You have had a loss. A moment's pause. *I know of loss.*

As only an immortal could, who saw the millennia pass. She knew this of Xido. But could the god truly feel it as did a human? *It—I don't know,* she confessed. *I have not lost anyone here before. Not someone I cared for like Tau.*

Had she ever cared for anyone so in Hirstel? Na couldn't recall such feelings.

You may have to become accustomed to it. The little god's voice was unusually gentle, with none of the sarcastic tone it so often held. *But not inured, my friend. Do not allow that.*

I feel—changed. She could think of no better word.

As you surely are. Im, as well.

He said he struggled with Torut last night. Um, I did too, for just a moment. Na considered mentioning her dream but decided it didn't matter.

I fear this will only make him more eager to deal with the two of you, and swiftly. He now knows he can not match himself against our Im. A crooked smile came to Xido's face. It made him look even more homely than usual. *I think I begin to understand why fate brought him here.*

And you, said Na. Hadn't Xido mentioned sometime he did not believe in fate?

And maybe even you. Who can say?

We could ask Banat.

I'd prefer not. Let his buddy Im do it. Xido's voice had grown sharper, only for a moment. The two gods might be friends but Xido sometimes seemed to resent Banat's influence over the boy. *Holos suggested that knowing Torut's darkness may have made Im more moral, so we can't blame all of the boy's priggishness on Banat.*

I suspect Atima has a role in it.

No doubt. But I think there is something to the chief wizard's thoughts.

A thought came to Na. *You have seen that darkness too.*

And worse. But even I would prefer to distance myself from what lies in the mind of Torut. Take care you never glimpse it, Na.

Again, the dream rose up. The sorceress pushed it back down. Something was going on in the room where she sat. Na turned a greater part of her awareness back to it, to see Cuna admitting a contingent of tailors.

I have visitors, she told the god, and left him.

29.

NA'S NEW ROBES WERE MUCH better fitted than the ready-made ones. For the first time, she felt almost comfortable in this Tesran formal wear. Yes, the sleeves that fell beyond the tips of her fingers were an annoyance, as was the way it wrapped almost twice about her body, secured with a narrow sash. Little of Na was to be seen when she donned these robes!

"I shall wear the yellow one tonight," she had informed Cuna, once the dressmaker and her many assistants had exited. Then she had napped.

Her apparel for the evening was laid out when she awoke. The robe was of silk—all the new ones were—and a shimmering deep gold. Na had turned down all the patterned cloth offered in the initial fittings. She liked this simpler look. The green facings, narrow bands, were nice too. Olive green, the tailor had named the color, but Na had no idea what an olive might be.

As the maid had suggested, a small knife and purse went into the left sleeve, an inadequate kerchief into the other. She decided to keep her familiar blade in its scabbard belted beneath the robe.

Should she just go down to this dinner Holos had planned? Or would someone come for her? She didn't even know how soon it was. Na had thrown the shutters open again, to Cuna's unvoiced disapproval, so she could see the sun falling into the Sea of Sanctuary.

There came a solid, unhesitating knock on the door, three sharp taps. Na waved her maid aside and went to open it herself. Holos stood there; two forms were to be seen behind him. "Resplendent, Lady Na, simply resplendent," he said. "Shall we go?"

"Certainly, Lord Holos." She could scarce keep from laughing at the formality of it all. As Na stepped out, she gave the soldiers another look. "Two guards?"

"Yours and mine. The prince thinks it best I too go guarded now. My life may not be so tempting a target as Im's but the Wizard-Lord would not be displeased by my demise and the turmoil it might cause."

"Our assailants did seek it in Phamahd."

"But I was most certainly not their primary target."

This Na knew. To her surprise, the chief wizard linked his arm in hers and set off toward the right, soldiers following. They did not, however, go down the usual stairs to the courtyard but continued around the corner and along the south gallery.

"Tuthinos's rooms are over here," said Holos. "My secretary's too."

"Catha."

"Ah, you remember her name. It would have slipped away from many. She and her husband dwell, um, here." He nodded toward a wooden door that looked like all the others. There were no windows along here.

Na saw no point in asking what the husband did. It was not something she would even have thought of in Hirstel but people attached more to such things here. "Will they be at your dinner?"

"No. Tuthinos can write down anything that needs writing down. My own suite is here at the end."

"Above your library."

"Even so. Will you come in?" Without waiting for the answer, Holos turned his attention to the soldiers, "Hmm, you'd best come in too. And wait over there by the stairs." He gestured toward them as they entered.

They would exit, then, by that wide staircase to the left. Na knew only it did not end in the library. She gave the room a looking over. Opulent and a bit messy. Like Holos himself. A divan. Rich hangings. Too many colors, too many patterns! As in the library, narrow paper panes allowed diffused light to enter. There might be proper windows in the rooms beyond, probably in the wizard's sleeping chamber.

"I've something for you," murmured Holos. For the first time this evening he sounded slightly hesitant. The wizard retrieved a box from one of the low tables and poured some shining object, some trinket, into his hand. Ah, the amber pendant from yesterday.

Of course, Tuthinos had purchased it at the chief wizard's behest. Na was both a bit pleased and slightly disappointed in this, and could not quite sort out all the reasons why. "May I?" asked Holos.

Na only nodded. He stepped behind her, moved her cascading curls aside to fasten the jewelry about her neck. The short golden chain left the gleaming stone visible at her throat—one of the few places she was not covered up!

The sorceress wished again for a decent mirror. The pieces of polished bronze in this house that pretended to be such were wholly inadequate. Maybe—

There. She reached out across and through worlds and retrieved an ornate, silver hand-mirror. Holos was apparently astounded as she looked herself over. "It's very nice, Holos. I thank you." Maybe she should thank Tuthinos as well. She placed the mirror on a table. "That will go home on its own in a while. I hope its owner doesn't miss it!"

It had been a bit of ostentation and not at all necessary. The pendant did look nice though. It matched her robe well. Satisfied, Na turned her mind elsewhere. She was not a vain woman.

No, she was not. Or, at least, less so than many of us. If anything, the sorceress Na was sometimes a little too pleased by the appearance of her body without clothes. That, my listeners, I shall leave to your imagination. What? Yes, I did say a little of it in my last tale of Na and Im. And maybe I'll say more, later on.

"You seem to have a special gift for that sort of magic, my lady," said Holos. "It is too fatiguing for me to use it often. Shall we go down to my guests?" The wizard chuckled softly. "Our guests, maybe I should say. They have come more for you and Im than for me."

They descended, one guard before, one after. The stairs turned to the left, halfway down, and a heavy wooden door hung open at the bottom, giving onto a hallway. To her left, Na could spy the library. "I brought very little with me from Hirstel," she told Holos, "but I did carry a few favorite books. Would you care to have them? They have proven to be of little practical use in this world." She did not mention they included her own grimoire, eighty years and more in the crafting.

"I would welcome the chance to look them over. Perhaps, though, they should go to one of our larger libraries. You wish to visit those, I am sure."

Na nodded. She hadn't forgotten the most important of all reasons for traveling to Tesra. Knowledge! "Someone's in there," she said. "Oh, Cory. So Im too."

The bulky demon was hard to miss, when it didn't stand in a corner or float up to the rafters. Whether Holos intended it or not, she turned and entered the room. The wizard followed.

"My, so shiny!" she said on getting a closer look at the great red creature.

"Zerc helped polish it up," spoke Im. "With his good arm."

"It has been long since I was burnished so," said Cory.

"Zerc jumped at the task. He begrudges the new servant I've been allotted." The young wizard was perched on the big table, legs dangling, booted feet protruding from a long geometrically patterned red robe.

Tuthinos occupied one of the chairs, going over papers. He looked up at the demon. "It is too bad there are none of your kind to see you."

"Does not matter," rumbled Cory. "It pleases me."

"They are not all of them red like you, I understand."

"We come in many colors, according to our caste." The demon offered no more than this.

"We have seen blue and black so far," said Im. "Is it time to eat?"

"I am afraid not," Holos answered. "Some guests have certainly arrived and would like to get a glimpse of you two. Only when you are ready. We can send Tuthinos to keep them busy for now."

"Certainly, sir," said the other wizard, rising from his chair. "I was doing nothing of import."

"Making up verses," said Im.

"Ah." Holos turned to the sorceress. "Tuthinos here has some renown as a poet." There was the trace of a self-deprecating smile. "In the newer style. I don't understand poetry myself."

"Will you give us something?" asked Na at once. This newly revealed side of Tuthinos aroused her curiosity.

He glanced at Holos. His master gave him no cue. A moment of apparent thoughtfulness, perhaps deciding on what to offer. Then Tuthinos recited from memory.

This poem has no meaning;
it's but a string of words,
dancing to some rhythm
I once piped up and lost.
And if that music's flown,
I do not weigh the cost,
for it has no meaning
more than the songs of birds.

Sheepishly, almost apologetic, he said, "That is in the, um, modern style of which Lord Holos spoke. Some accuse us of abandoning sacred traditions."

Im was the first to comment. "Hmm. I like it. You're not really saying it has no meaning, right?"

"Maybe. I don't strive to understand what any poems mean—especially my own!" A smile accompanied this. "You will find the meanings of some traditional poets painfully obvious as they drone on and on about them in the strictest of form and without a metaphor to be found."

Na suspected both the smile and the statement itself were practiced, for just such moments as this. "In Hirstel," she said, "we remained very strict about keeping to the old forms, but the poems are stuffed with obtuse symbolism and occasional nonsense. I think that was to be expected from a people whose minds half-dreamed in other worlds much of the time. I can see that now."

"There was nothing else happening to write about," observed Im.

"Tindeval fancied himself a poet," Cory unexpectedly announced. "I would have to endure his trying out verses on me."

"And you gave him an honest opinion?" asked Na. She knew nothing of this side of the Prince-Sorcerer.

The great crimson creature shrugged. "Your human languages are inadequate to true poetry. I was willing to tell him so." The low rumbling laugh that followed conjured visions of distant avalanches echoing down mountain valleys.

Im hopped down from the table. "Let's go meet your friends."

30.

NA GAZED UPWARD TO A vaulted, painted ceiling. She could not make out what the painting depicted, but it was certainly colorful. Almost bewilderingly so. Maybe it was meant only to be an abstract design, but that over there—a snake maybe?

She turned her attention back to the humans gathered below it. The gathering was not that large. Na had seen larger, had hosted larger, back in Hirstel. She had, after all, been the second most powerful person in that city, even as Holos was here.

And her home had been more impressive. This dining room, rising its two stories, this whole homely apartment building, could not compare with the imposing, soaring spaces she had occupied there.

Now she was little better than a beggar. She must do something about that. Getting to know these important people was a start, to be sure! Some were wizards. Some were priests. Some were simply wealthy.

Na suspected more than a few of them had finer, larger homes than the chief wizard. Holos did not seem to care so much about show. Not for himself.

Mursoazes spied them at once and advanced, a richly robed woman at his side. "Lady Na! May I present my wife, Elixane. You know Lord Holos of course, my dear," he told the woman. "And this is Master Im, with his, um, attendant."

Mursoazes's wife was quite young in appearance. Na suspected she was in years as well. Elixane also did not look particularly Tezian. She took in all of Cory's imposing height without comment nor any sign of surprise.

"Lady Na," she said. "Master Im? Surely it should be Lord Im, husband mine."

"Shush, my dear. It's liable to go to the boy's head."

The term 'lady' seemed to be applied indiscriminately to any woman of some importance, however modest. It was not a true title as mec seemed to be. Na wondered if mec might not be a suitable title for herself.

Lady could do for now. But Elixane was right—if she were to be addressed so, Im should most certainly be 'lord,' not 'master.' Not that he would care.

The pair fell in with them as Holos escorted them about the room, introducing where he saw proper. He now directed them toward a tall figure in a blue-green robe. The Mec Arana. A shorter woman all in white stood conversing with the priestess. That woman had hair nearly as long as Na's, though dark.

"Arana. I welcome you. Mec Huna, may I present Lady Na and, ah, Lord Im?"

Huna was youthful, in appearance, in her manner. Her robe clung to her trim, somewhat angular form, being apparently of a lighter-weight material than most. An athlete, Na thought at once. And a little vain.

No one could tell anything about Na's shape beneath this stiff voluminous garment she wore. Not her slender waist, her somewhat prominent breasts and buttocks. She might not have been conceited about such things but she didn't like hiding them either.

You see, I told you we might get back to that. Now stop giggling so we can move on.

But she was thankful her thin legs didn't show. Those ankles and calves sometimes seemed too spindly to hold the rest of her up, not that she was exactly large or heavy. "My regards to your brother," Holos was saying to this Huna.

He turned to Na and Im. "The mec is sister to our Prince Huenoziles, as well as high priestess of Trepais."

"Your hair led some to think you might be a priestess of Trepais yourself," said Huna. "It is a mark of our order. But Trepais is unknown to you."

Arana turned to her. "Your goddess has been speaking to you again?"

"It is so." She laughed rather loudly, loudly enough that some nearby glanced at the priestess. Mostly, they seemed amused, seeing it was the Mec Huna. "But the Lady Na knows other gods rather well."

Did the gods gossip with each other? When next she spoke to Xit she'd have to take this up with him!

"The Lord Hiul is not with you tonight, Arana?" asked Holos.

"Oh, he's about somewhere," was her offhand reply. "Far be it from my husband to turn down anyone's food and wine."

"Aren't there two other gods?" asked Im. "Are their priests here? Or priestesses? I'm not really sure which they have."

"All the gods have both male and female servants," spoke Arana.

"But Fasenais and Trepais have chief priestesses while Kerais and Zilais have male chief priests. I think I saw Wuil a little while ago." Huna looked around the crowded room, as if to spot the individual she had named.

"That would be the chief priest of Zilais. He shouldn't be hard to spy. He wears a red robe," said Holos. He glanced at the garment of that color Im wore. "And cuts a somewhat imposing figure. Thevros, the priest of Kerais, is busy at the temple, preparing for the Yule."

"That is the special feast day for the Earth Father," added Elixane. It was the first thing she had added to their conversation since being introduced.

"So it is," Holos said. "I am prone to forget my guests are not aware of such things. Ah, Tuthinos."

His aide approached. "We can serve dinner whenever you wish, sir," said he, after a formal bow to the women.

"Then let us be seated. Murso, I ask you and your lady to hold down the other end of the table for me."

The table extended almost the length of the room. Wouldn't it be more practical to have two or three shorter tables? Na asked herself. But there were undoubtedly protocols of which she was unaware. Maybe some would feel slighted being placed at a different table.

Ha, maybe some should and learn their place! Best leave that all up to Holos, eh? And to Tuthinos. Would he sit with them?

"You two, as guests of honor, shall sit on my either side," said Holos, leading them to the head of the table. Then he leaned in and spoke in a near whisper, "The Lady Elixane may seem demure when at the admiral's side but she is a most competent business woman when he is away. She comes of an important and wealthy provincial family." He let his gaze go for a moment to where the couple took their places. "Murso may be allowed to stray a little but never doubt that she still holds the reins. Here, Im, you at my right."

Na went to the highest place at the chief wizard's left. "No, my lady. Here beside me." The table was broad enough for them to sit side by side. She looked down its length to see the admiral and Elixane so seated.

"Na is to be your lady tonight?" asked Arana, taking the place she had just vacated. She, nor anyone else, seemed to question her right to the spot.

"There should always be a hostess," Huna stated, sliding in beside Im. Apparently she had no male companion. A smallish man, white-bearded, sat next to Arana. The husband, she assumed. His robe was of the same color as her own. A man of good taste! Na told herself, smiling inwardly.

There was some shuffling about as others claimed places further down the table. Some, she noted, purposely chose to be close to Mursoazes. Better than being stuck in the middle, maybe. The sailor was so far away! They would have to use wizard speech if they wanted to talk. Mursoazes had said he could speak from afar, hadn't he? But not well, or so he claimed.

A large, craggy-browed fellow in a red robe settled beyond Huna. His golden beard fell nearly to his waist. This must be the chief priest of Zilais. Wuil, right? And the woman he guided to the seat beside him must be the wife.

Too bad. He was rather nice to look at. In his way. She couldn't help make a comparison to her little Xit. Not so nice to look at but so vital. No mortal man could hope to match a god, in the long run.

Some of those beyond she had been introduced to. Na couldn't remember most of their names and suspected it didn't matter. The first course came, a soup of some sort, but no bowls were placed before Im and Na.

There must be meat in it. Na silently cursed her young companion and gnawed a radish.

31

"THE ADMIRAL INVITED ME TO go sailing with him," reported Im. "He says he'll teach me."

"He taught me. Long ago," Holos said. "You should know he has sent a message to Phamahd, to Captain Mak, about Tau. The captain would, I assume, tell the boy's family."

Na was not sure there was a family to tell. "Thank him for us," she said.

Im nodded an agreement to this, before nodding a goodbye to another guest. A few lingered yet. "It will be after this Yule celebration of yours," he said. "The sailing, I mean."

"A good night to you, Mec Arana," said Holos. "And to you, Lord Hiul."

"You must visit me at the shrine," said Arana, to no one of them in particular.

"Or at our house," added her husband to this. "I would know more of these new wizards of yours, Holos."

The chief wizard laughed. "I am sure you would! There will be time enough, Hiul." He sobered at once. "I hope there will be."

"Indeed," came Hiul's grave rejoinder. The two passed out into the lamp-lit courtyard.

"Are you two friends?" asked Im, looking after them.

"Friendly rivals. Hiul is a fine wizard. Once the chief competition for my office, but we get along well enough." Holos stopped short. Had he intended to say more but thought better? "Unlike his wife," he finally said, his voice lowered.

"She seems friendly toward you," said Na. "Or polite anyway."

"Beneath our banter we are—adversaries. There is no denying that." The wizard turned to his next departing guest, while Na wondered at the basis of their enmity. That was most definitely something she should know.

The Mec Huna lingered to the last, sitting and conversing with Tuthinos. Monopolizing the assistant wizard's time, to be sure; he probably wanted to be about his duties. "Is the mec, um, interested in Tuthinos?" Im whispered. "She's not married, right?"

"Her order does not marry. They are, in theory, virgins," replied Holos.

That surprised Na. Maybe it even astonished her. She had certainly never heard of such a thing before! "All the followers of Trepais?"

Holos chuckled at the idea. "Certainly not, only those who mind the temple. The high priestess is usually chosen from their number these days, though it is not required."

"Being sister to the prince probably helps," remarked Im.

"That is so. Huna is a little older than the prince, but both are young. Huenoziles came to the throne practically as a boy. In his twenties, he was. Ah, here she comes."

Tuthinos had not hurried off to supervise anyone, but ambled along at the priestess' side. Huna stopped and stared long and intently at Im, before saying, "Trepais has spoken to me of you." Her eyes went to Na. They lingered there in a much more friendly—and even frank—way. "Not so much of you, but I would like to learn more."

Oh, ho. So that was where Huna's winds blew. "If time permits, my lady," she said, attempting to sound as noncommittal as was possible.

It was Tuthinos, surprisingly, who broke into laughter. "I warned you, Cana. The Lady Na has a divine and quite male lover, from all I have heard."

Huna but laughed as well, saying, "We shall see. We shall see about both these wizards. They are important, but of course you know that! Is my girl out there?" she called into the darkened courtyard.

"Yes, mec!" A young priestess, a white hood and cloak concealing most of her form, at once appeared at the door; a moment later, both were gone.

"I trust she will report to her brother," commented Tuthinos. "I'd best see to things." With that he strode off to do so.

Holos led them back through the passage toward his library. "What's a cana?" asked Im.

Na had already tried to puzzle out the word. "That means something like 'the consecrated,' doesn't it?"

"It does, and so some speak of Huna as the Cana, because she is in communion with her goddess."

They entered the library. The dim lamplight shone in from outside. "No candle lit?" complained Holos. He sounded tired. "Ah, well, my people have been busy." He settled into a chair.

It was Im who found and lit a candle. And, yes, he pulled the flame to light it from another world. Holos but shook his head at this.

Na took a seat near her host. "A god speaks to me at times," she said. "Can I call myself Cana too?"

The remark was in jest and Holos took it so. "Wizard-speech with Xido does not count. Huna is no sorceress yet her goddess speaks to her, in dream." He sat thinking a moment. "It might have been so with her distant ancestor, Lacoazes."

"The first prince," spoke Im. "The one who foresaw Tesra."

"Then perhaps that talent is inherited even as ours is," said Na. It was possible, wasn't it? "Now we have that out of the way, what does mec mean?" she asked. "Something more than 'lady,' I assume."

"They who hold the title mec command. They are leaders."

"Definitely something more than 'lady' then."

"Indeed so. The word is found in Old Zikem, is it not?"

"Mech, yes, pronounced almost the same. I know it only from

books, as simply an old title of honor. It was not used in Hirstel." As all Zikem nouns, it had no gender. That was done with modifying words. Here, mec seemed to refer only to women.

"There should be a special title for you, Holos," said Im, after a moment of silence.

The man only smiled wearily. "Chief wizard is quite enough." He rose, stretched. "Tomorrow is the eve of the Yule. We'll all be busy. Best we get some sleep."

Na was entirely willing to agree and was at the door of her room a few minutes later. One of the soldiers had accompanied her from the moment she stepped into the courtyard. "I'll be outside as guard," he told her. "Should be someone else here when you wake up, my lady."

Of course, the ever-watchful Cory had also been with them, and Im's own human guard.

"What? Oh, my lady." Cuna rose from one of the chairs. She had surely been dozing. A single candle illuminated the bedchamber.

"You needn't have waited for me. Go tend to your husband."

"He'll be helping clean up the mess in Lord Holos's banquet hall, I dare say. Let's get you out of that robe. Will you want it cleaned for tomorrow?"

"I don't think so. Let's not worry about that now." Na allowed the maid to help her shuck her outer garment. "Now get out of here," she ordered.

"Yes, mistress." In short order, Cuna slipped from the room. Na snuffed the candle and collapsed into her bed, clad still in the under-tunic she had been wearing.

Tired. But maybe—yes, she wanted to speak with Xido. She called, reached out, looked into their accustomed meeting places, but there was no sign, no response. The god might be busy. He might be ignoring her. He might even be deeply asleep.

Na wasn't sure whether that last was possible. She truly knew little of Xido's god nature.

May I speak with you, Na? came an unknown voice.

It definitely wasn't Torut. She should be cautious none the less, should probably raise her barriers, cut herself off from this stranger. A stranger who knew her name. *Speak.*

A man appeared. His skin was the color of raw silk, his nose like the beak of a hawk. The hair was black as was the clipped beard. Dark eyes shone beneath raven brows.

I am Hurasu, he stated, in perfectly accented Ancient Zikem. Or what would have been considered perfect in Hirstel. *No, not the wizard who ruled the valley of the Tez—not exactly—but one of the infinite variations on that man.*

The Urathu we venerated in Hirstel?

Perhaps, my lady; perhaps not. And perhaps close enough it does not matter. The Tesrans consider me a minor god these days. The man laughed. It was a sharp bark of a laugh. *Or a hero who was taken to the heavens to become a demigod. The story varies.*

And you don't know the truth?

He shrugged. *I have always been.*

In potential, this Hurasu had always been. Xido had explained things well enough for Na to know this. Mortals did not create their gods; they discovered them.

Yet, he continued, *I have all the memories of the mortal Hurasu.*

Or believes he does, Na said only to herself. *So why do you speak to me?*

The Tetrad considers me the best choice to carry messages to a sorcerer, having been one myself. The best in this world during my long mortal life. Maybe the best since, too. It was hard to say how serious the demigod was. A slightly sardonic smile ever played about his mouth.

Another voice cut in. *I would not think so, old man.*

Perhaps not, Torut, but it is not you who rivals me now.

The Wizard-Lord showed himself. Too much of himself, as usual, felt Na. *You mean the boy?* he snarled.

Im certainly has potential. The mocking expression remained on Hurasu's face.

Which he will not live to see realized. Torut abruptly winked out.

My children must squabble, said the ancient god-wizard. *You too are among my children, Lady Na. You too have my heritage.*

So I have understood.

The Tesrans remain my people, the true inheritors of all I created in the Valley of Visions. I must ask you, no, must trust you, to defend them.

What of the other gods? The Tetrad?

They are unlikely to become involved. Even sending me was out of character for them. Nor— Hurasu for once hesitated. *Nor do they necessarily favor the side on which you find yourself. You would do well to learn more of them so you might understand this.*

Hurasu faded away. A few minutes late, a weary Na faded into the darkness of sleep.

32.

"Celebrations will start by afternoon," Tuthinos told them. "Not that the entire city is not already on holiday." Holos had other affairs to attend this day; his aide would again be their guide.

"Do we have to go?" Im did not seem at all eager to leave the comfort of the house. Outside, dark clouds hung low over the city, and rain squalls passed through with an appalling regularity.

"The prince has invited you. It would be well to show up."

"Will we meet him finally?" asked Na.

"It is possible but I expect him to be too busy. His sister too. Perhaps I should tell you I tutored them both when I was younger."

"I would guess that explains Huna's friendliness," said Im. He searched through the pastries. "Any left with raisins? Ah, yes."

"They consider me family, in a sense. Never doubt that goes only so far." A servant entered the library. "Yes?"

"Will you be wanting the carriage, sir? Or your chariot?"

"Make it litters, three of them. Oh, and make certain the bearers are armed." As the man left to attend to this, Tuthinos said, "Horses might be more trouble than use among the crowds that will gather. And we must hold to the pace our guards will set."

"And what of me?" rumbled Cory.

"Yes, what of Cory? Maybe I truly should remain here."

Tuthinos looked to the demon. "You can't be persuaded to stay behind?"

There came a chuckle like great blocks of stone grinding against each other. "Not unless you forcibly prevent me, wizard."

"Very well then, come along. But you won't be permitted within the temple. More lunch, anyone?"

An half hour found the three at the gates of Holos's home. Three litters awaited them on the street, with burly, sword-carrying bearers.

As they passed out, a deep grunt came from Cory. "Your wards are still up. I can not pass."

"Oh, Lord Holos must have forgotten to lower them."

Na couldn't help wondering whether he had already known this. "We could take them down, Im," she said.

"I'm not going to bother," replied the boy. He walked back into the archway to stand beside the demon. "We stay."

Tuthinos made no attempt to argue this time. "Take the extra litter back," he ordered. "We head to the temple. Side by side, where you are able. Oh, and a couple of you soldiers had best remain with Lord Im."

"Four of them," said Na. "He's the one who most needs protection." That would leave them the other eight, after all; the entire squad of twelve had been prepared to accompany them.

"Very well," said Tuthinos, nodding to the soldiers. Four detached themselves. The rest fell in beside the litters as they started forward along the wide brick street. There were already crowds, and much traffic seemed to move the same direction as they.

The embroidered curtains of both palanquins were open so they might converse. "There would have been wards in the temple precinct too," Tuthinos told her. "The demon could not have gotten very close."

"And Im would have waited outside with it. Probably willingly," said Na. She could actually imagine Cory tucking the boy under its arm to prevent him going in. "I once suggested finding a way to slay the demon, a thought Im immediately rejected. Never mind that Qu'orth-seth had been on the brink of killing him not so long ago!"

"Yes, I heard his story of their first encounter."

"I wouldn't think of saying something like that now. The two seem to have formed a sort of bond." Perhaps the creature had grown on her a little, too, though she knew it remained completely and utterly amoral.

Yes, yes, it protected Im but it was also the reason the demons of its world sought Im's life.

They were moving west, in the direction of the sea. "These are mostly public buildings along here," Tuthinos informed her. "The prince's palace is over that way." He waved an arm somewhat northward. Na noted, of a sudden, the brick pavement had changed to one of gray stone. Some of the buildings were of stone, as well, or at least their lowest floors.

"We go to a temple of Kerais?" she asked.

"It is the Great Luth, the Temple of the Tetrad," replied Tuthinos. "There are many more temples and shrines in the town and in the country dedicated to one or another of the Four, or to one of their aspects."

"Or lesser gods?" Na's memories of last night's visitor were still prominent.

"Yes, including some that seem to have come with the, um, common folk from our valley home and had nothing to do with the Tetrad, originally. Some from those who dwelt here before us, too."

Na nodded and thought for a moment. "What do you mean by aspects? I've heard them mentioned."

"Each of the gods has six named aspects. Some count even more." The wizard shrugged. "They remain the gods."

"But these aspects might not always agree with each other?" Was this what Hurasu had suggested?

"Some so argue. I am not versed in the finer points of theology, my lady."

Another rain shower rolled in from the great lake and both pulled their curtains closed. It was not at all cold. Still, one of her wool robes might have been a better choice on a day like this. It wasn't like she was going to another formal dinner, after all!

But she might meet Prince Huenoziles. Best to make the best impression, though she wasn't sure why.

The crowd grew thicker around them, allowing them no longer to travel abreast. The soldiers cleared a way ahead, mostly by shouting, occasionally shouldering someone aside. "There be the temple, my lady," said he who strode on the right side of her litter. It was one of the barbarians but not he to whom she had previously spoken.

This one had better Tesran, still strongly accented. Na looked toward the edifice they approached. Not really that large, and for the most part not high, it was of that same gray stone. The walls sloped inward a little as they rose. Squat towers stood at each of the four corners.

"A corner for each god," she breathed, speaking only to herself. But the soldier overheard her.

"So is it, lady. Four gods, four houses." He squinted toward the structure for a moment before saying, "Six highest gods have we in my birth-land, one for each direction."

That interested Na. "Six directions?"

"Those of the four winds, and up and down. Sky and earth."

"Well, that's sensible. Is Tuthinos getting down?" Again, she was speaking mostly to herself and the guard did not answer.

The wizard walked back to her. "We can't move forward anymore, can we?" Na called before he could compose himself to say anything. "So we walk in?" She slipped down from the palanquin.

"Yes. You bearers, stay with the litters until we return. Maybe move them out of the way if you can. Guards, with us. And one of you bring the rugs in my litter." Tuthinos offered her his left arm. His other hand held his staff. "The soldiers can't all come in with us but they can go as far as the gates."

"We shouldn't leave you, sir," spoke the corporal. He had his men already arrayed to clear the path before them.

"Oh, I am sure a couple of you will be permitted within."

That seemed to satisfy the man. For the moment only, perhaps. "One of the men has been telling me of other gods," said Na. "Oh, I don't know your name."

The barbarian soldier was directly ahead of her. "Jom, Lady Na," he said without turning his head nor neglecting his duty. "Of the tribe of Es. Ogit up there is of the tribe of Ger." That was the man with whom she had spoken before, in the house of Holos. He had taken the point position. "In our birth-land we would have tried to kill each other. Brothers are we here."

"Their nations dwell in the north," said Tuthinos, "and many serve in our armies. Most have little love for the Wizard-Lord."

Jom scowled at the mention of that name. "This wind I mislike," he said. "It blows from the enemy's realm."

Tuthinos nodded solemnly at this but did not speak to it. Rather, "One of your own gods shares this day, does he not?"

"Yes, lord. Orgum, he of the sky."

"You and Ogit will have to tell me all about your people one of these days," said Na.

"Tesrans are my people now," came the soldier's answer. They had arrived at the gate. Many were milling about, seeking admittance. Surely most had no reason to expect it. Vendors moved through the crowd, hawking their wares with loud voices.

"Make way for Lord Tuthinos!" called out the corporal as they pushed forward. "Lord Tuthinos and Lady Na!" Many eyes turned their way at the mention of that name. Tesra was curious about her.

"Two attendants only," barked the guard at the opening—arched, as were most in Tesra, a broad barrel vault. On noting with whom he was dealing, his tone became almost apologetic. "One each, my lord," he said. "So go my orders." He might have expected an argument. He had probably had more than one already today.

"Of course," replied the sorcerer. "Choose two," he told the corporal, "and the rest await us."

Neither guard who accompanied them in was a northerner but one looked more Bazu than Tesran. Did the army recruit from the south as well? It might be interesting to speak with him too. Knowledge was not found only in books.

"Show the lord and lady the way to their places," the guardian of the gateway told one of the liveried loiterers there. "Two tiers below the prince."

"In other words, ground level," Tuthinos informed his companion. "Lead on, mistress." Their guide was a woman of indeterminate age, somewhat stout with a heavy-jawed head. She bore some sort of official staff, crowned with a black globe. The black was naught but paint, Na could see.

Tuthinos, too, had carried a staff this day. That was fairly uncommon for him though the chief wizard Holos was rarely separated from his heavy rod. He had left it propped in the library during their dinner last night.

"Holos will be up high with the prince and all the chief priests," he continued. "Save Thevros, of course. He'll be busy at the altar."

They had emerged into the open and Na could see that altar, in the middle of an open-air cruciform enclosure. There were rows of seats on all four sides, except where the towers rose, their corners protruding into the space. All was built of the same great blocks of gray stone.

Great but not nearly so great as those of which Hirstel was built. Those were mostly of the same sand color as the rest of the world she had left behind. Less than a year ago still!

The guide led them to the west end of the space. Na doubted Tuthinos had needed direction. "Here will do," he said. The woman only nodded and held out a hand.

Satisfied with the coin that appeared in it, she said, "A Joyous Yule to you," and hurried off. The seat was of that same stone as everything else, nothing more than a ledge or deep stair-step, and surely uncomfortable. Three rows rose, as they did on the other sides, and the temple walls continued above them. They were thick walls. Thick enough for passages and rooms within them, Na felt. But not large rooms.

The towers were another matter. Maybe she could see inside them some day. "My rugs," spoke Tuthinos. One of the soldiers handed them to the wizard, who spread them on the stone. "You men sit too, on either side of us." He took a seat, and Na beside him. "Nearing mid-afternoon. We shouldn't have to wait long for things to begin."

"Is the prince here?"

"Not yet. I chose a spot where we can see him fairly well. He'll be center, top row. Holos, too." They were somewhat to the left of the center. Or right, now that they were seated and facing the other way. "I doubt anyone will ask us to slide either direction."

The altar in the middle of the space was not so large, nor was it of the same stone as the rest, being of a ruddy brown and apparently unshaped by human hands. Three wide steps of the gray stone led up to it. Was there—? Yes, a portal of sorts was conjoined with it in some way. Not one through which anyone could pass, but a thinning of the wall between worlds. "This is a place of power," Na remarked.

"I should not be surprised you can see that. The altar-rock was recognized as such a place by the first Tesrans and so they built their temple here. It has become hemmed in as the city grew."

Which might explain why the place was not larger. It was packed full of Tesrans! Na considered asking which tower belonged to which god but decided it was unimportant. Unimportant at the moment.

There arose a loud clatter, as of many flat sticks being banged together. Which was exactly what it was, realized Na, as a procession emerged from the archway opposite that through which they had passed. The northern side of the complex it would be. These Tesrans needed music lessons. Didn't they have gongs they could beat upon?

Everyone had risen to their feet. Na wasn't sure why but she did the same. Oh, that was Huna there, wasn't it? She couldn't make out the face but the long hair and white garment made it seem likely. And that just might be Holos at her side. Her attention shifted to the man leading the way as they proceeded in her direction, after taking a turn around the altar.

"Is that the prince?" she whispered to Tuthinos. There was no reason to whisper; the crowd was cheering loudly.

"It is, and his wife at his side." Na gazed in their direction and nodded her head. "Huenoziles married after becoming prince," the wizard continued. "There are children but they are still, well, children. They call me Uncle Tuthee."

Na thought she would like to hear that. She could make out the various individuals now. Huenoziles, as his sister, was somewhat compact but seemed broad of shoulder. It was difficult to be sure of such things with these Tesran robes. The wife looked young. So did the prince himself. Holos and Huna were right behind them, and then Arana and Wuil and their spouses. Some of the other faces might be familiar. She might have met some of them last night.

Most of the attendants and stick-clackers veered off as they approached the seats. The rest of the procession went right up the middle—a way had been kept clear—and settled themselves along the top tier. It started to rain again.

33.

AT LEAST SOME OF THE bad weather was blocked on the western side of the temple. "When does the high priest show up?" Na asked.

"Before dusk," replied Tuthinos, "but not too soon, as that is when the main rite takes place. Nothing is worse than dead time! He'll be emerging from the sanctuary of Kerais. That's the one over to our left."

There had been various goings-on over the past hour and more, speeches and ceremonies and awards that seemed to have nothing to do with any god. There were musicians and groups of singers. Tesran music seemed rhythmically complex but rather simple otherwise. There were none of the interweaving melodies she had known in Hirstel— sometime dozens at a time—nor yet the rich plaintive tunes she had heard and come to love during her short time among the Ildin.

Those folk had a goddess of music, the wife of Banat, no less. That's what these Tesrans needed!

Now, black-robed priests were circling the central altar, carrying bronze incense burners. That might be a sign something was about to happen. Aiee, what a stink!

Torches. She could see them through the open doorway into the tower of Kerais. The *ten*, the sanctuary, Tuthinos called it. It was getting nearly dark enough for them, between the sun falling low over the sea and the gloom of all this day. Here they came, marching out two by two, each black-robed priest bearing a burning brand. That must be Thevros. She couldn't tell much about him at this distance. All the more so in that he wore a hood.

As Thevros mounted the three steps to the altar, his torch-bearers dispersed to the four corners of the court, two disappearing into each tower. The high priest began to chant. Na could make out a word here and there, something about returning light and a new year and a plea for the blessings of Karais upon the earth and those who depended upon its bounty. Farmers and hunters, he named, and he prayed for those who now lay beneath the earth. Kerais ruled them too, didn't he?

One thing to be said for Thevros, high priest of Kerais, was that he had a strong voice. It carried all through the enclosure. Was he done? A gesture to one of his attendants and a torch was handed up to him. "Let the fire of Kerais burn through all this, the longest night!" the priest pronounced. "His people need not fear the darkness!"

With that he thrust the torch into a brazier before the altar-stone. Flames leaped up at once from it. Simultaneously, the priests atop the four towers lit bonfires there. The cheers from the crowd within the temple were matched by even louder ones from those outside.

"Fires will be lit all over the city," Tuthinos whispered. "All through the nation. Logs will burn through the night and the people will celebrate."

And undoubtedly drink too much, thought Na. Not that she was the sort to begrudge them their pleasures. Especially on a dismal night like this. She heard a sort of humming sound, almost masked by the noise of the crowds. What? Didn't anyone else notice it?

A shriek from one of the men atop the sanctuary towers. "Night-wasps!" someone cried out.

Na had no idea what night-wasps might be and didn't wish to find out. "What can be done?"

Tuthinos peered into the dark sky. A swarm of small objects darted back and forth there, above the light of the torches and bonfires. "We'd best get you to safety. Magic won't work here. The temple is warded against it."

So it was. Na looked the net of wardings over. What? So flimsy? She undid the bindings with something akin to disdain. Now what? She couldn't knock these creatures from the sky, not directly, or at least not without endangering the humans below. Na recalled the beekeepers she had seen across the sea.

Smoke. Smoke and smoke and more smoke. Great billowing clouds of smoke. That was what she needed and that was what she pulled from another world. She didn't stop to notice what was creating it. A forest fire maybe. No time to worry about that. Keep pulling it in.

Foot-long striped forms began to fall into the court, buzzing, crawling about haphazardly. The priests scurried from one to another, thrusting their torches into the dazed insects. She suspected the crowd would know how to deal with any that came down outside the temple. Na sat down hard of a sudden, exhausted from her effort. So much smoke! Never had she striven so hard, so long, at such a task.

"That was more than just opening a way," someone said. A woman.

"I don't understand how she did it," came another voice, a bit peevish. "I put up those wards myself."

"Perhaps you shouldn't remind people of that fact." Na looked up. Her mind was clearing, her dizziness passing. It was the Mec Arana and her husband, what's his name. Hiul. That was it.

"There was a loose thread," she said. "I pulled on it."

Somewhat to her surprise, the white-bearded wizard laughed, shaking his head. "And it unraveled, my lady?"

"I suppose no one noticed it before," spoke the mec. It was hard to make out how she felt about this. "Wizards simply don't question my husband's work."

Holos stepped forward. "And with good reason. Lord Hiul is an adept sorcerer."

"But not as adept as this young lady, it seems," remarked Hiul. "Take good care of her, Holos. She may be valuable to our cause."

"So have I thought from the first."

Na attempted to rise but her head swam. A hand on her arm

steadied her as she settled back onto the rugs. Tuthinos. "What were those?"

"Night-wasps. Very rare this far east and then only in the summer. Today's darkness and the winds must have brought them."

"Torut's winds," came a firm voice, a woman's voice. "Plagues have come on such winds. One struck down our father."

"It is so," came a surprisingly similar but masculine voice. That was the prince, wasn't it? And his sister. Na tried to get to her feet again but failed. Or maybe Tuthinos's firm grip kept her from rising.

"Would we had our bows with us, Huna. We could have had sport shooting them from the sky."

"They are dangerous?" asked Na. And wouldn't shooting arrows into the sky above these crowds have been also? Huna's brother seemed a reckless sort! Maybe Huna was herself.

"Their sting is sometimes deadly," spoke Tuthinos. "Always debilitating and extremely painful. Or so I am told."

"I'll fetch one," said Huna abruptly. The woman ran out into the court and scooped something up in a corner of her robe.

"A bit burnt," she said, exhibiting the insect on her return. "Squashed too."

It was a wasp or something much like one, fully a foot long, black with blood-colored stripes. A sharp barb on its tail still twitched though it was thoroughly dead. "They attack humans," said Huna. "We don't know why."

"Conditioning, maybe," commented Holos. "Or an instinct bred into them. Almost certainly the Wizard-Lord's hand, either way." He turned to Hiul. "We should get the wards back up soon."

"Get Im to help you," said Na. "The boy ought to do something useful."

34.

"I DO NOT THINK HIUL mismade his bindings," Na announced. "Someone had meddled with his work and created that way of quickly undoing them." She had thought on this in the night, had reconstructed in her mind the wards she had so quickly taken down.

"For use at some future time, perhaps to allow an attack. Your discovery of their flaw would not have been expected." Holos nodded at the logic of that as he rolled a small orange about in his hands. "The wasps, of course, are but animals and no bindings would have kept them out."

"But the temple was warded against the use of magic?" asked Im. "I've never heard of that."

"Nor had I. The opening of ways to other worlds was blocked. Hmm, I suppose that is related to warding against a being from another world."

"Maybe," admitted the younger sorcerer. "More abstract. I should learn it!"

"A waste of the altar stone, I think. It has some of the properties of your Jewels back at Banat's shrine, Im."

"Which is why it was warded," spoke Holos. "There are those who fear such power." He began to peel the fruit, laying out the pieces of rind neatly on the tabletop. "Your actions were quite impulsive, Na. You have a penchant for that."

"Good in an emergency," opined Im. "I'm too inclined to still be thinking when Na acts."

This was true. Sort of. Over simplified. Still, Na appreciated the boy's compliment. It was a compliment, wasn't it?

"Good last night anyway," said Holos.

"Did Torut actually send his stinging minions to attack us?" She asked.

Holos but shrugged. "Who can say?"

"I wish you'd brought one home for me to see," spoke Im. "Nothing exciting happened here. In fact, all your people seemed rather gloomy, Holos. Wasn't it supposed to be a holiday?"

"Yesterday, Yule Eve, is a time when we Tesrans show a special reverence for our ancestors and all who have lived in the past. We do tend to be a bit somber, at least until sunset. Today, with the new year, we look to the future. It is a day for family and children."

"Your children are grown." Holos had told them this.

"But there are grandchildren. I expect visits before this day is done." Holos sat, quietly thoughtful, for a short time. "I have heard of Im's family but not yours, Na. Have you parents in Hirstel? If you mind not the asking."

"No." she replied. Too curtly, she realized at once but chose to add nothing more. Na's father was an unknown, her conception the result of a casual dalliance. As for her mother, she had not spoken with her for decades. The chief wizard need not know any of this.

"We are cut off from anyone in Hirstel," said Im. "Speaking from afar was rarely practiced. There was no need for it."

"Ah. And so none there are attuned to a call from you."

"Most would not even recognize it for what it was," Na told him. And that was just as well.

"Though I'll bet we could get through to Tindeval," Im said.

"Why?"

"Hmm, no reason, I guess. Unless he wants to adopt me and be my dad today."

"Let Holos do that. Or even Tuthinos. Where is he, anyway?"

"With Huna and Huenoziles," said Holos. "They do see him as family of a sort. More so since their parents are gone. They sometimes refer to him as their big brother." He give Im a discerning look. "I believe a god has already adopted you, my boy."

Im snickered. "And abandoned me. About what one should expect from the Trickster."

Na was inclined to agree with that. Xit had abandoned her too. Well, they had abandoned each other. She knew that was for the best.

The secretary appeared at the door. She was not dressed so formally as they were accustomed to seeing her. "A message, my lord," she said, holding up a piece of paper. "From the admiral."

"Thank you, Catha. I do not think I will need you again today. Run along."

"Yes, sir." She scurried off. Na wondered for but a moment whether she had children, before Holos began giving them the contents of the letter.

"Come visit me this morn, he says. Meaning you two, not me. Murso says he'll take you out on his boat and show you the *bonya*." The wizard chuckled rather loudly over this.

"Merfolk, right?" asked Im. Na had never come across the word before.

"Indeed. It is an old word, a word from myth and the languages our people spoke before Hurasu taught them Zikem, it is believed. There are merfolk dwelling about the islands in the Sea of Sanctuary but they are unlikely to show themselves in this weather. For that matter, they are always pretty shy."

Ah, now I see expressions of disbelief among you, my worthy listeners! I have it on the unimpeachable word of my friend, the sailor Bandis, that mermaids of great beauty abound in the Southern Seas. In fact, he claims to have wedded one and fathered a number of fish-tailed children. No, no, I can't give you that story today. Go ask him down at the docks if you disbelieve—he can be found in one wine-house or another—but first leave some small token in my bowl.

Holos perused the rest of the page. "He'll be showing up here shortly."

"I wonder if Cory can fit in his boat," said Na.

"You know it can float along beside it in the air," Im reminded her, "if it's not too far. It could have done it all day back in Hirstel, where its powers were greater."

"It is formidable enough as it is," commented Holos. He popped the last orange segment into his mouth.

None could withstand the demon when it guarded Piras Tindeval's tower. Its powers were unimaginably beyond those of any mortal. Here it was strong but far from invincible. "We'd better find appropriate clothing," she said.

Both were ready and waiting in the entryway to the house of Holos when Mursoazes rode up in his chariot. He had no driver, handling the pair of stamping horses himself. Both were dark but unmatched in color. The admiral was not one to care about that sort of thing, she was sure. He looked the party over, without dismounting. "Cory too? I guess I should have expected that. You'll have to run alongside, demon."

The horses were giving Cory suspicious looks. Na doubted they would like it running beside them. "But not you Zerc, nor the soldiers," continued Mursoazes. "I don't care if the prince did assign you to watch these two. Now hang on."

The last thing Na glimpsed was Zerc's disappointed face as the admiral wheeled his chariot about and set off down the street at far too great a velocity. Would any of the Wardens of the Ways—so Tuthinos named them—dare stop and admonish so important a man?

The sky remained overcast, but there was no rain this morning and the wind had grown fitful. The unseen sun still lay low in the eastern sky. If there had been snow and cold weather across the sea it had stopped short of Tesra. Would the water be rough? If the admiral slowed down she would ask him; as it was, Na held on and held her tongue.

At the advice of Cuna, Na had donned trousers, and a thigh-length jacket rather than a robe. Im was dressed much the same. Those were Tau's never-worn clothes, weren't they? Including the wide leather belt. "I didn't know if you would wear the leather," she half-shouted over the clatter of the hooves.

"I wear it with respect for the creature from which it came. It would be wrong to discard it."

That was one way to look at it, she supposed. If faced with a similar ethical conundrum, she might have simply given the belt away, making it someone else's problem.

Then the Sea of Sanctuary lay gray before them. The wind, blowing first one way and then another, and never hard, raised but a light chop. A flock of gulls cried, wheeling overhead.

Mursoazes looked up at them. "A few seabirds winter along these coasts. Most go further south. That's my boat over there. I name her *Woran*. That's an old name for the rainbow. Pre-Zikem, I'm told."

"Some kind of god, too, isn't it?" asked Im. "I've heard the servants swear by the name."

"Oh, well, yes. I wasn't going to bring that up. The Rainbow Snake is a very old deity, its worship far older than that of the Tetrad. It's not a bad idea to have its protection for my little boat, is it?" The admiral sounded just a little embarrassed. Most unusual for the man.

Na remembered the snake she thought she had made out wriggling across the ceiling in Holos's banquet hall. She'd have to take another look.

"Any protection is good when surrounded by water," she said. "Will it be just we three? Or four, with Cory."

Mursoazes looked the demon up and down. "You must weight at least as much as two men, eh? Maybe three. We'd better carry no more crew."

Na wasn't sure of the three men weight. Perhaps if they were really large men.

"And I hope you can row as well as three, if need be!" added the admiral.

"I can get out and push," came Cory's response. There was no clue as to whether it was serious.

A groom took charge of Mursoazes's horses and chariot. "Come along," said the admiral, leading them onto a stone quay. Was it that same gray stone of which they had seen so much? It looked a little different, but maybe just because it was wet. No, it was a tawny color, and had a rougher, grittier surface. Probably less slippery! The boat itself looked like a boat. That was about all Na knew. There was a single mast and the vessel's length was perhaps the height of three men. Large men, again.

Na felt something, something quite unexpected. Someone had placed a hand on her buttocks. "That should not be there unless you wish to lose it," she whispered. "I *am* carrying my knife." Two of them, actually.

Mursoazes's paw slipped away far too slowly. "What would your wife think of this? And your mistress?" she asked.

"Mistresses," the sailor replied. He sounded not the least repentant.

The sorceress was not at all accustomed to such things. None would have dared it in Hirstel. She was far too important there, and far too powerful. So it had been since she was a talented girl first making her mark. Perhaps Mursoazes should learn it was going to be the same in Tesra.

"Let it not happen again," was all she said.

"Very well, my lady. Let's get on our way then. In you go." Mursoazes undid the mooring line and hopped in after them. "Take an oar, boy, and we'll get it away from the dock."

There came a subterranean chuckle from Cory. It stuck one broad hand into the water and paddled them out into the open. "I see you're useful after all," quipped the admiral.

To this, the demon made no reply, but Im said, "I reckon Cory wanted to get going. We take too long."

Cory's head went back and forth. "It is hard for me to see here," it announced. "My vision is not as yours."

Na had been vaguely aware of this fact. Cory sensed energies or something of that sort, not solid forms. Im knew much more, she suspected. There must not be much energy to see out here on the cool featureless lake surface. There wasn't all that much for human eyes.

"Keep watching for mermaids anyway," Im told it.

"They are not eaters of men here, are they?" asked Cory. "I have heard of such in some worlds."

"None in this lake," Mursoazes assured them. "Nor likely to seek human lovers, either, as those in the southern seas."

Na wondered about the truth of that.

Yes, as do some of you. Let's not let that get in the way of the story right now.

"They're not found near the city, anyway," the admiral went on. "Too shy of us. Some do live around my island estate, to the west." The slightest of a grimace. "My wife's island, I should say. It belonged to her family."

"And where is your wife today?" Na could not resist asking.

"With her sister's family. I'll see Elixane later. Here boy, help me get the sail up and I'll show you some things."

Apparently Mursoazes had wanted to show her some things too. He would not make the same mistake twice, Na was fairly certain, but there would be other men in Tesra. It was something she must deal with. Things could not be as they had been in Hirstel, empty, meaningless, the lovers who came and went. She would not let it be so here.

This world was different anyway. Na felt awake here as she never had in that lost desert city of dreams. She could have all she wanted here, couldn't she? She could be happy.

The boys—it seemed as good a label as any—had their sail up. "Mak told me you called up a wind from another world for him," Mursoazes was saying. "We'll try to get by with what this one provides today. There, pull the line a bit toward you. Yes. See? The wind doesn't push, it lifts."

"Ah. Like the wing of a bird." Im's eyes went to the western horizon. "So where shall we fly?"

What did Im know of birds? wondered Na. "You say there are islands?"

"Many dot the Sea of Sanctuary. The larger ones are all further west, too far for us today! There." The admiral's outstretched arm pointed somewhat northerly, Na thought. It was not a good day to make out directions. "See the isle?"

"Um, no," admitted Im. Na shook her head.

"So blind!" rumbled Cory. "It burns with power."

Did it? Maybe she could sense something when they drew nearer. "More than a few powerful folk have villas on one island or another," Mursoazes said, steering the boat more or less in the direction of the purported isle. "There are shrines on some, too."

"So which is this one?" asked Im.

"Neither, exactly. You'll see if this wind would decide to blow one direction for a while."

In time, Na could pick it out. They were already fairly close and it loomed large, but so near the color of the misted sky it was hard to differentiate. Hmm, yes, there was some sort of power here.

"A portal?" whispered Im.

"Could be."

Mursoazes guided the boat around a low headland and into a shallow bay. "This place belongs to the prince, in name, but he essentially holds it in trust for the nation. A museum, of sorts." Evergreens rose close to the shore, a welcome sight on this dreary midwinter day.

"Then no one is here?" Na asked.

"There will be some priestesses around, no doubt. They won't mind us." The boat came alongside a modest wooden dock. Cory reached out a long arm and pulled them close while the admiral tied up. No other vessels rested there. "Priestesses of Trepais. The Mec Huna's fond of the place." He gave Na a grin. "You may have to swat her hand away one of these days, my lady."

"And who says I'll want to?" she replied.

Mursoazes roared with laughter. Im looked perplexed.

35.

"You will find these standing stones here and there all around the eastern end of the sea," the white-robed priestess told them. "These ones have a special power to them."

Na could see that clearly now. "Raised by the people who dwelt here before the Tesrans, right?" asked Im. "That must have been a lot of work."

Especially without demons to help them. There were six tall monoliths, arrayed in a circle. And at their center—what? Na could not make it out exactly.

"We believe it connects in some fashion to the gods they worshiped," the woman continued.

"Ah!" said Im, of a sudden. "A portal of the gods. And only they can pass through it. See it, Na?"

Hmm. Maybe. "And they have no worshipers left here," she half-whispered.

"A few, my lady," said the priestess. "They are not completely forgotten. As for it being their gate, young sir, I wouldn't know."

But he was probably right. "We thank you for your time, my lady, and wish you a Joyous Yule," spoke Mursoazes, turning to his companions. "Now we had best get you back to Tesra before the prince and chief wizard both become too worried! Or Cory, for that matter." The demon had been persuaded to remain at a distance. It had seemed less than eager to approach the stone circle anyway. They took to the path leading back to bay and boat.

The way was not far. It was not a large island, only a rocky hill rising from the Sea of Sanctuary. Cory stopped, its head going back and forth, searching, and then tipping upward. "I have seen those before," it said. "On the ship. They mean you harm, Master Im, do they not?"

They all looked up. "That they do," said the young wizard.

"Rupa," breathed Mursoazes.

"I can destroy them," spoke Cory. It sounded sure of itself.

"Do you think we will allow you, criminal?" came a deep voice. They turned to see two great demons, identical to Cory save for their deep greenish-blue color, standing in their path. The demon police of its home world.

"We take the policemen!" cried Na. "I'll get the one on the left."

They would have to depend on Cory to handle the menace from above. Mursoazes had not even carried a sword onto this island. The demon police rushed upon them, hoping to overwhelm the two sorcerers before they could do damage—and, of course, kill Im if they could. They had learned and improved their tactics!

The creatures were perhaps slightly smaller than Cory. Nearly as strong and probably more agile, they did lack its acclimation to this world. They would be less certain in their movements, less trusting of their untested abilities. Suddenly, Cory barreled between the two humans, arms extended, and crashed into the demons, knocking them to the ground. "Gave you some time," it said, and turned its attention back to the rupa.

It was the time they needed. Im and Na both knew the best way to deal with these beings. Im had figured it out, realized they could be 'deflated,' part of their essence squeezed out of them and sent back to their own world. Like great bags, without internal organs to speak of, the demons were filled with some sort of 'ether.' They didn't know what else to call it. That ether could be sent back to their world, to which they were still connected. Both wizards knew the mechanics of it now. The police-demons began to wither and quickly winked out, drawn home before being permanently damaged. There were undoubtedly safeguards in play, placed by the demon sorcerers who sent them.

But the rupa—five of them, there were, red woman-like beings with wide leathery wings. They circled back and forth just overhead, eluding Cory's attempts to grab them. "Don't look at them!" cried out the demon. "They will bewitch you!"

Mursoazes already stood in a daze, staring at the creatures. There was something about them, as if they went in and out of focus. Oh, she understood. "They are moving in and out of worlds," she called out to Im. "Duplicating themselves!" She suspected Cory was immune, not seeing as did humans.

There was a sudden twang. One of the rupa fell to earth, an arrow through its chest. The priestess. She was calmly nocking another arrow. The four remaining rupa turned toward her, shrieking. The moment's distraction allowed Cory to leap high and catch one by a leg; in another moment it was dismembered. The other three sped toward the woman.

A powerful wind, a wind such as Na had never felt, struck her, sending her flat on her face. She could see it hit the rupa, sending them whirling, cartwheeling through the sky. The priestess fell to one knee to brace herself, drew her bow, and then, shaking her head, slackened the bowstring. There was no shot. Mursoazes sat on his arse, bewildered.

Then the wind was gone. At a distance, Na could spy two of the rupa come together, hover for a moment, and wing off toward the west. Where was the third?

"One broke its wing," spoke Cory. "Over there. Best I go finish it off." It stopped suddenly and turned to Im. "A bigger wind than you called for at sea, Master Im!" Its laugh was a thunderclap, as it strode off to find the injured rupa.

"That *was* quite a breeze," said Na, rising and dusting herself off. "I could have broken a wing too."

"A typhoon on some sea in some world," said Im. "I rather rushed to find it."

"And who was the impetuous one this time?"

The boy laughed. "You should be glad of it, Na! Let's check on the admiral."

Mursoazes was already recovering his wits. Not all of them, to be sure. "What happened?' They helped him to his feet as Cory and the priestess approached, side by side.

"Funny thing," said the woman. "The injured rupa fluttered into the circle and disappeared. No one has ever heard of that before and believe me many have gone in and stood there over the years."

"I think maybe I might disappear too if I tested it," stated Cory.

"So don't try it," Im told it. "We have much to be grateful to you for, my lady," he said to the priestess, "and know not your name."

"I am Alpisha," she said. Alpisha was not a young woman; she looked at least Na's age. She had Na's blond hair too and wore it just as long.

"We all thank you, Lady Alpisha—" began Na.

"Sister Alpisha."

"Sister Alpisha, then. We must get Admiral Mursoazes home before the prince and chief wizard worry too much about him. Farewell and our thanks again."

In a few minutes, they were at sea, with Im steering as best he could. Fortunately, Mursoazes regained enough of his senses to get them into port.

36.

"WE CAN HASH IT ALL out tomorrow," Holos had said. "Now is still the holiday." An abashed Mursoazes had returned them by the early afternoon. Na and Im had cleaned up, and rested now in their rooms, but were invited to join the wizard.

And his family. Na was both curious and nervous about that. Why the latter, she was not certain; the children and grandchildren of the chief wizard meant naught to her. She went out into the gallery and to Im's door, her guardian soldier following. He might not let her out of his sight again!

"Are you ready to go downstairs?" she asked, standing in the open doorway. Im was in a chair, leaning forward with his arms on the windowsill. The boy was gazing out over the city. The new manservant was busying himself with nothing of importance.

"I think I shall skip it," he said. "I suddenly feel quite worn out."

And his heart was far away. This city was not and never would be his home. Was it to be hers? "Resting is probably the smart thing to do," she replied. "I'll just go down and say hello." Yes, a brief polite visit. Nothing more was needed. "There will be pastries, I suspect," the sorceress could not resist adding.

"You can have mine." The boy wasn't fun at all this afternoon. He did sound weary.

A few minutes later she was at the library doors. The sentry there opened for her. That was a relief; she had been uncertain whether to knock or go in. Candles flickered but the room was unoccupied. Might Holos be upstairs? Na decided not to go looking, but took down one of the books and began leafing through it, not really paying much attention to the words. Something about cultivation. A moment later she noticed a diminutive form at the doorway into the hall.

A child, staring at her with wide eyes. A little girl? She bolted and ran back the way she had come. "Grandpa! Grandpa!" Na could hear echoing.

'Grandpa' was not long in coming. "Welcome, Lady Na," said Holos, "and a Joyous Yule to you. We are happy you chose to join us." The little girl peeked from behind his substantial form, wrapped in peach-colored silk. "Run back to your mama, will you, dear?" he asked. "The lady and I would speak for a little while."

He took a seat beside her. "My daughter's daughter. We would be pleased if you sat down to the Yule dinner with us."

"I would not wish to intrude," Na murmured. Yet she did wish it, didn't she? Going back to her room had not the slightest allure.

"Nonsense. You will eat with my family, my lady. Um—" Holos seemed to have remembered something. "You don't eat meat though."

"I might, if Im isn't watching," she admitted. She had to giggle at that. Im as her conscience!

Holos only raised an eyebrow at the remark and went on. "You have no problem with dairy, do you? Some Tesrans are more comfortable with it than others."

"None had consumed milk for many centuries in Hirstel but Xido said we had the heritage within us. We only needed the right, um, tiny creatures in our guts. He took care of that, as he did when he protected us from diseases." That was not very long ago. It felt like forever at times, while her lifetime in Hirstel seemed no more than a moment. "Im grew quite fond of milk with his morning cereal. And raisins." Na rather liked those herself.

"I have seen how much he enjoys raisins. I'll have to see about having milk delivered here." He paused just a moment to consider. "If the boy stays in this house. I admittedly can not handle raw milk but have no problems with yogurt. That was introduced to us by the nomadic barbarians of the north."

Like Ogit and Jom? That was probably whom he meant. "There seem to be barbarians of the south among your people too," she said. "I mean Bazu."

"Best they not hear you name them barbarians! Some have taken service. Some live here and have become Tesran. There is a Bazu city, Bitasa, that is part of the Unem. It lies south, where the coasts of the Great Sea curve back westward, and thus lies not so far away from our river routes, though mountains rise between. But this is no day for geography lessons, Na."

Before she could reply, the wizard seemed suddenly distracted by something. Was he speaking from afar with one of his subordinates? Maybe Tuthinos. She could join them and say hello but that wouldn't be good manners.

No. There was a presence of some sort. Here but not here. An elemental! Then Holos was back. "Pardon my momentary lapse of attention, my lady. I had to speak with an *anxem*."

"We used elementals quite a lot in Hirstel," she told him. "To carry messages, since we didn't speak from afar. You do the same?"

"Yes, the anxem are indeed minor elementals and it is sometimes safer to use them for messages. Less work, too."

That was certainly true. Na decided she should look into their use. It had been long since she had even thought of the little beings, although they were all about, floating from world to world. One forgot their presence. Holos was rising. She should too. Go and meet his family. She allowed the chief wizard of Tesra to link his arm in hers and escort her from the library.

She didn't mind Holos's touch. Why she might even have tolerated his hand on her rear end. If it didn't linger over-long! Into his banquet hall they proceeded. Altogether too large a space for only a few people. Wouldn't his private rooms have been better?

At least the long dining board was no longer there. Most of its sections were pushed to the walls and a smaller, more intimate table remained. Two adults, young adults, sat there sipping at drinks. The little girl climbed down from her place at once and ran to them, stopping short and shyly looking up at Na. "This is my granddaughter Turana," said Holos. "Can you greet the Lady Na, Turana?"

A quite solemn "Joyous Yule!" came from the little one, before she became bashful again and scampered back to her parents.

"My daughter Tennas and her husband Zerapules." There were polite bows of the head and polite murmured greetings.

They don't know what to think of me, Na told herself. They've heard rumors and some might be alarming.

"My sons are far away this year," Holos continued. "It is good of them to spend time with an old man."

Tennas snickered. "Do not take my father seriously," she confided to Na.

The sorceress took a place beside her. "Of course not. He's a politician. How could I?"

"Ah, at last a woman who understands you as I do, Father!"

Na doubted this was true. But she did think she knew something about Holos. She had dealt with other men like him. Piras Tindeval, Prince-Sorcerer of Hirstel, most prominently. He too was both a politician and a powerful magician.

Small talk and family gossip followed. Zerapules, it seemed, was some sort of bureaucrat. The missing sons were both in the north, one a soldier, the other a merchant. Na's attention wandered as did her eyes, about the great mostly-empty hall. The large hearth at the far end held no fire tonight, as it had during Holos's party. A bronze brazier, filled with coals, provided them a modicum of heat. She looked up to the painted ceiling. Yes, that definitely was a snake and it might well have the colors of the rainbow. Tesran art seemed crude to her.

"I knew nothing of snakes before coming to this world," she said.

The others followed her eyes. "I forget that's up there sometimes," admitted Holos. "Painted before I took residence in this house."

"We used to live up in the hills," said Tennas. "My parents had a villa."

"No longer practical." Holos didn't seem to want to dwell on that subject. "The snake is an old motif in Tesra."

Tennas shook her head. "Much more than that. In the oldest myths of our people, those that go back even further than Hurasu, the Rainbow Snake was the creator of the world, the offspring of the Sun and the Water."

Na had to smile. "She sounds like Tuthinos," she told Holos.

There was sudden silence all around. Little Turana looked from one adult to another, wondering what had happened. It was Zerapules who spoke first. "My wife was once betrothed to Master Tuthinos." He gave them a lopsided smile. "They avoid mentioning him around me. As if I might be jealous!"

Maybe he should be. Tuthinos had the highest of friends while Zerapules was a mid-level functionary. But when it came to his wife? "Tuthinos should be jealous of you, Master Zerapules." Na, too, could be a politician.

"I hope so," said Tennas, with perhaps a little too much enthusiasm. Her husband only laughed at the remark.

"And I think I'd best signal for the first course," Holos said.

Perhaps inevitably as the evening and meal—surely the best Na had tasted in this city—progressed, the conversation came back around to myths. "I understand you visited the standing stones on the prince's isle today," said Zerapules. It was unlikely he had been told of what else occurred there. "There are quite a few such in the countryside."

"Erected by the earliest inhabitants, I understand."

"Maybe not the earliest," said Holos. "But here when our people arrived."

"And their builders are still with us. You can see their blood among our people," added Tennas. "They were a dark folk but not so dark as the first Tesrans, and sometimes light of eye."

Yes, she did lecture like the chief wizard's aide. They would not have made a good couple, Na decided. They might have driven each other mad. Was there singing somewhere? Outside, maybe.

"My people," said Holos. "Would you like to go listen to them?" Turana hopped down at once and took her grandfather's hand. The rest followed him out to the courtyard. The sky had cleared, in part, and stars shone through, here and there. A choir of the house's servants and attendants sang beside the fountain. As Na had noted before, the singing was simple in melody—at times it seemed to have none at all—but highly and sometimes complexly rhythmic.

Holos stood listening, the little girl in his arms. Na looked up toward her room across the court. Was Im there on the gallery, taking this in? She could make out forms in the shadows but not who they were. Maybe just the soldiers.

She *could* see the tears in the eyes of Holos. He was not really like Piras Tindeval at all, was he? She had let her memories of the ruler of Hirstel color her perception of this man. This good man.

This man who loved his family, his people. After a time, they turned back to the dining room. "We have gifts yet to open," announced Holos. "Before Turana falls asleep."

These they did open. It was another Yule custom of which Na had been unaware. The bulk of these went to Turana, and when she was done examining each and every item, she turned to her grandfather, asking, "What did you get for Na-na?"

"That's just Na, my dear, and you should probably call her Lady Na," said her mother.

"I am afraid—" began Holos, but Na broke in.

"Your grandfather gave me this lovely necklace," she announced, pulling back her collar a little to better show the amber pendant. What had led her to wear it this evening, Na wasn't sure, but she was glad she had.

The girl gazed at it, with a quite serious expression. "That's pretty," she decided, and turned back to her own haul of presents.

It was dark but not late when the family left. After all, these were the longest nights of the year. Holos's eyes were again misted as they made their farewells. Then he turned to his remaining guest. "I think my children are not sure what to make of the Lady Na. You have an air of command about you. They are unused to that from my intimate guests."

Not if he ever invited the Mec Arana to dinner. But they weren't quite friendly, were they? Holos wouldn't invite the priestess to sit down with his family. "Perhaps they should become used to it, Holos. I would not object."

"Nor I," he admitted, perhaps a little too cautiously. She would have to do something about that.

"Do you wish to return to your room now, my lady?"

"I don't see why I need to return anytime, my lord," said Na, taking him by the hand.

37.

"As you well know," spoke Tuthinos, "there are beings—creatures—who haunt the ways and gates between worlds and prey upon those who travel through them."

It was Na who commented. "Yes. The sphinxes, the ghalun."

"So are the rupa, too, though their main concern is capturing human males with which to mate."

"They breed with mortal men? Then these rupa are in some sense human?" This from Im.

"No more so than gods. Or demons, for that matter. Many of those can mate with humans."

If they so choose, thought Na. Xido had explained that to her and also that he had chosen not to. She had been entirely all right with it. She did not need to be carrying a child, even one fathered by a god.

"It is said," continued Tuthinos, "they carry them to their nests in the high crags and once they become pregnant their captives go over the side."

"As do any male offspring," added Holos. "If one can believe the treatises." He waved an arm toward his bookcases.

Catha listened to all this a bit wide-eyed. Talk of such monsters was not an everyday thing. Never mind that another red monster was standing peacefully in the corner. She was used to it by now.

"Of course, the Wizard-Lord brought them here. Maybe not the current one."

"Invited is more likely, my boy," said Holos. He seemed unusually mellow this morning. Na knew why. Did anyone else? "Through one of the portals we know exists in the Rift."

"Do they need portals?" asked Im. "They seem to, ah, exist in more than one world at once."

"A bit like elementals," Na appended to this.

"To establish themselves here, yes," said the chief wizard. "The creatures haven't dared attack the city itself but they do take travelers in the west, disrupting trade. Fortunately, they are not too numerous and do not need that many mates.

"A few have been bold enough to appear over the Sea of Sanctuary in the past but never have they mounted an attack like yesterday. I trust my friend the admiral has learned a lesson."

More than one, I hope, said Na only to herself. But did Mursoazes's unwelcome attentions set her on the path to Holos's bed? Maybe she should thank him!

She hoped too that no one noticed her entirely inappropriate smile at the thought. Holos would put it down to something else, as would any man.

Don't deny it, gentlemen. You know it's true—and so do your women.

"We knew about it right away, of course," Tuthinos was saying. "The priestess Alpisha is a sorceress and was giving her tale before you had left the island."

Holos chuckled. "She referred to you as her twin sister, Na."

"If I were half-again as broad in the shoulders, maybe. Sister Alpisha is a sturdy woman."

"And a famed archer. She was high priestess of Trepais before Huna, but chose to retire to the island."

"Speaking of high priestesses," said Im, "the Mec Arana has invited me to visit her."

"At her villa?" asked Holos. He glanced toward Tuthinos who would undoubtedly have known of this. "Hiul would desire to speak further with you, I am sure."

"No, some shrine. She wants to keep me all to herself!"

"So I'm not included, I take it," said Na. "Not that I mind." She but stole a quick look at the chief wizard. Holos, her lover. Perhaps even her seducer, though not consciously. "I'd as soon stay here."

"But the breakfast is all gone so let's allow Holos to get to his work," Im said. "I can go visit the priestess later if you think it's, um, appropriate."

"Make sure he has six of the soldiers with him," Holos told his aide. "No, eight. And yes, I'd best have some time to attend to things."

Two of those soldiers accompanied them across the courtyard, along with Tuthinos and, to be sure, Cory. Im leaned in and whispered, "If you wish to talk about anything, I'll be in my rooms for a while."

She just might. If anyone was to be her confidant, why not the boy? She gave him a noncommittal nod. "By the way," he went on, "I've heard Mursoazes is already on his way back to Robon. Cut his vacation short."

Na looked at him with mingled suspicion and curiosity. "Where do you hear things like that?"

"Zerc. He roams around this place picking up bits of gossip all day." There was something akin to a giggle. "Including that of you and the chief wizard." Im's expression became a bit wistful. "I'll miss the admiral. Now I'll probably never learn to sail properly."

Na might miss him herself, despite everything. They climbed the stairs silently, side by side, and parted at her door. Cuna gave her odd looks as she entered the apartment. Maybe everyone would this day. Or seem to.

Tuthinos had gone on to Im's room. Maybe working out the logistics of a visit to—where? A shrine, Im had said. That could be anywhere in this city, or even outside it.

She rested a while and then returned to the library. Holos was gone. Na had actually hoped it was so. Catha was there, writing out letters, and told her the prince had called for him. Books were what she had come for, to the library and to Tesra—the city's great store of knowledge. These books of Holos were as good a place to start as any.

Around noon, Im stuck his head in the door. "Holed up down here, huh? I'm off to visit this temple or whatever it is." He only glanced at Catha, still busy with the correspondence. "You can tell Holos if someone else doesn't." With that the boy was gone. She might as well go to her own rooms and read there.

No sign of Cuna when she arrived. She stepped back out into the gallery. Im's guard was gone; her own remained. The Bazu fellow, it was. She didn't feel like talking to him right now. Oh, there was Zerc. He hadn't accompanied his master. Na waved to him.

She didn't really feel like talking to him either. In time, Cuna returned, bearing a tray. "I saw you comin' and hurried down to fetch some lunch," she explained. The woman was more competent and more conscientious than she had been giving her credit for.

"I'll just be sitting here and reading for a while," Na told the maid. Or maybe she would take a nap. She didn't get quite enough sleep last night. "Take care of whatever needs taken care of, will you?"

"Yes, mistress. I'll come get the tray later."

The sorceress attempted to read but could not concentrate. Her mind strayed elsewhere, mostly to Holos. He was nothing special as a lover, certainly with nothing approaching the skill of the immortal Xido, nor his lean muscular body. Na did not mind at all. She might be in love. She wasn't completely sure; she *was* sure she never had been before.

Nor had she ever truly had a family. The priests and priestesses of Banat at their shrine in the hills had come close to being one. Im? He had become her brother, hadn't he, as surely as if they had been born of the same parents? Even more so.

And now Holos. Could she become part of his family? *Be* his family, and he, hers? Whether it was love or no, the wizard offered stability and normalcy. She need no longer feel rootless in her new world.

Or it was but an illusion. She fell asleep, still debating, still undecided.

"My lady." It was Cuna. "The master asks you to dine with him." The woman was attempting to stifle a broad smile.

Na felt like breaking into one herself. "I'll be there shortly. Help me dress. Oh, I'd better wash first." The girl who had delivered the request was sent off. Na followed as quickly as able.

They were eating in the library, speaking of nothing much, when Im came breezing in. She could see it had grown completely dark outside; the lanterns were being lit around the courtyard. Na scowled at him as best she might but he didn't seem to get the message.

"Back from the luth," he reported, plopping down on one of the chairs. Cory took up a position by the door. "It's a pretty place. On a hillside with lots of cedar trees. Hmm, I'd better have some supper sent to my room," he said, looking over the mostly-empty dishes.

"The mec didn't feed you?" asked an imperturbable Holos.

"When I got there but she sent me away without any supper." He leaned forward. "I think she had other appetites on her mind."

Arana?

"We talked for quite some time about little of importance. Or it didn't seem very important to me. She was rather curious about the Jewels. I didn't realize most people even knew they existed. And then— well, she tried to get me into her bed."

Na tried not to laugh. It wasn't so ridiculous, really, was it? Im was a healthy and personable lad, if not exactly a handsome one. She had once toyed with the idea of having designs on him herself!

"You turned her down," said Holos.

"Of course. But before I got out of the place, one of the younger priestesses also propositioned me. And with Cory standing right there! I, um, think maybe the mec put her up to it."

"Surely not," objected Na. She couldn't believe that of the aristocratic high priestess. And she liked the woman, even if she didn't get along with Holos.

"That seems somewhat suspicious," was the chief wizard's only comment. "Did she speak of aught else?"

"Well, there was a lot about preserving Tesra and putting the nanem back in charge of things. Like I care—no offense intended but I don't plan to stay here, Holos. I'll help bring down Torut but your politics mean nothing to me."

"Nor should they." Holos looked to the sorceress. "I suspect our Lady Arana was trying to woo young Im to her faction."

Na still found any of it hard to believe. Im rose. "I believe I'll go to the kitchen myself," he announced. "I bid you a good evening." He might have smirked just a little.

As the servants began clearing away the meal, Holos said, "And I believe I would like to go upstairs. Will you accompany me, my dear?"

"Never doubt it," she replied.

38.

"THE PRINCE AND HIS SISTER have asked us to visit," she informed Im, before Holos had a chance. The pair had not attempted any pretense this morning as to where she had spent the night.

"It is so," said the sorcerer. "Huenoziles is going to invite you to stay in his palace. You only, not Na."

"I would assume I should accept." The boy considered the sorceress for a moment. "And I believe I should leave Zerc with you, if you are staying. He'll be more useful here."

"If he wishes," Na replied. She would not mind having the sailor with her.

"There will be a chariot or coach coming shortly to convey you," Holos said. "Best grab a few things you'll need and the rest can be sent along. Hmm, you might too, my dear, in case they ask you to stay the night."

She certainly hoped not and was certain the wizard felt the same. In short order, both Hirstelites were waiting by the gateway into the house of Holos, not knowing what sort of conveyance was coming, nor when. Two chariots came charging up the street. "They're even more reckless than Mursoazes," Na whispered.

The rider of the first hauled back on the reins, bringing his team to a quick stop. Her team. That was Huna driving. Na looked to the second chariot. Sure enough, Huenoziles held the reins. An armed man rode with each but no other guards. These men leaped down and held the horses while brother and sister strode their direction. Or they might have swaggered or even strutted. They seemed full of themselves, whatever words she used.

"Ho, Im," called Huna. "Are you ready to come stay in a real house?"

Her brother's glance was not entirely approving. His eyes passed across Cory and came to rest on Na. "We would invite you too, my lady, but we know you have reason to wish to stay."

"You do?"

"*Every*one knows, dear," said Huna. She sighed rather dramatically. "It seems I missed my chance." Then she snickered. "So did our Aunt Alpisha!"

"Grandaunt," came Huenoziles's correction. "Not with you, Na. We happen to know she's had a thing for Holos."

Oh. That was even worse, maybe. "Isn't she supposed to be, uh, celibate?"

"Not since she retired. Released from her vows, right, Huna?"

"So it is. I'll never need worry about that sort of thing!" A quick frown. "Unless maybe I wanted children some day. But never mind that." She brightened again, almost instantly, and turned to her brother. "Im would make an excellent father, don't you think?"

"Im intends to return to his promised beyond the sea," he told her. The object of their discussion stood bemused.

"Oh. Well, there is certainly no hurry!" She turned to Na. "Do you want to come now? You can visit anytime, you know. It might be better when Lord Im has settled in. And you can bring your boyfriend!"

Huenoziles shook his head. "My sister doesn't even live at the palace," he said. "Well, some of the time."

"I come and go," the priestess interjected. "No one can hold me! Hey, is our big brother here?"

"Tuthinos? I haven't seen him this morning, Mec."

"Holos is keeping him busy, no doubt. Doesn't want him around you." Huna leaned in, confiding with a stage whisper. "He would have been a competitor if you'd encouraged him at all."

"That would certainly have complicated matters," commented the prince. "Well, so you're staying, Na? Which of us do you ride with, Lord

Im? By the way, I'm pleased to meet you. First time we've met, I'm pretty sure!"

"Then let him go with you and get acquainted," said Huna. "We'll see you later, Na!" With that, she vaulted into her chariot and grasped the reins. "Beat you home!"

At the speed Huenoziles pursued his sister, Na doubted he had time to converse with Im.

There was no need for this bag she had packed now. Maybe it should go to Holos's chambers instead of hers. No, she wouldn't suggest that yet. She would have to do something about the wizard's rooms. About his entire apartment. That too could wait. Na took the narrow stairway up from the storerooms. She could see the door to Im's rooms hanging open.

No longer Im's rooms. That was no longer Im's guard that had followed her upstairs, either, in company with her own. Cory, of course, had run along with the prince's chariot, as it had that of Mursoazes. It didn't appear to have any trouble keeping up. The demon would certainly create something of a sensation at the palace. And in the streets before they reached it!

Huenoziles had quite ignored Cory, perhaps at his sister's advice. Na suspected he relied on that quite a bit, despite their apparent competitiveness.

Zerc stood in the center of the room, supervising the packing of all Im's belongings. He came to Na as soon as he spotted her in the doorway. "Master Im says I'm to follow your biddin' for a while, m' lady," he said. "He may call for Zerc later on."

"You know he will leave Tesra eventually." How soon? Na had avoided thinking about that so far. The boy would surely sail away one of these days. She might never see him again, though both live centuries more.

Centuries. "How old are you, Zerc?"

"Why, I reckon I'm somewheres about a hundred and ten, mistress."

She was not all that surprised, not really, though she hadn't expected Zerc to be quite so long-lived. How much of that life had been spent at sea? No matter. It was time for him to retire from a sailor's life. "When Im does go, I would welcome you in my service," she said.

"Thank you, m' lady. The boy, Im I means, spoke to me of it." He turned back to the pair of Holos's servants. "I'd best finish gettin' his things packed and sent after him."

"Yes, carry on. You can sleep in my antechamber when you vacate this room. No one is using it." She had to smile at that thought. "Any of it."

"Yes, ma'am. So I've heard. Um, if I might make bold to say, the wizard is a fine man. I seen that right away."

It had taken her longer.

39.

NA LOOKED TO THE HIGH vaulted ceiling. This room actually rivaled the greatest Hirstel had to offer. Her eyes returned to the company gathered below it. A council of war, that's what it was, though no one had used that term. And here sat Im and herself, a part of all this. A part of Tesra.

She had considered speaking to Im from afar these past three days. No, it was better, she decided, to wait and let him get settled. There were other things going on to divert her. Na had begun to delve deeply into her lover's library and now thirsted for what knowledge might be found in other collections of lore about the city.

She was delving a bit into Holos too, learning more who he was, and was generally pleased with that knowledge. A cautious man—she had known that almost from the first time they had spoken from afar, while Na was still on the other side of the Greater Sea. Yet he had reached out to her, even then, knowing she and Im might be valuable allies. Or at least that he should know who these two powerful sorcerers were who had unexpectedly appeared in his world.

It was good that he had. He would probably bring up marriage sooner or later. Holos was being cautious there, as well. Afraid of scaring me off, she told herself. And of alarming his children.

Now they sat side by side in the palace of the prince, in his audience chamber. All four chief priests were there, and a handful of lesser ones. Some of these might be attendants, some seemed to hold authority of their own. Several wizards, of varied age and both genders. Hiul was among them. Military men, some of these must be, and advisers and functionaries. Most of them wouldn't matter and needn't be there, she was certain.

That was Alpisha sitting beside Im, wasn't it? And Huna on his other side. Every woman had an urge to mother the boy, she had come to recognize. She'd been guilty of it herself. Of course, some had other interests in him. She looked across the gathering to where Arana sat, serene, paying neither her nor Im the least attention. Had she really tried to seduce the young sorcerer? Na still found it hard to swallow.

Huenoziles rose and began to speak without preamble. Na was only two seats away, with Holos between them, so she had to lean forward to see the prince.

"All have heard of the rupa daring to attack the Isle of Standing Stones," he began, "and attempting to slay our two visiting mages. Or maybe take them. With rupa, who can say?"

"Indeed," someone said. Na thought it was one of the generals.

"We assume the enemy was behind this," he continued. "The question is how to respond."

It was Holos who spoke, almost at once. "By adding those two powerful mages to the defense of the Unem, my lord."

"Defense only, then?" came a question. "As ever?"

"We haven't the strength for more," said another, a weather-beaten sort with a closely trimmed dark beard.

"That is true, Admiral Punos," said Holos. "For now. We may grow stronger."

"If you can make your subordinates behave," commented Alpisha.

Holos answered that at once. "I take responsibility for that, my lady. I allowed my old friend Mursoazes too much leeway."

The admiral laughed. "I've made that mistake myself."

Huenoziles was clearly disinterested in all of this. "How goes your wizard war, Holos?" he asked.

"I shall permit Lord Hiul to speak of that, sir. He is closer to its everyday events." He whispered to Na as the other sorcerer rose, "Tuthinos knows more of it, in truth. He should be monitoring our network even at this moment."

"Things change little, my prince," spoke Hiul. "We sometimes manage to spy on the enemy's wizards. They sometime overhear ours, despite our barriers. It is—it is the Wizard-Lord himself who remains the greatest threat, when he deigns to bother with us."

Holos spoke up. "If Torut finds a wizard, he is always vulnerable. Few are strong enough to keep him out."

"Even so," admitted the older sorcerer. "Worse, from time to time he manages to corrupt one and turn him to his service."

"Or her." That was Huna's voice.

Hiul nodded. "I am told our visitors are strong enough to withstand him."

"They are," said Holos, and no more. The conversation then went into specifics, of wizards here and there, of distant bases on the northern seas and skirmishes upon those seas. Voices rose in support of more aggression against the Rift. Others rose in favor of attempting to make peace. Arana's was among the latter, though her arguments were subtle rather than fervent.

At last, the prince signaled for silence. "So things will go on much as they have, it seems. At least for a while." He glanced toward Im. "But we do have a new weapon. Two new weapons. What do they think of all this?" His gaze turned unexpectedly to Na. "My lady Na?"

There was a quick drawing in of Holos's breath. He had not expected this! She rose deliberately, not so much to compose her thoughts as to appear serious and steady to this assembly. "My lord, I have chosen to make Tesra my home—a home I have sought all my life, it seems. I shall do all I can to defend it. Whether my abilities can add anything, I do not know, but I promise to try." With that she sat down, just as deliberately.

"By the Old Lizard, you are a politician," murmured Holos.

She didn't understand the oath but was willing to agree with the chief wizard otherwise. "Well spoken, my lady," said Huenoziles, "and we both welcome you to Tesra and accept your service." His eyes went to Holos. The prince might have wanted to say something more about the two of them but apparently chose to hold his tongue. "The wizard Im and I have already spoken at length," he continued. "Although he does not choose to make our Unem his home, he does have a personal quarrel with the enemy. We can depend on him to lend us his power."

She heard Im calling in her head. Now? Oh well. She went to their usual meeting place. *What is it?*

Hueny and me are buddies now, he said. *It looks like I'll be staying with him and his sister. We've—already parted, haven't we? I wasn't expecting it this soon.*

It did happen when we weren't looking. But it will be a while before you go back across the sea.

Yes. I suppose that depends on what happens with Torut. I haven't much hope of destroying him, seeing how things are here.

Holding his ambitions at bay for a time would be a victory, spoke another, uninvited voice.

Who are you? demanded Im.

Hurasu, isn't it? I didn't know if we would speak again.

Hurasu I am. I am also Old Lizard, by the way. In a sense. So my people called me—that mortal version of me—an age ago. The lizard is a figure from their ancient myth, as is the snake. Ha, perhaps I am no more than an aspect of him!

I take it you two are already friends. Sarcasm was not always easy to express when speaking from afar but Im managed it well.

Allies, she replied. *I think.*

That seems accurate, said the demigod. *I'll not butt into your speech any longer now but know I am paying attention.* With that, his form melted away.

You'll have to tell me about him later, said Im. *I think he is right. Winning the battle against Torut would be enough for now. The war can wait.* He abruptly blinked out. Na returned to her place by Holos. He hadn't seemed to notice she had left.

That sort of thing would happen. She was the better sorcerer of the two. Would that bother Holos? And should she—let him in sometime? Take speaking from afar the step further, share their minds, the way Im had with Atima? Or with Xido, for that matter. She wasn't sure it was even possible for the two of them. Maybe in part.

Stop daydreaming, woman, and pay attention! Debate was apparently at an end. Im and Huenoziles were already gabbing about something. Huna, standing at Im's shoulder, laughed loudly. The boy *had* left her. She wished Holos would embrace her, right then, but he was already moving off to speak with someone.

"Your Holos will often be busy," came a voice from behind her. Na rose to greet Alpisha.

"That I was aware of, my lady—or should I say sister?" Not twin sister!

"Ali will do. I assumed your eyes were open."

Na had to laugh. "At least partly. I did not expect to see you here. I thought maybe you didn't leave that island."

"There is a time for solitude and a time for companionship. Ah, you were speaking from afar with Im just now, were you not?"

Someone had noticed. "He did call to me." She would not mention Hurasu's presence.

"The boy has shown me the little world you two use. Do you mind if I reach out to you there sometime?"

"Not at all, Ali. Although we might want to find one he doesn't know about!"

"Perhaps so. We both may wish to speak with him when he has

returned across the sea." She glanced toward where Im still conversed. "My niece and nephew will miss him, I am sure, and have no sorcery."

But it does run in the family, as Alpisha demonstrated. "They grew fond of him rather quickly."

Holos's children, too, would carry that heritage, even if it had shown itself in none of them. Maybe Turana would mature into a wizard someday. Maybe she wouldn't. The heritage might not have carried to her generation at all.

"My ladies."

"Lord Hiul." Alpisha only nodded to the man. Her attitude was notably cool and she did not try to conceal it.

"My wife and I would invite you to visit us," he told Na. "Our house, not the shrine of Fasenais, as she did Lord Im."

Na thought that might be a good idea. She needed to know more about what was going on in Tesra and these were two important citizens. And she was curious about Im's tale.

"I would certainly like to do just that," she replied, "and I thank you and the mec. I'll have to see when I could manage it."

"If you can, tomorrow evening would be excellent. I shall let you discuss it with Lord Holos."

Who apparently did not share the invitation. "I shall," she promised.

"Fine, my lady, fine. We hope to see you then." His nod to Alpisha before turning away was every bit as cool as her own.

"At least you're safe from Arana's advances," remarked the priestess. Na wasn't particularly surprised she knew about that.

40

AGAIN, NA WAS UNSURE WHETHER it was a dream arisen from her own mind or if Torut had whispered to her in the dark.

When I have swept all the world away, I shall rule the infinite void, he said. *With you at my side.* The void lay all around them, black, vast. She hung suspended in the middle of—nothing. *There would be peace at last.*

Peace. Yes, she would like to be at peace.

And be nothing? It was another voice, intruding. Had it been Hurasu? She couldn't remember now.

Existence is strife, whispered Torut.

And that is good, said the other.

Good? The word is meaningless. Meaningless. The voice echoed, faded into the darkness of the sleep from which Na awoke. Holos slumbered beside her.

Existence is good, she whispered to herself, before slipping back into sleep. She dreamed no more that night.

She saw little of the chief wizard that morning; duties took him away once again. But he had been agreeable to her visiting Arana and Hiul. "Stay the night, if you wish," he told her, "though I shall surely miss you." With a kiss, he was away to wherever he was needed that day.

A litter was brought out after lunch. It seemed the most sensible way to travel. She must learn to ride or drive a chariot! "I ask you to stay and look after things," she told Zerc. It might not be a good idea to show up with him in tow. Four armed men was a sufficient escort, acting both as guards and bearers. Holos might have ordered a larger one. Tuthinos wished to but she vetoed him.

Eastward through town, through the rolling hills. Apartment buildings gave way to patches of farmland and grove, to villas and houses, some large, some modest. There were clumps of shanties, too. "Squatters," said one of the bearers when she asked about it. "Not all the poor are willing to be jammed into the public houses and rely on the public allowances."

So that was found here. There had been hints of it. Na was in no way bothered by the knowledge; there had been similar arrangements in Hirstel. But no one could leave that city and squat in the lifeless desert!

She should learn more, she decided, and tucked that resolution away, to be retrieved some other day. There were more pressing matters. They left those hovels behind as they climbed higher into the hills. Here there were only well tended gardens and groves, screening the villas. "The next one to the left, isn't it?" one of the bearers was asking another.

"That it is, mate." He turned his head around to look at Na. "We'll wait until you decide whether you're stayin' or not, m' lady."

"Lord Hiul's a good one," said the other. "He'll see we're fed and comfortable. We've been up here before."

"And if you stay, we'll come back in the morning. Here we go, boys." They turned up a road, paved with a paler brick than the street they had left. It had taken perhaps a little over an hour to get her here.

Yes, a Tesran hour. Make it mid-afternoon.

There was a humming, buzzing noise coming from the right. At once, Na thought of the night-wasps. Surely not—

Hiul came ambling from among the trees. "Greetings, Lady Na. I was tending my hives. Bee-keeping is one of my passions since I, uh, stepped back a little from wizardly duties."

Retired, in other words, though obviously his counsel was still sought. And his wife remained actively important in the affairs of Tesra. That wife appeared a few seconds later, coming from the direction of the still largely-unseen house.

"It's good to stay busy, Lord Hiul. I'm growing a little bored," she admitted, slipping down from the litter. "There are a great many books for me to read and study, but I would like to do something more active."

"Holos undoubtedly has some duty in mind for someone of your abilities. Something more than passing along messages, I'm sure!"

"That would be a waste indeed," agreed Arana. "Come along to the house and we shall talk of such things."

"And you boys head around to the kitchen," Hiul told the bearers. "Tell them I'm ordering unlimited beer for you."

That might lead to some meandering on the route home, thought Na. She did not think much of the idea of staying overnight.

She might not have minded some beer herself but the servants brought wine to a table on the veranda. It wasn't a bad day to sit there, reasonably warm, sunshine enough, though it would soon grow dark. She did hope they intended to let her into the house!

"What sort of duty would you set me, my lord?" she asked.

"Hmm, spying, I would think. I'd wager you could find your way past warding pretty well, my lady."

"But would she attack if she did find her way?" asked the priestess. "Could you bring yourself to act upon another's vulnerabilities?"

"An enemy? Certainly. It's no different than using a knife on them, is it?"

The couple looked at each other, perhaps a little too knowingly. "Somewhat different, my dear," said Hiul. "A vulnerable, frightened fellow wizard is different from someone who attacked you on the street. Even if he or she is an enemy."

Na considered this a moment, sipping the wine. It was nearly colorless and rather tart, unlike any she had in Tesra before. Or anywhere else. "I guess I wouldn't know until I had to, would I?"

"Well, I doubt Holos sets you to such a task," felt Hiul.

Arana smiled thinly at that. "Nor would you, husband."

"It's not going to be for me to decide, is it?" The old wizard sounded just a bit testy.

Arana smiled yet again. Na didn't completely like that smile. "You probably know Lord Hiul and Holos were rivals for his position."

Hiul held up a hand in dismissal. "Oh, I have been envious of Holos, I'll not deny. I've no rancor toward him."

"Perhaps you should."

"I had no claim on the title of chief wizard, my dear, so there has been no injury, just some misfortune. That comes to all of us." He suddenly smiled as well, a benign smile intended for Na. "Even to Holos, but it seems his fortunes have turned. The loss of his wife hurt the man badly."

Arana did not seem willing to leave it at that. "It should have been one of true Tesran blood in the post, a nanem like you." She turned to Na. "You also are of the nanem, although your ancestors wandered to another world."

And that entitled them to—to what? Rule over everyone else? Did she dislike Holos because he was not of that blood? Or hate him, even? Too many questions! These too should be set aside to examine later.

"I thought anyone who served Tesra was considered a Tesran," she said.

The woman only snorted at this. Delicately, true, but snorted none the less. "It's getting cool," she said. "Let's get inside."

Arana led the way, through wide double-doors. Hiul took Na's arm and whispered, "My wife and I are both of the party of the nanem, but she can be a bit fanatical. I try to avoid such subjects and it greatly helps my digestion!"

The house, like that of Holos in Phamahd, was all of one level. Maybe wealthy Tesrans liked to show they had the room to spread out in their country villas, unlike the cramped vertical spaces of the city. The talk turned to matters of lesser import. Both Arana and Na avoided any mention of Im's visit to the temple.

But that fitted in with the things she said to her, didn't they? Arana wanted both of them on her side, supporting her cause. She did feel that she was being wronged by those not of her pure blood. She did feel Holos had stolen the position rightfully belonging to her husband. Na was unable to banish these thoughts completely from her mind.

Inevitably, the talk came back around to wizardry. Arana might even have steered it that way, Na realized. "My wife could have been a top sorceress herself, if she hadn't entered the priesthood," Hiul confided.

"Top? Competent, maybe," objected Arana.

Hiul only shook his head at her. It was obvious he did not agree.

"What called you to become a priestess?" Na asked.

"The advice of one I trusted. One I admired. He lived far away but we wizard-spoke—ah, what am I going on about?" The priestess poured herself another goblet of wine.

There was altogether too much wine. Before dinner, with dinner. That meal was simple and a bit bland. "As my husband implied, his digestion is not of the best," Arana confided. After the meal she suggested they return to the now lantern-lit terrace. The sun was just sinking below the horizon. There was a good view of the sea from here, a sea fading into the dusk.

"Will you send your bearers home and stay with us this night?" asked the priestess. It was time to decide on that, wasn't it?

"Ah, thank you no, Arana. They'd best be told to prepare to bear me home." Home. Yes, the house of Holos was home and that was where she wanted to be this night.

Hiul nodded knowingly. He understood, perhaps. More wine appeared as the darkness gathered about them, the trees falling into shadow, the golds of the sky fading to an orange-gray and then to black. The wine was a deep red and cloyingly sweet. Na thought there was an odd flavor to it, one she could not place. Some spice the Tesrans used maybe. There were a great many of those, somewhat bewildering in their variety and uses.

Whatever it was, it must not bother the stomach of Hiul. The old man had nodded off in his chair. Na felt sleepy herself. She'd best be on the way back into the city. What was that sound, that flapping, flapping, flapping? Above her—winged figures.

She tried to rise but was too sluggish to move. The last Na saw was the face of Arana, without expression, as clawed hands grasped her and lifted her into the air.

41.

THE SEA OF SANCTUARY SPREAD beneath them. Was that the far shore Na had glimpsed? She had been wrong about the hands. The rupa gripped her with taloned feet as they winged westward. Another soared nearby. Na attempted to reach out, to speak from afar with Im or Holos or anyone, but she was too befuddled. She could not concentrate.

It was too late anyway. She had no doubt they were on their way to Torut and none could stop them. Her captors were no more than silhouettes, dark forms against a dark sky. The clouds had closed over them as they traveled; there would be no light of moon nor stars. Na would not know when they crossed that far shore.

She was not even certain of the direction they traveled. Tul Sunac, the Great Rift, was as much north as west, wasn't it? These rupa nested in the rift. She thought they did. Someone said it—or did they? She drifted away into blackness, a dreamless sleep.

And awakened to sunrise and water once again beneath her. Na was fairly certain this was not the Sea of Sanctuary but one of the other great lakes. Her head was clearer. Maybe she could speak to someone now. Damn, it was cold!

"Noooone of thaaaat, weeez'rd-wooom'n," hissed the rupa bearing her. "Rooopa feeeel yoooou caaaaalling." The creature shook her vigorously. It called out in its own language to the other; a moment later Na felt herself released and falling. The second rupa caught her and carried her onward.

"Seeeester get tiiiir'd," she explained. "Nooo taaalk nowww!"

Na might have had a moment's contact with Im before the rupa stopped her. Or with someone. She had called out in their accustomed meeting place, the little world they used. Xido or Holos might have been listening. For that matter, Alpisha could have. There would surely be opportunities later. Best she not tempt these rupa to drop her now.

The beings were of a red color all over, not a bright red but that of mature wine, with a subdued brownish tinge. At least at the moment. She recalled that the color varied some as they danced above them, casting their mesmerizing spell, on that island. Their arms were wings, bat-like, but with only one long finger supporting their webbing. The others ended in claws, as did their grasping feet. The body between these extremities was human enough and feminine, though the breasts were small and the chests deep.

And the heads—they were beautiful, if alien. The rupa's expression never seemed to change. They were like statues standing in some temple, forever serene. Tangled, inky hair flowed back from those heads, and hair grew in most of the other normal places. More than usual, perhaps, on the shins, above the sharp talons.

A number of small objects suddenly appeared in their way. "Niii-ight waaasps!" called out the other rupa. "Weeeee neeear hommme!"

"They steeeeng weeez'rd-woooom'n!" cackled the one bearing her. "Goood tooo eeeeat. Nooo tiiiime nowww!"

They climbed away from the swarm and continued. They were not so much flying over the inland sea as paralleling its coast. The water lay to their right; shining white objects floated here and there on its surface.

Some of you appear as baffled by them as Na, I see. Ice, my patient listeners. Great chunks of frozen water found in the northern seas. I advise you never to travel there and look upon them—it is much safer to listen to my tales.

Ahead, a towering torrent of water poured into the sea. They passed above it and followed the river feeding its flow, through a broken, rocky land. A smaller, narrow lake, more a widening of the river, came and went. Ahead lay mountains, a huge, high range, far grander than any Na had ever seen. Admittedly, she had not seen much of mountains, in this world or any other.

"Hommme!" called out one of her captors. She wasn't sure which. So this was where those 'high crags' lay, and the nests of the rupa. How would they cross them? They would cross them, wouldn't they?

A pass. Na could see the notch in the mountains. The rupa winged toward it, ever climbing. Her carrier called to the other and she came and grasped Na's legs. It must take the strength of both to get her across. Or the men they were more accustomed to carrying. Na was certain to be lighter than most of those.

Her head swam and she might have blacked out for a minute or two. Na had no idea how long. The air is thin, here, she told herself. She had read of such things. She wondered if any of those vast peaks went all the way up to where there was no air at all. Probably not—that she had not read of.

Then they were gliding downward and the one rupa released her legs. Off to her left—the south, right?—lay another large lake. Maybe it could be called a sea too. A deep valley lay before her and more mountains rose beyond. The rift, at last.

They dropped toward a strip of broken land lying between two broad rivers or maybe arms of the sea. Rocky, jagged spires stood there, amid a range of colorless, high hills. Little appeared to grow. Smoke billowed from cones or fissures. A dark keep appeared. The rupa fell toward it with their captive.

Carved from the rock itself, she decided. There was power here. Na could feel it. Every wizard knew that places of physical power, such as volcanoes, sometimes coincided with gateways. Her own people had passed through a gate beneath a great cone to reach Hirstel, ages ago. Lava from that cone had obliterated the gate, leaving them with no easy way to return.

Humans stood below, peering up at her and the rupa. She could make out little more than their shapes at first. Spears in their hands? Or staffs. They might be either warriors or wizards! It proved to be the former when the rupa finally set her feet on the rocks. The pair flew away, swiftly, without a word.

A man addressed Na in badly accented Zikem. "Our lord asks us to welcome you, great sorceress," he said. "We shall escort you to your rooms."

"Not my cell?" She couldn't resist asking this. Na was in no good mood after her flight. And she was ravenous and maybe even hung over.

"Of course not, revered one," he answered. The man was quite pale, paler than even the Charcha across the sea. Or a dwarf, for that matter. Long blond hair, almost white, hung in a single braid down his back, protruding from a bowl-shaped helmet. And the head within that helmet! It was oddly shaped, like a loaf of bread stood on its end.

The other soldiers were the same. The sorceress was slightly surprised to note that at least half of them were women. Of course women could fight but she had never been among a people where it was common for them to be warriors. Maybe it was just a quirk of the Wizard-Lord.

He would be here somewhere, Torut himself. She shuddered at the thought and followed this captain into the keep.

42.

"The rupa, Lady Na? Some say they are demons of another world, invited here by our master's predecessor. May his name be forgotten and cursed."

Wouldn't both be difficult? This woman was a sorceress, of that there was no doubt. How powerful? There was no telling. Wards here seemed to prevent magic, even as those placed on the great temple in Tesra. She would attempt to examine them more closely later.

"I can tell they enter other worlds somehow but little more." This meal was unappetizing. She might even have said disgusting if she weren't so hungry.

"Oh, they send parts of themselves away to many worlds and bring them back, displaced. It is largely an instinctive skill. It can bewilder and entrance those who stare too long." The woman snickered. "So do they entrap the men they carry to their nests, and make them pliant."

Na did not think it at all amusing, but it was a clear description of the rupa's power. She picked at the decidedly too-old eggs, swimming in rancid fat, yet on her plate. "Am I a prisoner in this room?" she asked.

The woman seemed quite surprised. "Why of course not. You are the master's guest." Did she really believe that?

"Then I can wander about."

"You can, my lady. Anywhere in the keep. Not outside. It's dangerous!" She reflected for a moment. "Hmm, *not* anywhere in the keep. There are private places, to be sure." For a moment, Na might have glimpsed fear in her. "The Smota will let you know where they are."

"Smota?"

"The soldiers who guard our home. They are of the tribe of Smot."

Obviously a very different people than the barbarians who took service with Tesra. "Oh. What is it with their heads?"

"They shape them so when they are little, with binding and boards.

They think it is beautiful!" The woman shook her head, as if perplexed. "It isn't, is it? I'm not always sure about things."

"Not beautiful at all," Na assured her. "What do I name you?"

"Oh, I don't have a name. The master took it away." She leaned in and whispered. "I didn't need it, you know. Shall I remove your dishes?"

Na nodded. A moment later, her visitor was gone. The addled sorceress seemed to be of her own Tezian heritage. As, to be sure, was Torut. Were many so here?

If her movements were to be unrestricted—largely unrestricted—she could go out and investigate. First she should investigate those wardings. Test them. She sent a part of herself out to look at them, a web spread through a number of worlds. It was not surprising that she was able to do so. As at the temple, they raised a barrier against the outside but those within the wards could still use some of their abilities. As was she. Not speaking from afar. That required sending too much of oneself to another world. Na was only looking. She could do no more than that, sending a part of herself out but having no place for it to go, leaving it suspended *between*.

It might be accurate to say she was reaching out and *feeling* the bonds some skilled sorcerer had put in place. Torut, most likely. It might be possible to pick at those bindings a little but she doubted she could accomplish anything. Learn something, perhaps. Hmm, there was another doing even as she. They couldn't speak, to be sure, but she could sense him touching the bindings. Him? Maybe not. Whoever it was, they felt somehow alien. Not human.

She turned her attention back to the chamber she occupied. There was water for washing. Clothes were laid out, of a cut quite unlike those made for Tesrans. Long skirts. That was how the nameless woman was dressed, with no top. It was how Na had dressed in Hirstel. It was surprisingly warm here. There would be no reason to bundle up.

Yet it seemed odd to go about so now, go as she had less than a year ago. There were loose sleeveless jackets among the clothes. She slipped one of these on. The clothes in which she arrived were much the worse for wear, and the talons of the rupa.

There was a guard in the hall, one of the Smota. A woman. She was not armored as had been those who greeted her outside, but wore a leather skirt and a top not unlike her own, except that it extended down only to her midriff and fit more snugly. The skirt was shorter too. A short curved sword hung at her side. Na wondered if the woman—a girl really—would follow her but she remained at her post.

She was kind of pretty, despite her head, wasn't she? Only a leather band had encircled that, holding back her golden hair, a shade or two lighter than her own. Maybe Na would try engaging one of these Smota later. How had they come to serve Torut?

The Smotan left her mind as she encountered Tezians further along the way. These hurried by, giving her quick furtive glances. Yes, both genders went without covering their upper bodies, for the most part. She noted that they wore their fingernails long. She could not bring herself to look down and see whether toenails were the same, but she remembered Torut's curling to preposterous lengths.

This place was cut from the solid rock, a dark gray, almost black. Volcanic, undoubtedly, and maybe not that hard to carve. It would be too easy to get lost in these bleak, featureless passageways. More so in that there seemed to be no logic to them. They curved here and there erratically, as if at the workmen's whim. There were crude carvings, randomly placed and inferior to any art of either Tesra or Hirstel. The scenes some depicted were rather disturbing.

You're getting nowhere, Na told herself. You'd better get back while you still remember the way. She stopped where another tunnel opened onto this one. It would be a good place to turn around. Then she looked into that tunnel and changed her mind.

Coming toward her was a demon.

43.

IT WAS A FOOT SHORTER than Cory and of a golden color all over. Otherwise, this creature was the same.

"You are Lady Na, I think," it said. "I felt you earlier and came looking. This Wizard-Lord said you would be coming."

Although the demon's tones were somewhat flat, there was certainly just a bit of contempt in them. It did not think well of Torut. Wait—it felt her? "You are a sorcerer?"

"I am of that caste," it replied.

"Then it is your sort that send police to kill my friend."

It hesitated. "We only, ah, open the ways for them. And provide some protection."

"And so you consider yourselves blameless." She knew that way of thinking.

"We would do you no harm, sorceress. We are not murderers, only seekers of justice."

"Yet you would murder Im."

"He is an impediment to that justice and must be removed." Its sigh, like a wind from the depths of the desert, rumbled and echoed along the stone walls. "Officially. The magistrates are, um, stiff-necked as you humans put it. The rest of us do as they order."

There was no arguing on those points. "And so you ally yourselves now with this Wizard-Lord." She did not tone down the contempt in her own voice. Maybe they could find something on which to agree.

"Again, we follow the instruction of the magistracy. Whether I approve matters not at all."

"Well, you should know I do not approve, neither of your magistrates nor of Torut. So, with that out of the way, we might as well be friendly. Are you alone here?"

"I have a bodyguard. One of the reds, as is, what do you name it? I know only its name in our language."

"It's been answering to Cory lately."

"If Cory turned itself in it would solve many problems."

That was most unlikely but there no sense in saying so. It would also be tricky because of the demon's geas to 'someday' kill Im. That would probably pull it right back to the boy if it did go its own world.

"I suppose there's no point in asking your own name. Not pronounceable by humans, I'd guess."

"Probably not. It might even hurt them."

Na had to smile slightly at that. She'd heard Cory make the same joke. It must be an old standard among demons. "I'll call you Lord Gold," she decided.

"Not a lord," it demurred, in a surprisingly small voice. "The magistrates would not like that at all."

"Goldie, then." The demon sorcerer raised no objection. "I'm heading back to my own quarters."

"And I to mine. I trust we shall meet again."

She started away when a sudden thought came. "Oh, Goldie," Na called, turning back toward the demon. "How do you feed in this place? Aren't you blocked from connecting to your world?"

"I must go outside from time to time."

"Ah, I see." She would never be permitted. Maybe though, she could use Goldie somehow. Na nodded another farewell and set off down the hallway. The Smota still lingered outside her door when she reached the room.

"Do you guard the room, whether I'm in it or not?" she asked.

The girl yawned. "I'm supposed to attend you, mistress." Her accent was somewhat better than that of the warrior who had greeted her arrival. It had that same old-fashioned feel that Torut's did. Maybe all Zikem speakers here sounded that way.

"Then why did you stay?" She went into her chamber. The girl lounged in the doorway.

"You didn't ask me to come along."

"Oh. That's sensible. Just follow me next time, unless I say otherwise. You might keep me from getting lost in this place."

"My friend Tacor go lost here once. He wandered for days until he ran into himself, coming around a corner." This was said with a completely straight face. Na was halfway inclined to believe the young woman. Well, maybe not quite halfway.

"I hate to admit this but you make more sense than anyone else I have run into this day. I don't know what to think of the woman who was here earlier."

Her guard—or guardian?—took a seat on the bed, without invitation. "Her mind is broken. So are many here."

Na nodded. "I can see this, despite the barriers this Wizard-Lord has put up."

"I know nothing of wizard things, mistress. Mistress is right word?"

"Call me Na. If need be, put 'lady' in front of it."

"Yes, when others are around. All right, Na. I am Duxi. You are like the Tezians here but unlike them. You are from Tesra? I have heard much about Tesra!"

"I live in Tesra now. I came from another city, far away."

"And the people there are like the Tezians," Duxi concluded. "Right? The Wizard-Lord's people. There aren't so many of them but they all have sorcery. The people outside are mixed. They call them mongrels in here." She perhaps snickered before adding, "The people of your Tesra, too."

"There are some in Tesra with similar ideas." Na's mind went to Arana and the last sight she had of her. Was the priestess all right? For that matter, what part did she have in all this? She could not begin to sort that out. "Your people, um, serve the Wizard-Lord?"

"We have for many generations. Even before Torut." She appreciably lowered her voice before speaking that name. "We were promised new lands. But there were already tribes in them! Some we have pushed east."

The Esa? The Gera? It would make sense and help explain Jom and Ogit's hatred for the Wizard-Lord. "It seems I am here now, but I've no intention of serving Torut." She spoke the name loudly. Defiantly, she hoped.

What Torut's intentions were, she was not willing to even guess.

44.

IT WAS INEVITABLE THAT TORUT would call her to him. Her guide, a blank-eyed Tezian man, led her up stone stairs, through galleries that reeked from volcanic activity. The walls felt hot here and there. At last, they entered his tower room. Na glimpsed the first sky in, what, two days? Or could three have passed? It was deep blue and clear beyond slits of window. She reached out to find the wards extended to this room.

A cloying incense floated atop the stifling, brimstone-scented air, its bluish smoke wafting from braziers on either side of the chamber. The naked, nearly-emaciated form of Torut sat in a black high-backed chair. Not that much of that form could be seen, as his unkempt and centuries-untrimmed hair and beard fell across it.

"All right, I'm here," she boldly announced. "What now?"

"What indeed? That might be up to you, my lady."

So much for that approach. They stared at each other for a moment before Torut rose. "Come," he said. "Stand beside me and look upon my realm." An attendant opened a door and the Wizard-Lord stepped onto a shallow balcony. Na followed.

The barriers were up out here too. The Great Rift lay below and all around her. A wide river or maybe a lake—that was to the west, wasn't it? And vast mountains beyond, higher even than the ones across which the rupa had carried her.

"How did I get here?" she asked. "Yes, I know the rupa carried me but why was I unable to resist them? My limbs would not obey me."

"You imbibed the essence of the poppy. Many of my people here use it to dispel their weariness, to bring peaceful dream."

"Then Arana put it in my wine."

"She did. We have spoken since. There are suspicions but no accusations." A sly smile. "She can claim the Rupa hypnotized her and her husband."

"Until I tell my story," she reminded him. Oh, and she would!

"You can not while you remain within my walls. But you will join with me and then it will no longer matter."

Torut believed that, she was sure. It would do no good to argue the point. "The mec is your agent in Tesra." She stated this rather than asking it.

"One of many. I warned her of your coming and she went to do my work in Phamahd. It was she who undid the alarms at the house of Holos there, and set the fool Azil into action. He has no idea whose hand moves behind Arana's, whose shadow she is."

The attack in the streets of Phamahd. The difficulties crossing the hills to Tesra.

And all that had happened in Tesra since. Na much doubted Arana had directed everything herself but she certainly was aware of what was going on. Could she have been involved in the attack at Holos's gate? If so, she owed her for Tau.

"It was she who sabotaged her husband's warding of the temple, wasn't it?" That was one time she had stymied the mec!

"Yes. Being the wife of old Hiul has certainly helped her in the tasks she has been set. I believe she truly cares for him." One bark of harsh, bitter laughter. "Once she would have killed him out of hand had I ordered her. Long has she served me but I see the treason now in her mind. She seeks to bring Im to her side and use him against me."

As she had hoped to use this mad man for her own cause in Tesra. If ever Arana had been devoted to him, it was long past. Torut hadn't seen that. He might be unable to.

"She played along, while she could," Na remarked. "Attempting a balancing act."

"And now she falls. Arana never had within her what was needed to stand at my side." He turned his golden eyes to her. "Unlike you." When there came no answer, Torut continued, gazing again upon his valley. "There are many points of power within Tul Sunac. It is the ideal place for a sorcerer to make his base and his fortress."

"For what purpose?"

"What purpose has anything but to *be* a short time and disappear into the void? But until then I could bring peace and order to a chaotic world. Tesra has grown corrupt and decays from within. Barbarians roam the wastes of what were once great nations. The nation from which you and I sprang, Na." He waved a crooked, clawed hand toward his wasteland realm. "I create a new Valley of Visions here."

There was truth to what he said. Tesra was declining and those who ruled it were aware of the fact. The rich were becoming more oppressive, the poor becoming more restive. It would be good to set things straight, wouldn't it? She and Torut, using their combined power for good—and her own good, too. A benevolent Queen Na. Flashes of a dream with armies chanting her name passed through her mind.

No! What was she thinking? She stood beside a madman, a nihilist who wished to tear down, not build. A man enamored of the great void. Why shouldn't she rule here herself, cast him down, be the Wizard-Lord? That dream rose up like a bubble and burst. Na could never match the power of Torut. Only one man alive could.

She had to admit that Arana was right in trying to bring Im to her cause. He must be the hope of all of them.

"There *is* power here," she stated, "within this keep of yours. What lies without I can not sense through your warding."

Torut threw back his head, laughing wildly. "I should remove it so you can see! Not now, my lady, though it would do no harm if you spoke to those in Tesra. I mind not at all if they learn of Arana's actions."

Na assumed a thoughtful expression. "She could still be of use to you. She does not know you are aware of her perfidy." It was a gamble to say this. Had she remained silent Torut might just have lowered his barriers but Na felt somehow it could prove best to keep the high priestess in play.

"Quite true. Let us simply say it's far too much work to unbind everything right now. Though it is also inconvenient to go outside when I wish to communicate."

She wondered just where he did this. Not where Goldie did, she was sure. The demon sorcerer went out the front entry, the one through which she had been brought into this place. Na had made sure to speak with it these past days. If only to relieve the boredom.

It was better company than Duxi. The girl and she had exhausted most topics of conversation early on. Still, she was Na's best source of information and seemed to be assigned to her permanently. Permanently and constantly. Tezians still brought unappetizing meals but interacted little otherwise.

Torut turned from the view without further words, entering the audience chamber. Na followed. He settled into his chair, regarding her for some time before speaking. "Return now. We will speak again."

So nothing much was going to be resolved this morning. Her guide escorted her to her room. Both Duxi and Goldie waited there. What could those two find to talk about?

And there was another. Two others. The slightly acrid and not too unpleasant scent told Na of them before she spied the two forms reclining on the carpets. Both rose, crouching semi-erect. Ghalun.

Duxi said something to them in an unfamiliar language. Not the Smotan tongue, which she had heard a few times around this keep. It did not even sound human. Nor was it, for one of the ghalun replied in what was surely the same language.

"These are Yarni and Smasi," she announced. "They're good boys. Aren't you?" She scratched one of them behind his ears. An appreciative whimper came from the creature. A short tail wagged.

"I'm sure they are," Na said. Smotan names, weren't they? Possibly the girl had named them herself. Na had no problem with sentient— somewhat—canines. There had been some quite intelligent dogs back in Hirstel. Some were even competent magicians.

"The demon has news for you," Duxi told her. "He thinks it is very important. I mean, *it* thinks it is. That's right, isn't it?" She glanced toward Goldie.

"It is, girl. We have no gender. Can you give us privacy?"

"All right. I shouldn't, you know." The pair of ghalun followed her into the hall.

"News?"

The demon got right to it. "I went outside this morning to replenish myself, as usual. I also sometimes speak to my people when I am out there, other sorcerers. My superiors are eager for good news."

The magistrates, undoubtedly. "There is little to tell them most days. Torut says only that he has plans in motion, when he deigns to speak to me. None of that matters much at the moment. What is of import is that another reached out and spoke to me from afar. I think he was a god, but also a sorcerer."

Not— "Hurasu?"

"So he named himself. He said even though he was divine he could not penetrate the Wizard-Lord's wards. We spoke of you."

"Has he told any of my friends where I am?"

"He did not say. The god was more interested in how I came to this place."

"Through a gate, I assume." It and its companion would not have traveled here through wizardry, the way they sent their police after Im. That was temporary. They would be pulled back home in a short time.

"You assume correctly, wizardess. I gave him an account of the roundabout route we traveled. I think he intends to come here himself."

45.

SHE WOULD HAVE PREFERRED XIDO but any god should do in a pinch. That there were gates, permanent portals, in the Great Rift, Na had been aware. The rupa, the ghalun, would have come here through them, most likely.

But did a god need portals? Xido hadn't. He had brought her and Im to this world via gates, but the dark god was able to travel at will through the worlds himself.

Goldie did not seem to care in the least that she was plotting with Hurasu. None of its concern, it said, nor that of its people. Their alliance, such as it was, with the Wizard-Lord concerned only Im and Cory. "If one of our sorcerers acted like this Torut," it said, "it would long since have been cast into a river of molten iron." It lowered its voice some, though it was still loud. The demon didn't really seem to understand human hearing very well. Cory had been around them long enough to figure things out. "As did we cast out our gods, eons ago," it told her. "They abused their power over us."

Xido had filled her and Im in on those gods once. Cory too, who had only legends to go by as did, most likely, Goldie. They sounded a thoroughly nasty bunch who had created the demons to serve as slaves —and food.

Now she waited. Torut no longer ignored her presence but called her to him every day, sometimes in the high room where first they met, sometimes in what she suspected were the sorcerer's private chambers. Though they spoke of little of importance, Na could feel the undercurrent of tension between them. Torut was wooing her, that was certain, and never failed to mention the power they would wield together, the good they would do. Would, he said, not could. Sooner or later, he would act. Perhaps not rationally. His moods and madness came and went.

Duxi and her pet ghalun were lounging in her room, when

abruptly the humanoid canines sat up and growled. They were worried, baffled growls, more than ones of menace. Their muzzles turned back and forth as if trying to catch a scent.

"I can hide from the eyes of men but not from the noses of ghalun," spoke a voice from a shadowed corner. Why were there shadows there? They began to dissipate, revealing a lean, light-skinned man of somewhat average height. "In this place, with its dark walls and dark corners it was not at all difficult to slip in. Though holding shadow around me all the way in was not easy! I can't pull any more once inside the wards."

Duxi's jaw hung open but she had enough presence of mind to reassure the ghalun. "Lord Hurasu," said Na. "I would guess you did not come alone."

"But my companions did not enter the keep with me. I warned them to stay hidden for now. Not that they have enough skill with shadow." Na might not herself. Im's mastery was unmatched in her experience. Even Xido had been a bit in awe, though the god tried not to show it.

Then Im was not among these companions. She would learn of them sooner or later.

"This place is more like your gate-riddled Hirstel than anywhere else in this world," Hurasu remarked. "There are several portals nearby, some rather new. Most go nowhere good."

"New? I thought gates were, um, permanent."

"The rift is physically in turmoil and the doors open and close even as the earth here moves. I think the one we came through is old and stable. Stable enough." He took a seat on the bed beside Duxi. One of the ghalun sniffed his hand. Satisfied, it reclined on the floor.

"I told my companions to come to me on their Isle of Stones and I opened the gate there, then guided them here through a number of other worlds. It would have taken weeks of travel otherwise, and it is unlikely then we would have gotten past the Wizard-Lord's borders."

Na managed to smile, though she felt weary. She had been lethargic these past days. "Unless you got the rupa to carry you, Lord Hurasu."

Duxi scowled at the mention. Even the ghalun growled.

"I think not! Of course, I can come and go to this land on my own, though not into this hole of Torut's with its warding."

"Traveling so is tiring. Xido has told me this. I don't suppose you brought him along."

"No. It's better he remain where he is, though I should say he does know of your, ah, predicament." He appeared to be considering whether to say more for some while. "I am a better sorcerer than Xido in any form. That is simply a matter of natural talent. As powerful, as knowledgeable, as the Crocodile God is, he might come up short in a battle of wizardry against Torut, and he knows this." She thought him done then, but he added. "I believe Im could likewise trounce your little god, given a few years more growth and practice."

Xido had said much the same himself. "I understand," Hurasu continued, "that you were once able to bind Xido yourself and Im had to release him."

She had to smile at that memory. It was her first encounter with both god and boy. "He has proven he can block Torut," Na said.

"That is his strength and his cunning at work." Hurasu spread his arms. "But that is not what we need at the moment." He rose. "I but wished to make contact with you, Na. We shall consider our plans and I'll return soon to speak again. Take courage."

"I'll try. I've not felt up to much of anything lately."

"Too much poppy smoke in the air," stated Duxi. "Not here but where you go visiting. They burn it like incense in the braziers."

"Ah! That is good to know, my young woman. I thank you, and may your gods watch over you"—he smiled thinly—"and your furred companions."

"Gods," said Na. "Do these followers of the Wizard-Lord have gods? Can we speak to them?"

Hurasu shook his head. "Few follow any gods at all within these walls. Many outside reverence the Rainbow Snake still, but some have turned to the deities of the Smota and other barbarians who dwell among them."

"Hey, who are you calling a barbarian?" objected Duxi.

"Better a barbarian than a mad Tezian," he said, wrapping a voluminous cloak about him. "I can't pull any shadow to me so I borrowed this cloak on the way in." With that, he slipped out the door.

Duxi looked to Na. "He's right. It's better to be almost anything, anywhere, than staying here with all these crazy people."

"Would you like to come back to Tesra with me? You could even bring Smasi and Yarni." Why not? Ha, she was assuming she *would* get back to Tesra.

"I'll have to ask them. They have a pack, you know."

Could it have been the pack that attacked them? Duxi could probably ask them but it might be best not to know.

And there was something more important she was wondering about. "Poppy smoke, you said. I see people sometimes smoking pipes here. Is that the poppy essence too?"

Duxi nodded somewhat vigorously. "Mostly. We Smota and the other, uh, barbarians sometimes smoke certain herbs." Her face became long. The girl had a facility for quickly changing her expression. "And a few have fallen into the vices of the Wizard-Lord's people."

"I've seen the Bazu of the south smoke pipes. They use some herb they cultivate."

"I saw a Bazu man once. He was brought as a prisoner and Torut had him crucified. The crows went for his eyes before he was dead. Sometimes they get the manhood too but this one had already been castrated during his torture. It's time for lunch, isn't it? Should I call someone?"

"Later, Duxi." Maybe much later. "I want to rest a while. Could you leave me?"

"Certainly, Na." The girl sounded a little hurt. Let her.

Na turned her mind again to Torut's wards and bindings. They were too complex for her to undo but she had picked at them from time to time, learning about them if naught else. As she went looking into them, something caught her attention. An elemental, a little harmless elemental that floated from world to world, universe to universe, attached to no place particular. What Holos had called an anxem, and used to convey messages.

She had done so herself, and frequently, in Hirstel. Could she turn this one to her service? Surely there were more about. Na had simply not thought to look for them.

And they were not bothered at all by Torut's barriers. The little beings passed right through them. She reached out, enticing the anxem with soft words, and brought it to her.

46

"I FELT A PRESENCE," SAID Torut.

"Here? Is that possible?"

"No. No, of course not." He turned from the narrow window. "But it reminds me I can not relax my vigilance nor turn from my course. I have waited for an answer from you, Na, waited patiently."

The game was over. "And I must choose between you and Tesra. You and the man I have come to love, and the people I have made my own? You must know the answer to that."

"There comes a day my armies will burn Tesra and put its people to the sword. If they are fortunate!" His harsh laugh changed mid-note to a snarl. "Your Holos—yes, I know it is he you speak of—shall suffer the most painful death I can devise. And as he lingers, before passing to his gods he shall see you at my side. He shall see me take you like this!" His arms snaked out, grasped her. Na was surprised by the strength in them. She could not break away. "Ha, his gods. They too I shall destroy. Their temples will become brothels for my troops. I will be the god of all this world before I destroy it too!"

Na continued to struggle but there was a weakness in her. Her limbs would not do as she wished. The poppy again, in the wine she drank with him or in the very air. The face of Torut appeared twisted, monstrous, that of a beast.

"All this you will share with me. You will not reject my gift." The Wizard-Lord grasped her, one arm around her waist, and half-dragged, half-led her toward a massive iron-bound door. "Not any longer."

Up steep stairs, cut from the rock, to a spartan chamber. Nothing but a sleeping mat and untidy stacks of books could be seen within it. But outside—tall windows all around let in both the light and the cold air of winter, and a vista of Torut's valley lay on every side. They must be above his wards. Yes. She reached out, trying to bring things into focus, clear her mind enough to speak with someone.

It was Torut who answered, from some world he had chosen. She was pulled toward it, into it, unable to resist. Only blackness lay there. No sky arching above, no ground supporting below, the two of them suspended. *I have found no world closer to the ultimate void*, hissed the Wizard-Lord. *Someday I shall take the final step into it.*

That was impossible. Being was as eternal, as infinite, as nothingness. Na knew this with every part of her own being. Didn't she? Or did her own being even exist now, in this place? Her mind reached out again, sluggishly, but only Torut was there. Maybe this world was Torut. It was so dark.

I search yet. This world I found when in the embrace of the poppy-essence but I no longer use it. What need have I of its illusions? I seek the true peace of annihilation.

She felt his breathing rather than hearing it. No, that wasn't right. She shared his breathing. *It is near, I know. Let the emptiness into you and yourself into it. We are poised on the edge of the void! Be one with it. Be one with me!*

Now she was truly falling into the mind of Torut. A piece of her rational consciousness still worked well enough to know they had physically merged in some sense here, a part of each of them occupying the same space. Im had done that with Atima.

Torut's mind was opened to her, opened completely. She felt it floating, floating among the infinite worlds, floating, floating, and finding never the rest it sought. For only a moment she felt pity for the man and his madness.

Then he took control of her. She could feel his body, her body, still in that tower room, where the sun shone upon them, and here too in the darkness and Na could not tell the one from the other nor why she fought. *Be one*, the voice told her. *Be one.*

Be nothing.

She screamed endlessly into the blackness.

47.

SHE WAS IN HER ROOM when she awoke. He will do this again, she told herself. Over and over until he has broken me.

She must leave before he had the chance.

Na reluctantly revisited events. Much of what had happened was fragmented, like bits of nightmare. Her thoughts were moths circling a candle flame. But she had seen into the mind of Torut, even deeper than Im and Xido and, yes, Atima had. She knew his secrets, if she could bring them out into the light.

The warding. That had been near the surface. She could undo it anytime, a few minutes work at most. It must have been on the Wizard-Lord's mind. What else had been troubling him? Ha. She had. There had been a jumble of thoughts, mixed desire and anger and hatred and even, yes, admiration. Na immediately backed off when she looked a little deeper there. Memories of what happened yesterday lurked there and Torut's were much clearer than her own.

What was this? Something about the demons of Cory's world. He had been making some sort of treaty or deal with them. Na had thought it only an agreement to help each other end Im's life but there seemed to be more. Allies in some way? Did Torut hope to use them in his wars? Deeper. Na gasped and put all the memories aside.

Goldie should be told of this.

She sat up. One of the ghalun slept on the floor. Duxi must have told it to stay with her. They weren't bad beasts at all, were they? Certainly not creatures of evil. Just wild hunters that followed their instincts.

Then the truth hit her. Another truth. Torut had been in her mind even as she had been in his. He would know Hurasu was here. He would know of the elemental, maybe, and the things she had spoken of with Goldie and Duxi. Or perhaps he had paid no attention to them, consumed by his own needs at the time. But they would be there, in his mind.

All the more reason to be on the move.

Why? Was there any point? Darkness would swallow them all and none of it would matter. No, no. That was Torut's mind. She was not going to stand beside him and greet its coming. She was going to destroy him. Destroy him utterly, as he deserved.

Something impinged on her consciousness. The elemental had returned. An elemental. She had left a little bit of herself outside her body to watch for it. Yes, it was the same one. *Hello, little fellow. You have done well.* Na wasn't sure it really understood such things but it would respond to her tone. It probably wasn't as bright as the jackal-man sleeping on the floor.

Message, it announced. *Tell?*

Speak. It would have it by rote, something short and fairly simple.

This is Tuthinos. Holos is not here, it said. Na had sent the anxem to Tesra, to the chief wizard. *He is near you. I have spoken to him there, with the others who intend to bring you back. I can relay messages if you wish.* That was all.

Holos had come with Hurasu? How could he be such a fool? *I thank you, little one,* she told the elemental. *I may ask you to bear messages again.*

Fun, it said, and floated away.

But probably not, if Torut knew about it.

The door opened, just slightly, and Duxi peeked in. "Oh, you're awake. And all right?"

"I seem to be," Na lied.

The girl pushed the door wide. Goldie stood beside her. "The woman thought you were drugged," it said. "She worried."

"I was." And worse. "You and I must speak, Goldie. I have seen something of interest to you and your magistrates."

The other ghalun came in on Duxi's heels, semi-erect. Both of the creatures sort of embraced before settling together on the floor, one lying like a dog, the other sitting in a manlike fashion. "The boys are brothers of a litter," Duxi told her. "Old enough to leave their family unit so they are willing to come with me." She giggled. "They hope there are bitches where we go."

"We must go soon," Na told her, and turned to the demon. "I have been inside the mind of Torut. There I saw gods, evil gods—the gods who once ruled your world."

"They were destroyed," Goldie replied.

"No. Gods can not be destroyed. That is part of what makes them gods." Na was not at all sure of that fact but it wouldn't hurt to tell this demon it was so. "They were imprisoned and Torut is seeking a way to release them." She sighed. "I could show you if it weren't for the warding."

"My superiors must know of this. But evidence will be needed."

"Yes. I can even show you where your ancient gods are locked up. After I get out of this place." She did not like the glimpse she'd had of those gods. She didn't like remembering it. They were human, in a way, yet terrible and alien, brutal chaos-creatures of flame and hunger. And it had been long since they had fed.

Said Duxi, in a very small voice. "You were in the Wizard-Lord's mind?"

"And he in mine, so he knows far too many things he should not. That is why we must hurry."

A clatter arose in the hallway. Voices and running and the sound of metal on metal. They looked out to see Hurasu, a long gleaming sword in hand, battling a group of barbarian soldiers. Two lay already on the black rock of the floor. Na was fascinated. Never had she seen a man— nor god—wield a sword so adroitly, so cunningly, so overwhelmingly.

But he himself must be overwhelmed by the number of his adversaries. With Torut's bindings, he could not access his powers as a god. Hursau was trapped.

"It has to be now," Na breathed, mostly to herself. She looked into that web of wardings with new understanding. There. And there. She reached out, undid that one, that one, and the others began to collapse, unravel, and she pulled here and there until the whole thing fell down. "Fly, Hurasu!" she called out.

A moment later he disappeared, a rather jarring montage of images fading in his wake. "We'd best fly too," she told Duxi.

"I'm ready. I even brought you clothes. Something better than these Tezians wear." She went to one of the shelves and picked up a bundle. "A Smotan outfit."

Why not? "Bring them. We should hurry now."

Torut would be quite aware his wards were down by now. Or he should be. What if he slept deeply? What if he still used the essence of the poppy, even though he claimed otherwise? Those were only slight chances. They must get out of here.

"I know a good way to the outside. Not through the main entrance." The soldiers paid them no attention as they went down the hall. They seemed still baffled by the disappearance of their foe, peering into rooms and passageways.

Narrow stairs opened off that hall a little further down, and they descended into dank cellars and ill-lit passageways. Was anyone after them? Did anyone even know they had taken off? That odor—were Yarni and Smasi smelling even more ripe than usual? They passed around a corner to be barraged by a chorus of yips and howls. "The kennels," explained Duxi. There must have been dozens of ghalun. "I wish I could set them all free."

"Why don't you?"

"They won't go. Like my own people." Duxi hurried on through the room, her own ghalun close behind. "We are near. You should change."

Na hurried to slip into the outfit. She tried not to notice the curiosity of the two ghalun. They had undoubtedly seen other naked humans. The clothing, all of leather, fitted fairly well. There was a skirt and jacket, as Duxi wore. The hem was cut at an angle, one side falling below her knee, and fringed. Fringed, too, were the calf-high boots and the arm bands. From a distance she might pass as Smota, especially with her blond hair. No one would be fooled close up.

Duxi handed her one more item of apparel, a hooded cape, all of white wool. "It's cold outside, Lady Na. Snow's moved in. And this will help conceal you."

Indeed it would. The posted sentry barely noted them as, a minute or two later, they stepped out into the sunlight through a small door, set among the rocks well below the keep. It was bitterly cold.

48.

NA? ARE YOU THERE? IT was Holos, calling from her familiar meeting place, the world where she so often spoke with Im and Xido.

What do you think you are doing? she scolded. *You shouldn't be out running around in the Wizard-Lord's realm!*

Hurasu asked, and I came. He thought I was the right wizard for the job.

And he thought the same of me.

Arana? That was too much. *You two are the companions he brought? Anyone else?*

No, we're it. He ordered us to stay close to the gate while he scouted.

Obviously neither knew how that scouting had gone. Unless Arana was in contact with Torut. What side was the woman on? *I don't know where the gate is,* she admitted. *Can you see the keep? I haven't traveled too far from it yet.* She spied a form ahead of her, materializing dark against the new-fallen snow. *Oh, never mind. Hurasu just showed up.* Maybe she shouldn't have told them that. Na broke off their communication. It was perhaps dangerous to speak from afar anyway. She might need an elemental again.

"Hurry," the demigod commanded as soon as they reached him. "Torut will pursue us with both men and magic." He looked toward the snow-covered terrain ahead. "I should have thought to bring snow-shoes."

"Or skis," said Duxi.

Na knew not what either was. Moreover, they did not have them so it mattered not at all. "We are glad to see you anyway," she said.

"The Tetrad came close to forbidding me to return. Not that they could prevent me but it's best to be on good terms with them, or at least most of their aspects."

"Why, my lord?" asked the Smotan girl. The ghalun bounded along at their side, frisking and chasing each other in the snow. At least they seemed to like it.

"They were not pleased with me fighting in Torut's keep. Calling attention to myself."

"You had no choice," Na stated. "I should contact Goldie as soon as possible."

Hurasu stopped at once. "Then we do it now. I'll show you where." He directed her to a nondescript little world, dim-lit by a ruddy light. Na suspected it was hot there but not enough of her was present to tell. She didn't even need to breath the air if she didn't want. *This is where the demon speaks to his colleagues. I'll call to him.*

Goldie materialized almost instantly. *This place is abuzz! At least I won't be bored for a while.* His chuckle sounded like only a slightly smaller avalanche than Cory's.

There was no time to waste. *Come with me*, said Na, and led him to another world, a world she had glimpsed in the mind of Torut. Hurasu did not follow. She suspected he had returned all his attention to where his body stood in the snow. *This is the prison of your gods*, she announced. *There are powerful bindings holding them here.*

I see them. Na could too. She had known they were in place but now it was possible to examine them. Alien, they were, and stronger than any she could ever have imagined. She could not undo them in millennia.

Nor could Torut, not on his own. If he held the Jewels of the Elements—who could say?

It was a steaming volcanic landscape, but not searingly hot like the world of Cory and Goldie, with its red sun filling half the sky. Even this little piece of Na could not survive in that place! Figures were running toward them, humanoid, misshapen, silhouetted against a churning yellow sky. Huge. They bellowed in a language she could not comprehend.

Go! cried Goldie. They were back in their initial meeting place.

Do you know what they were yelling? she asked.

Food, was the reply. *I must show this place to my fellows and you must run, Na. I thank you for this.*

She wasn't sure whether he remained, for she returned then to her companions. "Done?" asked Hurasu. "Then let us be on our way."

"How far?"

"Two leagues, perhaps."

"A negligible distance, were it not for the snow," said Duxi. "I think I know which gateway you mean. There will be guards. My people, most likely."

"Yes," agreed the demigod as they trudged forward. "We were able to conceal ourselves with shadow and night coming out. It may not prove so easy to enter."

"Especially if Torut has warned anyone there. Would there be a wizard?"

"No. There is some warding but that can be raised and lowered by servants within the keep." The man chuckled softly. "And by me."

Probably by her as well, if low-level sorcerers were assigned that duty. Na groaned at a sudden pain, despite herself.

"Are you hurting, Na?" asked the Smotan girl. "Can you continue?"

"There is some soreness," was all she was willing to admit. "I'll be all right." Soreness, indeed, and bruises—not all physical.

"Torut did this," stated Duxi. "I should go back and put a spear through him."

"You would not be the first to try," spoke Hurasu, not bothering to look back at them. "Better to save your spear for those he might send after us."

Men? Rupa? Or might the Wizard-Lord have monsters unknown in his service? Duxi did carry a spear, using it as a staff to help her traverse the snow. Na wished she had one herself.

"I've certainly gotten you into trouble, my girl," she said.

"I asked to be your attendant. I thought maybe it could change my life."

Na hoped it would. Duxi was a seeker even as she had been, leaving her own world in search of a better one.

"We head toward those rocks there," called out their guide, pointing. "That's where I left the others, in concealment."

Close. She would be happy to reach them and rest a bit. It would be a cold place to wait! Poor Holos must be shivering there among the boulders.

A sound, distant, behind them. Faint, hard to make out. Men crying out perhaps? They topped a low ridge—most of this land lay fairly flat—and Hurasu halted to gaze back the way they had come.

"There," he said. "Our pursuit."

Ghalun. A pack bounding across the snow fields, steadily gaining on them.

49.

THERE WAS NO RUNNING FROM them. They would have to stop and fight. The ghalun numbered at least a score. Even with two sorcerers to face them, it was unlikely they could be overcome. They spread into a semi-circle around the fugitives.

Duxi stepped forward and spoke to them in their language. There were answers from here and there. No one ghalun seemed to be the leader. The conversation went on for some time, the ghalun sometimes yipping at the girl, sometime at each other. Duxi's own ghalun crouched on her either side, looking from her to the others, perhaps uncertain whether to follow her commands or to act as part of the pack.

Then Hurasu spoke to them in the same tongue, a few words only. The pack came together in a clump, turning away from them, though now and again one would roll an eye their way. There was barking and growling and whining for some while. Na wished the delay would be over, one way or another, and they could be on their way before other pursuers showed up. Duxi's attention was on the jackal-men, listening to their speech.

"Duxi reminded them how she treated them better than anyone else in the keep, befriended them where others might kick them aside, brought them treats in their kennels." Hurasu smiled grimly. "I'd best not repeat what some of those treats were. And she invited them to come with us. They are debating that now."

"I don't think things are going our way," whispered Duxi. "Their blood is aroused and they are on the hunt. That is hard to abandon."

Especially with easy prey. Apparently easy. These ghalun might learn otherwise.

What was that glint beyond the pack? The sun, still high, was shining on something. Two somethings, one red, one golden. Goldie and his attendant. They did not walk but were hovering, gliding above the snow. They must not like it any better than Cory.

This set up a new chorus of yips and whines as the demons joined them. Tails drooped and were tucked between legs. "They have faced one like those two before," Duxi informed them, "and do not wish to again. I think most have decided to leave." She bark-spoke to them again, then shook her head. "But they fear to leave Torut. They will not come with us."

Most wouldn't. As the others wheeled and began to trot or amble off, depending on how many feet they chose to use, two bitches detached themselves from the troop and came to stand beside the humans—and Smasi and Yarni.

Goldie watched them go for a moment, the gigantic Red standing stolidly behind it, before turning to the humans. Did it know what it had just averted?

"I have shown others what you have shown me, and the magistrates have ended any alliance with Torut. So we too must leave this place." Its voice remained flat as it added, "Know that they will still seek the life of Im."

"You should let *them* know the Wizard-Lord seeks to take the Jewels of the Elements and use their power to release your ancient gods." Na was not completely certain of this but it seemed likely. The demons needn't be aware of any doubts. "Im will return to the shrine of Banat and guard them. He is your best hope against this."

"Of course," murmured Hurasu. "I should have seen that. It helps explain some of the Tetrad's interest."

"Pardon, masters," rumbled the red demon. Na had neither seen nor heard it before today but could find almost no difference between it and Cory. It could possibly be even taller. "Why does the wizard wish to free the old gods?"

It was Goldie who supplied the answer. "He thinks they will re-enslave us and provide him with an army."

"Army? Oh, to bring here." The massive head shook back and forth. It spoke something in Demonese.

"It says all humans are mad," Goldie reported. "I might agree. Shall we get moving?"

They tracked on toward the rocks where Arana and Holos supposedly waited. The snow lay thinner here but they were working uphill, so they progressed no more quickly. "I will not chance speaking to them from afar," said Hurasu. "Torut might have power enough to listen in, even if we raise barriers against him."

The sun stood overhead, bright yet not warming them much, when they reached the hiding place. There was a sheltered circle among the rocks. No, not just natural rocks but the ruins of some old strong place, many of the cyclopean stones still in place.

Hurasu pointed through one of the gaps. "You can see the gate over there. It's one of those that manifests as a cave."

Na wasn't interested in the gate, not right then. There stood Arana and Holos. At least they were practically and warmly clothed. It was so good to see the wizard, the man she loved. She fell into his arms. He was surprised, she could tell, but she wasn't going to let go of him until she was completely ready!

"So Hursau got you back on his own. We feel as if we came along only as spectators," he said.

"I hope you remain only a spectator," came her vehement reply. "The idea of you traipsing off to the Great Rift!" Her eyes turned to the priestess.

"I have told him I was involved. No more than that, at this time," she said.

"It can wait," declared Holos. He looked more carefully at Na. "You have been hurt," he said. "Hurt badly."

"That too can wait. Whatever possessed you to come here? How could Hurasu convince you to come? You knew nothing of him!"

"Huna told me to trust Hurasu. Trepais had vouched for him in one of her dreams."

Her eyes went back to the demigod. "So the Tetrad is willing to involve itself some."

"But they have commanded me not to take Torut on myself. Or strongly suggested I not."

As Xido, he might not be able to defeat the Wizard-Lord on his own turf, guessed Na. It was only a guess, she realized, and there could be all sorts of other reasons. One thing she did know was that Hurasu could and probably would abandon them, disappearing into another world, if things went totally awry.

But all they had to do was get into that gate down there and go home. Wasn't it? Forget Torut and what he had done to her. For now! She went and gazed down at the cave-like entrance. The most stable, the most easily traversed, gates often looked that way, Xido had told her. The one that had brought her to this world was completely invisible from outside. No one could enter unless they knew exactly where it opened.

The broken walls stood all around them. More broken some places than others. There were a few stone steps on the far side. Up she went to a tall narrow doorway in the rock. Now it was a window, opening to a vista of the east. The lintel stones were long gone. Torut's keep stood out clearly in the distance on its dark, broken ridge, framed by this ancient entryway. Smoke rose beyond. There was power there.

And there was Torut himself. Na could feel him reaching out, trying to make contact with her, searching through the worlds. No, keep him out. Don't acknowledge—then he was with her, one brief onslaught before she was able to raise her wards and shut him out. She fell backwards, onto the unforgiving stones and into darkness.

50.

"So the Wizard-Lord knows where we are," spoke Arana

Hurasu seemed unperturbed. "He would have guessed we headed for this gate anyway. His desire was to bring Na to his will, not to simply find her."

"I lingered a second too long, trying to see—see the forces around his keep," Na said. "That will not happen again."

"There should be no need to use your powers at all," said the demigod. "It is a fairly short dash to the gate. When you have recovered your strength we will attempt it."

Arana nodded at this. "The sun is falling. That will help."

Na stared at the woman, her enemy whether she had come to help or not. "I could show you some of the things Torut said about you." She would rather enjoy that.

"You shared his mind." The priestess seemed to be looking somewhere far away. "As I was never permitted. I resented you and your power, Na, from the first. I resented you taking my place in his favor, though I had come to despise him."

"Your husband was not involved in any of this." Na hoped he wasn't. She like old Hiul.

"Hiul was bewildered by it all and had no idea what had happened," reported Holos.

"You slipped him the poppy-essence too."

"I did. Best he not be involved. Nor anyone else. I had already sent your bearers home. Im heard you call out as the rupa carried you. That was the first any knew aught was amiss." Arana gave her a small and weary smile. "He was most unhappy he couldn't come to help."

"Young Im is too important to risk. The world could afford to lose any of us, but not him," Holos stated. "And I could not afford to lose you."

"Nor," stated Hurasu, "could we chance Torut turning you to his side." His eyes turned to Arana. "As once he did you."

"Once I was enamored of him, I admit this. He overwhelmed me when I was young and ambitious and very foolish. Since then, I have tried to—use him."

"That was foolish as well," observed Holos. Na almost laughed at her lover's pompous tone, despite the seriousness of all this.

"More than foolish. Insanity. I had hopes of bringing peace under the leadership of the nanem." Arana became suddenly vehement. "Wizards should not be fighting wizards!"

"Now," said Hurasu, "you must help us undo the wrong by repudiating and fighting Torut. And," he added, with slight but grim smile, "it is expected that you will name his agents in Tesra when you return." Arana but gave a small nod.

"The Tetrad wished to give you this chance. You *are* beloved of Fasenais," he said. "But now the Lady Na is recovered and we must go. There are surely soldiers on the way. The sooner—"

"Not on the way," rumbled Goldie. "They are here."

Holos stood beside the demon, looking eastward. "There will be at least one wizard with them, to report to Torut. Not the equal in power of any of us, I would think."

"I would not want to fight my own people," said Duxi. That was understandable, even though she had chosen to leave them. "Nor endanger my companions. It is not their fight." The four ghalun crouched around her.

"We would not ask you to," Hurasu replied. "Take them and run for the gate. We will join you later. Lady Na should go with you. The demons too."

Leaving the three sorcerers to bar the way, fight the approaching troop of Smota. They would not survive. Oh, Hurasu would, of course, and probably reappear at the portal to show them the way home. "I will not go," Na stated, as emphatically as she could.

"Nor shall we," said Goldie. "We are together in this."

"I finally get to fight?" asked the big red. "It's about time!"

Even without the help of Duxi and the jackal-men—and jackal-women—that certainly helped even the odds. The Smotan girl sighed. "We stay too."

There was a narrow, readily defended way up through the rocks. Na could see most of it from the high broken doorway. The approaching troop was not large. Sent quickly, perhaps with more to follow. They stopped at some distance to remove something from their feet.

Yes, snowshoes, to be sure. No one would want to charge up a rocky, narrow path with them still attached! Na knew nothing of this nor, aside from Hurasu and Duxi, did any of the others. And it matters not the least to our story.

"Do they have bows?" she asked, addressing mostly herself, but loud enough to be overheard. She could not see any.

"Not these men," said Duxi. "The Wizard-Lord does not permit them for the guardians of his keep. Maybe he is afraid one will shoot at him!" She snickered at that pleasant thought.

Na could use magic against them, rain down something from another world. That would open her to Torut.

Hurasu's sword was in his hand. "I and the red shall fight them in this world," he said. "You do what you think is possible."

"I too shall fight," spoke Goldie. "I've not the training of a warrior but I am bigger and stronger than those humans."

The red demon did not seem pleased but would not attempt to give orders to its superior. "Remain behind me if you can, sorcerer. My first duty on this mission is to protect you."

Na could not imagine Cory being so conscientious of any duty. Demons seemed to come in all sorts and Cory's was, well, criminal. A robber, it had implied, and sometime hired muscle. She wondered briefly what was worth stealing in its world.

"We should all go together," said Arana, pulling her thoughts back to their situation. "Holos and I can keep Torut busy so you can turn your attention to fighting." Holos but nodded gravely to this. He would never give up that sort of thing, would he?

One given in magic was that two weak sorcerers were not much better than one weak sorcerer. That is, they could not combine their powers. Of course, they could spell each other or lend some support or maybe attack from different ways, though that, more often than not, was impractical if possible at all.

Neither Arana nor Holos had the strength of Torut. Nor did she, though she came closer and had the added advantage of knowing his mind—if anyone could know the madness within the wizard. Yet Na was also the most vulnerable to him for the same reason. The Wizard-Lord knew her and the way into her.

There was nothing to do but plunge in, all three of them into the accustomed meeting place—a place Torut would know. He would surely attempt an onslaught at once, turning his attention from the fight below them and the wizard reporting it. That wizard was of no immediate concern to them. At once, Na put up her defenses, allowing Holos and Arana to engage while she went looking elsewhere, in other worlds, for something she might use against the Smota. They were already closing with the demons and Hurasu. It might be tricky.

She could just feel a touch of the Wizard-Lord's rage as she ran and hid from him. Then it was gone and she was completely elsewhere. What? More snow. Look into another world. Fire, no not now. Wind, smoke, all the things she had utilized before. Shadow was useless. Unless—she recalled how Im had built an illusory monster of shadow to frighten the Charcha barbarians. But at this distance? No, she hadn't the skills anyway. Something more direct.

A world of drenching, inundating rain. If she could direct some of that. All this was taking but seconds, but she should act. It was far but she opened a way, let the torrent through. It was almost more like a waterfall than rain!

And she was pleased to see that some of it froze even as it fell. That would add to its effectiveness. Na was able to hold the way open only briefly. The distance between her and the Smota was a factor there; if she'd wanted it to rain on her, she could have held it much longer!

Someone came searching through the dark. The wizard below, a slender wild-eyed Tezian woman, hoping to find her, attack her somehow. I can't be bothered with this, she told herself, and went to her. All that Torut knew rose up, flooded her. She entered the woman, blasted her mind, saw her fall away into blackness.

What have I done? Without a thought, she had destroyed another sorcerer. Was she no better than the Wizard-Lord? Was she fated to be at his side? Why was she fighting him? No, no, that was the Torut within her speaking. Push him down. Don't listen.

The soldiers had been no more than inconvenienced by her down-pour. They had fallen back a little, regrouped. Some were standing about the fallen figure of the wizardess, gesticulating to each other. That might have disconcerted them more than anything else.

Torut could do what she had just done. Na could only hope Arana and Holos were able to resist him. They were strong, far stronger than the woman she had struck down, but they had boldly opened themselves to his attack.

She looked again for weapons, weapons she could use here without endangering her own friends. What was that? A gas, noxious. Flammable? That didn't matter. It flowed from vents in the ground, in an empty land, beneath a gray sky. The wind was behind her, from the northeast. If she could direct it properly. She'd been able to point the rain at the attackers, why not this?

A moment later the Smota below were retching and gasping. Only a faint odor of rotten eggs wafted back to where Na stood. No worse than some of the meals in the Wizard-Lord's keep! But the wind that kept her and the defenders safe was carrying it away too quickly. Could it be ignited? She reached out to a world of storm—maybe the same she had used in the Greater Sea—and brought lightning. Na was a little disappointed nothing exploded but the lightning itself proved to be enough. With a cry that probably meant 'retreat,' the Smota ran.

Na sagged. She hadn't realized how her effort had drained her till now. But she couldn't leave Holos and Arana. Dare she take on Torut, already at less than her best? She looked out across the snow at the fleeing soldiers and beyond to the dark keep. There was power there; this she knew. Could it be seen, maybe, if she went roundabout, beheld it from *elsewhere*?

There. Yes, she could see the walls between worlds were thin there. She could also see the fires beneath, the fires of *this* world. In a way, they were the same. And she could see Torut's tower, the tower where he had violated her soul and her body. Surely he crouched there now, the hideous naked beast he was, attempting to destroy he whom she loved.

Could she direct her power so far? Could she attack the mad ruler of Tul Sunac? High up, higher than ever she had reached, she opened a way. A way to that same world of endless, titanic storm. Let loose the lightning! The sky was ablaze with the power she released, directed toward him she hated more than anything else in this world, more than she could ever have conceived of hating. Spears of lightning crashed against the keep. Na could not aim them, direct them toward Torut himself, no matter how much she wished it. She could only open a way.

He struck her hard. In her concentration, Na had let down all her guards. *You are the mightiest woman I have known,* came his voice, a menacing, rasping, whisper. *You could have ruled but now I must destroy you.*

He would. She was helpless.

What is this? You—no, I see you must live, Lady Na. Look within yourself and know why. With that, his presence was gone.

She did look, and understood, before passing from consciousness.

51.

"YOU DID A GREAT DEAL of damage to the Wizard-Lord's keep, my lady," said Hurasu. "It was as mighty a conjuring as any I have seen."

She didn't need to hear this. "Holos?"

"He remains unconscious, as does Arana. Your actions may have saved them both." He rose. "Whether you can walk or not, we must go. Torut has certainly sent more troops to pursue us."

Yes. He would still want to keep her here, even if the insane sorcerer had chosen not to destroy her. "I can walk," she claimed. She could try, anyway. "What of Holos?" And Arana, though she would as soon leave her.

"The demons have said they will carry them. All the way to Tesra, if necessary." He extended a hand. "Come now."

Her legs would not support her. The world became nothing but darkness when she attempted to rise. "I must carry you, it seems. In truth, my lady, I am a good bit stronger than either of our demons, being a god." He scooped her up. "Even as a mortal, I was the strongest man I knew. In this world—I was born in another." He chuckled almost under his breath. "The mortal me was. It can be confusing."

"Xido is at least as strong as Cory," she murmured. "Did you know Xido? I mean when you were mortal?"

"His path and that of the wizard Hurasu, the Lord of Visions, did cross. I would not be surprised if his memories of the valley of the Tez were more accurate than mine."

She slipped out of consciousness again then. They were in another world when she regained it.

"Ah, you're awake," crowed Duxi. The ghalun seemed enthusiastic about it too.

The first thought in Na's mind was the wizard she had blasted, a pang of guilt at having done so terrible a thing. The second was Holos. "How are the others?"

"The Tezian lady has roused a little. She's still very weak." Duxi shook her head. "Nothing from the man. He is your man, isn't he?"

"He is. We passed through a gate, didn't we? I think I roused a little when we did."

The girl only shrugged. She knew nothing of such things.

"You did, Lady Na," said Hurasu. "We had no difficulties coming through. The two guards ran at the sight of us and the bindings on the entry were easily swept aside. Now we are in the first world one reaches on the other side.

"Oh, a little elemental followed us. I think it is attached to you. I sent it on with a message to Lord Im. Best not to speak afar with things as they are. Even with us in another world."

"I don't like this world," proclaimed Duxi.

"Well you shouldn't. It is the one that gave birth to the rupa. We have a league or so to travel to the next portal. I would prefer them closer together but we have no choice." He looked the sorceress over. "Best I carry you again."

Na remembered little of that journey, through a dark land, in the shadows of trees so high she could not spy their tops. The gate was nothing but a place of shadow within those shadows. It led into a vast cavern with innumerable tunnels leading off it. "A construct of our minds," explained Hurasu. "So we see this nexus of worlds." He led them unerringly to an entrance and plunged in.

And they were immediately in a different world. "There are roads, so to speak, among the worlds," the god explained. "Worlds where gates are conveniently close, allowing easy travel. Relatively easy."

"But evil creatures also are aware of them," said Na. "I know of this."

"Yes, and lurk to attack travelers. The sphinxes are the most pesky." He glanced at Duxi's furred companions. "The ghalun too. We are probably safe, being numerous and some of us rather large."

Goldie and Red still carried the unresponsive blasted wizards. Holos. She longed to go to him but hadn't the strength. And they must get home. That would be best.

The next stop was volcanic, swelteringly hot, the air noxious to breathe. Hadn't she seen this world when she traveled with Xido? It could be one much like it. Na had no way of telling. She might have missed a world or two as she continued to slip in and out of consciousness.

They were again in the cavern. "The next world," announced Hurasu, "is the last before your home, and perhaps the most dangerous. It is the world of the ancient gods worshiped by those who dwelt where Tesra now rises."

"They are evil?" asked Duxi. She took a quick look at the demons. "Like theirs?"

"No, not particularly. Or not more so than most gods! It is their world that is deadly, a place of primordial forest and beasts. They are half-beasts themselves."

Well, wasn't Xido part crocodile? That didn't seem too bad. "They don't, um, resent the Tesrans, do they? I mean, for displacing their people?"

"It wouldn't occur to them," he assured her. "You're sure you can walk now?"

When she nodded a yes, he led them into the gate.

A monstrous antlered creature stood stolidly watching them on the other side. "Hmm, not divine, is it?" asked Hurasu. "No, just some of the local fauna. It's sometimes hard to be sure here. Lion Man likes to hunt these great elk from time to time."

"I've heard of him," came a barely audible whisper from Arana. "There are still those in the countryside who revere him and the other ancient gods."

The elk lowered its head, returning to its grazing. "Let us hope he doesn't show up," said Hurasu. "He would as gladly hunt us as any other prey. Ha, he would want your skull hanging in his cave, Red. And wouldn't know you don't have one!"

Arana was conscious but not Holos. The woman had been badly blasted. Na blamed her still for all that had happened, for the wounding of Holos. Worse than wounding? No, she would not think of that. She would help the priestess return home anyway. Arana had not redeemed herself but she had taken a step in the right direction.

Na would be watching whether she stayed on that path. She was able to walk now, no longer exhausted either physically or mentally. Oh, but she hurt so much, in so many places! She stumbled along with the others. This world was indeed all forest, at least what she saw of it. Some of the trees were familiar. Bigger though, weren't they, than the ones she knew?

It was like being in a great temple, its ceiling arching over them. Of a sudden, a voice echoed from that ceiling, a woman's voice. "Too loud, my queen," called out Hurasu. "The mortals here have tender ears."

A woman came from among the trees, a quite large, quite naked, and exceptionally fat woman. "I greet you, Great Mother," spoke the demigod.

She looked them over, somewhat disinterestedly. "It's a good thing you didn't run into any of my husbands," she said. "Have you decided to become one of them, little godling?"

"I only escort these ones back to their home, Queen of All. We may need to pass back through soon to get the, um, shiny ones over there where they belong."

"You are always welcome but stay with me a while sometime, all right?" She waddled over to peer at Holos. "This one is no longer with us."

The red demon nodded. "I felt him breathe his last as we entered here."

"Then we bear his remains home to rest." Hurasu turned to Na. "I am sorry, my lady."

"Your man, little woman? I am sorry too. I weep for you." And she did, great tears. A moment later, a rain shower started. "The Great Mother *is* this world," said Hurasu. "It feels even as she does."

"Thank you, my lady," Na managed to choke out. Holos gone. She wanted to blame Arana, blast her even as she stood there, but the image of another wizardess she had destroyed rose up before her. No, she would not seek vengeance on the priestess.

It was Torut who was to blame. He and only he would she seek to destroy.

"Pass through," said the Mother Goddess. "The way is not far. I will make my mates behave if they wander by."

As they went on, Na heard Duxi whisper to the sorcerer-god, "How many mates does she have?"

"Three. Lion Man, Horned God, and Great Bear. Not that she will not lie with any other male that chances by."

"She is dark, like the Tezians."

"As were the people who worshiped her. Here's the final gate."

Na could see nothing. Oh, on the ground. Or *in* the ground. It was identical to what lay within the circle of monoliths on the Isle of Standing Stones. "This portal is warded against human entry but not other beings," said Hurasu. "That way the gods were able to visit your world but you couldn't come and bother them. Being at least partly a god, I can pass, as can our demon friends. Hmm, I suspect the ghalun would have no trouble either. Those who are human need simply be in contact with one of us who is able."

So would he have brought Holos and Arana. Hurasu held out his hands to Duxi and Na, and stepped into the portal. A moment later they stood in another world.

"So there you are," said Alpisha.

52.

THE DEMONS WERE GONE. HURASU had returned at once through the gate with them, to guide them to their home.

"Im said to expect you. He is on his way with a boat." Alpisha suddenly embraced Na. "I mourn with you, my sister. All Tesra will."

For the first time, Na let herself cry, cry over the loss of Holos, cry over every loss. The two wept in each other's arms.

This is only the beginning of my grief, she thought. The memory of Holos will follow me all my days. But there will be days and I will go on, and I shall see Torut thrown down and destroyed. I shall serve Tesra and it will be my home, even though I dwell alone within it.

And Arana—what of her? That might be up to others.

Im did arrive shortly, with the promised boat. Cory was with him, of course. It was perhaps just as well it missed running into its fellow demons. Im handled the sails himself. The boy must have learned something from Mursoazes. Ah, Mursoazes, the man who was the best friend of Holos, the man who had once taught the wizard to sail. This would hit him hard too.

But not as hard as she would hit him if his hands again strayed. She smiled inwardly, despite her grief, at the thought. Mursoazes was a good man, at heart. Good enough.

As was Im. He saw to it the body of Holos was loaded, and Arana, still weak, was assisted aboard. The priestess gazed for a little while at the still form of the wizard before saying, "I too mourn his passing and my part in it. I thought once I hated Holos, but that's not true. I hated what he represented and the fact that he was chosen chief wizard over my husband. I hated that we of the pure blood slowly lost our power in Tesra, slowly were being overwhelmed and fading into the mongrel masses." Despite all, Arana remained true to her nanem beliefs.

"He was a great man, and a great wizard," she continued. "He deserved all that came to him, save this." She spoke no more on the short voyage to the mainland, clearly visible from the island. It was cold and the water rough, a wind howling from the north.

All save this. What had been accomplished by the death of Holos and all the rest? Torut's power has been diminished some. Not nearly so much as might have been hoped. Some of his schemes had been balked.

And things went on.

53.

NA SAT PROPPED UP IN her bed in the house of Prince Huenoziles, playing a game with Im. The game involved moving tokens of varied appearance and capability about on a board. Im was exceptionally good at it, Na not so much. She hadn't managed to beat the boy yet. Neither, apparently had Huna nor Huenoziles, since first introducing him to it.

"Xido doesn't like these sorts of games," Im told her, as he captured another of her pieces. "He says he works hard enough at thinking already."

She hadn't heard him say this but could believe it. Her Xit had preferred games of chance, games where he could give up being in control of things.

"Lord Xido could cheat if he wished," observed Cory. As usual, he had been quiet so long she forgot he was there. A chuckle rumbled from deep within the demon. "I would."

"Winning that way probably loses its allure after a time," she said. "Oh, Tuthinos."

The wizard hovered in the doorway. "Hi, Tuthee," said Im, cheerfully taking another of her tokens. "I think I've won again."

"Why do you play him, my lady?" asked Tuthinos, pulling up one of the chairs to her bedside.

"I'm bored. I'm getting up tomorrow no matter what anyone says. What brings you by, other than the pleasure of my company?"

"Isn't that enough?"

As usual, laying it on a little too thick. "I've news," he continued. "Hiul has been named the new chief wizard."

He had spoken this calmly, making no mention of the former chief wizard. People would continue to tip-toe around her for a while yet.

"I doubt he holds the office very long."

"Yes, everyone recognizes it as an interim appointment, Hiul included. Oddly, his wife announced her retirement from being high priestess of Fasenais. Arana says she will spend some time in one of the country shrines and meditate upon her life."

Na and Im could not help exchanging knowing looks. If Tuthinos saw, he discreetly ignored them.

"He is of the party of the nanem, but his prejudices are more a matter of attitude than action," he continued. "Also, several enemy agents have been rounded up. I don't know how they were discovered." He turned an inquisitive eye to Im. "And I suppose you won't share the prince's confidences."

Im but smiled smugly.

"I have news too," Na announced. "I am pregnant." She had known this but had hesitated to share it. The presence of another had been evident when the Wizard-Lord ordered her to look within herself. That was why he had spared her. She continued, her voice steady, as flat and matter-of-fact as she could manage. "I am certain the child is Torut's but none need know that. You two only. Oh, three. I almost forgot you, Cory! Tesra will think Holos is the father."

"Perhaps you should stay abed longer," spoke Tuthinos. There was concern in his voice. Two facts had been revealed to the wizard—he had not known till now of her rape by the Wizard-Lord. He could certainly be trusted not to speak of it.

"If I don't get some food soon I'll be too weak to get up," she complained. "Why doesn't one of you go get me something?"

"Vegetarian?" asked Im.

"Absolutely." Na had been strictly vegetarian since her return. She intended to remain so.

The young wizard cleared the board, returning the pieces to a silk bag. "I should go find Duxi. She's the only one around this place who can challenge me."

"The ghalun are more at my level," Na told him.

Im rose. "I have some news too," he said. "Mursoazes has promised to ferry me back across the Great Sea when the winter breaks. I shall have to say goodbye to all of you. But I'll be with Atima again." The boy was far away for a moment, already beside his beloved in his mind. "Oh, by the way, Cory, you won't have to become a statue again."

Cory's sigh of relief was like the winter wind across the sea.

And so we leave Na to live happily ever after, as we storytellers like to say, or at least until the next time I can gather a crowd. She became an important person in Tesra, a mighty sorceress, mother of a beautiful girl, wife of a good man. Oh, I didn't mention the husband?

That, of course, was Tuthinos. He loved Na quite a bit and I like to believe she returned the sentiment, though her heart sometimes turned to her lost Holos.

It is likely that Im was happy too.

AFTERWORD

I hope you have enjoyed CITY OF WIZARDRY, the sequel to THE WAYS OF WIZARDRY. These tales are set nearly a thousand years before the events of THE EYES OF THE WIND—where I introduced the god Xido —and serve, in a sense, as a bridge to that novel from my Malvern and Mora series.

As those novels, it is set in the world of my DONZALO'S DESTINY sequence. The technological level is meant to be similar to the early Iron Age. The magic, however, is the same.

It is not necessary to read any of those other novels to understand this one. Of course, I hope you will!

Expect to see more of Im and Na, both in a sequel (to be set many years later) and as a presence in other novels. Xido, to be sure, will show up as well.

Stephen Brooke

Author Stephen Brooke lives in an old farmhouse in the Florida Panhandle. He is the author of more than twenty books, as well as an artist and musician.

Visit the Arachis Press at http://arachispress.com for more of his work.

www.ingramcontent.com/pod-product-compliance
Lightning Source LLC
Chambersburg PA
CBHW030033030726
47500CB00001B/84